TREASURE BY POST

David Williams was born in South Wales. After Oxford and the Royal Navy, he pursued a highly successful career in advertising before becoming a full-time writer. *Treasure by Post* is his fifteenth Mark Treasure mystery. He and his wife live in Surrey.

Critical acclaim for Mark Treasure mysteries:

'Clever sleuthing and genteel social satire provide the pleasure.'
New York Times Book Review

'Inventive, baffling and funny.' *Guardian*

'As usual, the writer salts his tale with humour: but, also as usual, you leave the book with the sensation of having read more than just another thriller.' *Financial Times*

DAVID WILLIAMS

Treasure by Post

Grafton
An Imprint of HarperCollins*Publishers*

This one for Philip Ursell

Grafton
An Imprint of HarperCollins*Publishers*,
77–85 Fulham Palace Road,
Hammersmith, London W6 8JB

Published by Grafton 1992
9 8 7 6 5 4 3 2 1

First published in Great Britain by
Macmillan London Ltd 1991

ISBN 0 00 647253 2

Set in Times

Printed in Great Britain by
HarperCollinsManufacturing Glasgow

This one for
Philip Ursell

Chapter One

Sister Mary Maud squinted through her round, wire-framed spectacles at the wording on the red letter-box. The box was a vintage VR model, set into the churchyard wall at the residential end of the pretty Chiversley High Street. It was dark already, and the boughs of a stout if leafless oak were blocking the light from the street lamp on the corner of Steep Street. The diminutive nun produced a half-century-old pocket torch from the recesses of her voluminous black habit. With the aid of this, she finally satisfied herself that it was safe to post Sister Patricia's letter.

After stealing a glance to left and right, Sister Mary Maud pushed the envelope halfway through the opening with one hand, gave it a distinctly playful sort of tap with the other, then listened for the plop as it landed inside. Her eyes, the lift of the shoulders, and the little backward movement of her body all indicated how much this performance had pleased her. Her palms stayed upwards in front of her for another moment – but not, as it might have seemed, because she was actually blessing the postbox. From childhood – and her two-handed posting method dated from then too – she had never ceased to marvel that, for the cost of a few pence, letters could be carried to the very ends of the earth, and by air if one chose, which made the concept even more romantic.

The fact that Sister Patricia's letter was destined to travel only the eight and three-quarter miles from Chiversley to the Wessex market town of Shaftsborne was neither here nor there. Sister Mary Maud had not read the address on the envelope, nor would she even have dreamt of doing such a thing. But she had never been carried anywhere by air herself, and at eighty-eight years of age it was decidedly unlikely now that she ever would be. It was wonderful to imagine that the letter could be.

As Sister Mary Maud had hoped, the disc in the door of the postbox had shown that the five-thirty collection had not yet been made, even though the illuminated church clock gave the time at two minutes to six. She was not concerned that the Post Office had failed to do its duty at the contracted time. The half-hour lapse was as nothing to someone whose mind was turned regularly to a confident anticipation of eternity. What had bothered her was the possibility of Sister Patricia's letter lying lonely all night in an otherwise probably empty box. And getting damp. Sister Mary Maud waged a ceaseless campaign against dampness corrupting animate and inanimate objects alike. A letter seemed so very vulnerable – especially when rain was forecast.

She turned, and, with the east breeze at her back, paused to give an affectionate glance at St Timothy's in the centre of its broad and flattened churchyard. The old tombstones there had long since been uprooted. Most had been laid down as paving, except Sister Mary Maud never really cared to tread on them.

St Timothy's magnificent east window was illuminated from within. The soaring tower, further away at the west end, was silhouetted defiantly against a blustery night sky. The largely fifteenth-century building always invoked wonderment in the Sister's mind – even more than the postal service did.

Giving a sigh in appreciation, Sister Mary Maud folded her arms into her sleeves, and with the wind helping her, she padded off along the pavement in her stout sandals, her head bobbing in concert with her step. Soon after she turned into the churchyard through the lichgate. The path from there led up to the north porch where she would turn right along the narrower way that skirted the long north side of the church, and then around the tower and west end. The convent lay beyond the imposing building's south-west corner.

Today was Monday. At six p.m. on all the other weekdays, the sisters of the Society of Blessed Mary Magdalene assembled for vespers and devotions in the Lady Chapel of St Timothy's. But Monday was Canon Stonning's day off, and since the parish no longer had a curate, there were no services at all in the church. So on Mondays the sisters, led by the Reverend Mother, held their corporate evening worship in the private chapel of the convent

8

at the later time of six-thirty. Of course, it was no longer a large gathering: quite the opposite.

There had been a time when more than forty nuns, plus novitiates, had been present at every service, accompanied by as many patients. Now there were no patients at all, and very soon, Sister Mary Maud had just been musing, there would be no nuns either.

Recently she had taken to slipping across to the church at five o'clock on Mondays to listen to the regular weekly choir practice, with Dr Picton's organ practice to follow. Sister Mary Maud loved music. So she would have been in church now if Sister Patricia had not let slip after tea that she might have a letter to post later.

That letter had immediately given Sister Mary Maud an overriding purpose. Sister Patricia could not go to the post herself. It was not her age that prevented her (she was fully a year younger than Sister Mary Maud), it was her arthritic hip. Again, in time past, letters from the convent had, by unofficial arrangement, been taken away by the postmen when they made deliveries. But these days postmen seldom had occasion to come to the convent at all, and when they did they were often new to the job or the route and didn't know the custom. So Sister Mary Maud had taken it upon herself to post the convent letters. It was not an arduous duty. There was a letter to go rather less often than once a week – but that made the event more momentous when it did happen.

Sister Mary Maud had been aware that Sister Patricia's letter might not have been ready for some time, not even perhaps that day. Sister Patricia was as notably vague as her dear Sister in God was dutifully patient.

Sister Mary Maud had been content to wait, reading the works of St Thomas Aquinas from a volume she had taken at random from the overflowing bookcase in the narrowed corridor outside the basement printing room. Happily, Sister Patricia had limped out with the letter in only a little over an hour. Sister Mary Maud had been relieved at this, as much because of the errand it provided, as because she had been finding St Thomas Aquinas a bit highbrow.

It was good to be of service to Sister Patricia who still

did useful artistic work, the exact nature of which often went unspecified. Sister Patricia, in addition to being vague, was also testingly uncommunicative. Sister Mary Maud did put both *those* characteristics down to age, but in a perfectly charitable way.

And because Sister Mary Maud looked forward to hearing the choir practice, denying herself the pleasure today, by helping someone else, accounted a little for the extra colour in her still cherubic face – that and the east wind now propelling her back down the church pathway.

'Well, did you ever?' she said, quite loudly to herself a little later, when she caught sight of the two motor-bikes. They were cunningly parked to the left of the substantial, protruding north porch, and would have gone quite unnoticed by anyone without a torch. Sister Mary Maud had produced her own torch again because the porch lamp had been out. It normally lit the path up from the gate. She was careful always not to deviate from the path which to this point was all cement and no tombstones. The beam of her torch showed also that the bulb in the porch light was not just faulty. It had been removed. She tutted again.

The motor-bikes had been placed hard up against the porch wall, or, more accurately, against the upright tombstones set along the wall, as they were around almost the whole of the church. Sister Mary Maud preferred to see the old uprooted memorials used in this way, and not as mere paving. But propping heavy machines against those fragile lettered surfaces was nothing short of sacrilege. Apart from that, all motor transport was banned from the churchyard, hearses not excepted. The Parochial Church Council was adamant on the point. There were notices at all three gates.

'Tch!' expostulated Sister Mary Maud, who was seldom irritated by anything, as she prepared to move off to the right. She supposed the bikes belonged to the temporary male members of the choir recruited at festival times. Even so, such people should be told the rules – or better, taught to read.

Her indignation faded quite quickly as she moved down the outside of the church, listening to the faint strains of the singing from within. She knew the music well enough. It was called Vulpius, an old, bold setting to the Easter hymn 'The strife is o'er'. It had been one of her clerical father's favourites

– number 192 in the old Anglican hymnal she remembered: she hardly ever forgot numbers. So, Easter would soon be here again with its message and its revelations. She moved along humming.

And without knowing it, in all this Sister Mary Maud had just sown the seeds for several future revelations herself.

'Alleluia!'

Inside St Timothy's, the singing of the small choir, in the brightly lit chancel, rang through the big and otherwise darkened Perpendicular interior.

'. . . *Alleluia!* . . .'

The volume of the unaccompanied voices increased as the end of the last verse approached.

'. . . *All-e-lu-IAA!*'

The unison crescendo had built up strongly on the ultimate long note.

'And one, two, and OFF!' cried Dr Ambrose Picton breathlessly, calling as well as beating the time on the last extended syllable. His frail body did an involuntary half spin as he brought down the conducting baton with an extravagant final sweep – arms, head and shoulders following through with careless enthusiasm as he very nearly propelled himself into the sanctuary.

'That was splendid, everybody. Splendid. We'll definitely do it unaccompanied,' the aged Picton, choirmaster *and* organist expressed his delight, while regaining his balance. He also straightened his bifocals which had ended comically askew on his long, skinny nose. His benign gaze ranged over the adults in the second row of the choir stalls, then upon the children in the row in front of them. The four small boys and the two even smaller girls added more to the look than to the sound of things, but they were keen enough – and they responded to encouragement as surely as the grown-ups. The choristers smiled back at the Doctor.

But the general air of bonhomie in the chancel would have evaporated soon enough if choirmaster and singers had known about the three youths in bomber jackets and trainers who had earlier slipped in through the north door, and who were now busy in the darkness at the very back of the nave.

11

The oldest of the three intruders had been in a choir once – at the chapel in his first detention centre – but the experience was not even a memory to him now. His name was Sean Ribble. It was he who had wrenched the three metal alms boxes off the wall near the door, the noise of his action masked by the singing. Sean still hadn't been able to force the lock of the last box, but he was working on it with a small wrench. The box was marked 'Famine Relief'.

'Shows they knew we was starving for it,' Sean sniggered hoarsely to the others, angling the box so that the painted letters caught some reflected light from the chancel. The youngest of the three, who went by the nickname Knuckles, gave a low, uncertain laugh. He expected the joke was a sexy one, like most things Sean said, but he couldn't be sure: Knuckles didn't know what it said on the box because he had never learned to read properly.

So far the other alms boxes had yielded less than two pounds between them, for 'Church Upkeep' and 'Hospice'. Sean wasn't sure what a hospice was – only that it didn't seem to pay.

Joss Sutters, the third youth, knew about hospices: he and Knuckles Crabbe had once broken into a hospice and lifted a TV set while a bedridden patient had been watching it.

Back in the chancel Dr Picton looked at the time. 'Goodness it's nearly six. That'll have to do for this evening, I think,' he said, regretfully. 'It's still three weeks before Easter, of course. We'll have another go at the anthem next Monday. With the organ. Thank you, all of you. See you on Sunday, I hope.' Then came the afterthought, 'You can't manage the ten-thirty this Sunday I suppose, Mr Sedge?'

' 'Fraid not, Doctor. On the wrong shift, see?' Stocky George Sedge was a bus driver.

'Quite so. Pity.' Picton closed the music on the collapsible metal stand in front of him and pocketed his tuning fork. As in many big churches, it was impossible to conduct a choir practice from the organ keyboard: the organ loft here was high above the chancel on the right.

'All the ladies'll be present and correct though, Doctor. Well, present, at least,' offered the ample Mrs Edicomb with something unintentionally close to a leer as she gathered up music copies. She was the usual spokeswoman for the five women members, and the mother of Peter and Esme, two of the child choristers.

'Glad to hear it. Very glad. Well, good-night all.' Picton forced a warm smile for Mrs Edicomb who he found wearingly fatuous, and absently patted Peter's head, delaying the child's departure. Peter was an angelic-looking ten-year-old, given to tormenting his younger sister, such as by cutting up live insects in front of her with his pen-knife. Peter glanced up innocently at Dr Picton, ducked, then clattered off down the chancel steps after the others.

'Quietly Peter,' called his adoring mother. 'And take Esme's hand when you get outside.'

Esme glowered at the prospect, and wished she wasn't in the rotten choir.

Thirty years before, the choir of St Timothy's would have filled the carved, three-tiered stalls on both sides of the high chancel with its exquisite coloured fan vaulting. Tonight the group, which had clustered on the left side only, had numbered fourteen in all. Two of the three men were volunteers just for Easter Day. Still, it was a robed choir every Sunday, which was more than they had at the other two places of worship in the town.

'You'll be locking up later, then, Doctor?' Graham Brown enquired pointedly. He was the only permanent adult male chorister, a pale and earnest young bachelor, prematurely balding, with large, translucent ears and a wispy beard. He was the Honorary Treasurer of St Timothy's, and worked at a bank in the town.

'Thank you Graham, yes. I have my keys safe.' The seventy-two-year-old widower, a retired GP, had nearly forgotten to lock up on one occasion several weeks before, after temporarily mislaying his keys. The zealous Brown was not letting him forget it.

Sean at the back was spry enough to capitalise later on what he had heard of this not very loud exchange. He hoped his companions had been listening. All three ducked lower behind the last pew in the nave as the choir members left by the door some yards in front.

Dr Picton went across to the organ loft. It was under the arch that separated the chancel from the south chapel. He opened the door and moved unsteadily up the narrow spiral steps. It was a steep and awkward climb at the best of times, and the more so for a man with a heart condition who had been overexerting himself and who was clutching a cumbersome music stand. Of course, he should have collapsed the stand, but it was a complicated business, and never seemed worth the effort. When he was nearly at the top, the baton slipped off the music rest and clattered back down the stairs.

'Blast,' said the Doctor under his breath. He planted the stand in the loft, then went back down for the baton.

'Clumsy old fool,' he said, remounting the stairs, straight backed in defiance of his age and condition. He took out his handkerchief and wiped his brow, then his chin. He rubbed the chin again with his hand. Had he really missed all that beard when he shaved this morning? He moved across the loft to look in the mirror over the organ keyboards. Evidently he had. Not that anyone would remark or care if he walked about with a two-week growth. It had been different when his wife Joan had been alive – like most other things. It had been a full two years now. He bumbled along well enough, he thought, still absently making faces at himself in the mirror. Mrs Scott came in daily, cleaned the house, did his laundry, prepared his meals. He couldn't grumble. He was lucky to be able to afford such attentions. And life still had its satisfactions – the choir and the organ being major ones, along with the fishing and the bridge club. He ought to give up being a convent beneficiary though. There had been hints – even a veiled one tonight from Graham Brown. It was only responsible to let the others pass the privilege to someone younger, of course. It was curious how loath he was to do it though – or perhaps not entirely curious. He had serious misgivings about the motives of Charles Utteridge-Flax.

He put the music stand out of his way to the right, and unlocking the cabinet on the other side, took out the bottle of Scotch from the back behind the music. He poured a generous measure of the liquid into the glass he kept beside the bottle of Malvern water on top of the cabinet. He sank onto the organ bench, facing the manuals, and swallowed from the glass gratefully. Then he poured out another measure, again without adding water. Whisky wasn't strictly good for him, but if it set his heart racing, it also staved off the melancholia that threatened if he was alone at this time of day.

'Don't mind if I do then, Dad.'

The snide voice behind his ear gave him a serious shock.

Glancing round it seemed to him that the small space was crammed with people – rough, busy men in black leather clothing. There was something wrong with their faces. When he realised that they had nylon stockings over their heads, his stomach sank.

Sean, the one who had spoken, snatched the whisky bottle and dropped it into a shoulder pack. Joss began searching through the music drawers, emptying their contents on the floor. Knuckles, who was immense, dragged the Doctor backwards off the seat, called 'Catch,' and propelled him hard toward Sean who pushed him back again just as hard. Knuckles then grabbed the old man at the neck by his tie and shirt, making him stand on tiptoe, while holding a clenched fist up to the ashen face. The fist was armed with an ugly steel knuckleduster.

'One of these the key to the safe, Dad? The safe in the room with the nightshirts?' asked Sean. 'We just been in there, see?' He took the key-ring from where the Doctor had left it in the cabinet lock.

'The safe key isn't there. I don't have one,' Picton croaked. 'And please tell this lout to loosen . . .'

At a nod from Sean, Knuckles hit the Doctor in the nose and eye before he could finish the sentence. Picton felt the nose bone crack. It had happened to him before – playing Rugby more than half a century before. It was bizarre that the memory came back so clearly now.

'Your safe key, Dad. Where d'you keep it then? Better tell us or he'll bash you again. Worse prob'ly.' Sean was pleased with the way it was going.

Knuckles was standing over the Doctor who he had let crumple to the floor, grazing the back of his head on the organ seat as he went down. Picton took several deep breaths, willing himself to muster his strength and keep his self-control. 'The key to the vestry safe is kept by the churchwarden. There's only one,' he lied hoarsely, sitting up, and feeling for his handkerchief to stem the blood now coursing from his nose.

'Pull the other one, Dad. And give us the key,' insisted Sean, delighted with his own performance. 'We know you got it. Heard you tell someone. We was listening. So where d'you keep it then?' He nodded again at the others.

'I didn't say I had a safe key. I couldn't have.' He wiped his face, the eyes coming alert again, measuring the scene. 'I remember saying my own keys were safe, that's all. You misunderstood.'

What happened next was something Picton wouldn't have attempted without the two whiskies, and because he had no illusions about what was in store for him otherwise.

Steeling himself, he made a sudden dive forward, grabbing Knuckles' right ankle, and taking him off balance. At the same time he reached for the base of the music stand with his other hand. As Knuckles went down with a curse, Picton levered himself off the floor, thrashing out at Sean with the jagged metal stand. Sean jumped aside with a laugh, cannoning into Joss.

A split second ahead of all three intruders, his adrenalin peaking, the Doctor desperately lunged for the stairs, meaning to hurl himself to the bottom and lock the others in behind him.

His plan might just have succeeded – except for the devastating pain that sliced into his chest as he reached the top of the stairs, stopping him in his tracks. It was the onset of a massive heart attack. He fell forward towards the stairs, and died almost instantly, mouthing the words, 'Oh, Joan.'

16

Chapter Two

'Quite ravishing still,' pronounced the mellow-toned John Larpin, Bishop of Shaftsborne, about the woman in his arms.

'I don't believe I've ever been ravished by a bishop. Not a tall one anyway,' said Molly Forbes, the celebrated actress, allowing him to kiss her enthusiastically on both cheeks while hugging him back. Since she had gone to some trouble over her appearance she had been charmed by the compliment.

'He's still only a suffragan bishop,' cautioned Mark Treasure, Molly's husband, kissing her too in passing, and much less elaborately. 'Let him ravish you when he gets promoted, the damages could be astronomical.'

'I read the Bishop of Guildford's retiring. Could you be offered the vacancy, John?' Molly questioned seriously, holding onto Larpin's arm and leading him toward a sofa as Treasure went to pour drinks.

'No idea. You can start a rumour if you like,' the Bishop replied with a grin, sitting himself beside her. He was a slim, angular figure, with longish fair hair brushed very flat, and a high forehead with inquisitive lines above lively, tolerant blue eyes. At forty-five he was a year older than Treasure: they had played golf for Oxford University together more than twenty years before. Later, as a young priest, John Larpin had officiated at Mark and Molly's wedding.

The three were in the first-floor drawing-room of the Treasures' regency home in Cheyne Walk, Chelsea. The room ran the width of the house, with long, graceful bay windows at both ends. It was furnished pretty much in period, only some of the paintings were modern.

The time was just after seven, and the two men had arrived

at the house a few minutes before. Larpin had been attending a Synod committee meeting in London, and was staying the night before returning to his Wessex sub-diocese next morning. Treasure, Chief Executive of Grenwood, Phipps, the merchant bankers, had collected his bachelor friend from Church House, Westminster, on his drive home from the City.

'Anyway, I'm perfectly content at Shaftsborne for the time being,' Larpin went on, accepting the glass of dry sherry his host had poured for him. 'There's so much to do there. Problems, of course, but it's a rewarding area. Incidentally, your staying down the road from me next month could be providential.'

'So that you and Mark can slope off to golf and fish while I'm sweating in front of a hot camera?' Molly sat up even straighter, crossing her shapely legs and rearranging the folds of the crisp yellow dress. A slender enchantress, with an aristocratic bearing and a high register voice, she was more striking than notably beautiful, her innate attraction scoring the more for that – like her enduring public appeal as a high comedy actress.

Molly was about to play the lead role in a lavish new television version of Noël Coward's *Blithe Spirit*. She had appeared the year before in a successful revival of the original play on the London stage. Although most of the filming was to be at Shepperton Studios, near London, several weeks' location work was planned, using the interior and gardens of a country house between Shaftsborne and Chiversley. The production company had rented a smaller house for Molly on the edge of Chiversley with a stretch of the trout fishing River Wibble flowing through its grounds. This was one of the reasons why her husband had promised to join her there for part of the time.

'I'm hoping to be down for the weekend of the May bank holiday, and at least part of the week after that,' he said, standing with his glass before the Holland fireplace. 'But Molly's right about the fishing and the golf. Can you take some time off, John?'

'Sure. But it wasn't sport I meant when I said the visit was providential.' The Bishop frowned, rubbing a thumb along the black cord of his gold pectoral cross. 'You read about Ambrose Picton's death perhaps?'

'The Chiversley organist? Yes,' answered Molly. 'Nasty business.'

'There was another report in *The Times* yesterday,' said Treasure. 'Despite the assault, it seems now that he died from natural causes.'

'Aggravated natural causes. That's what the coroner's court decided,' said Larpin bitterly. 'There'll be criminal charges against the two young thugs involved even so.'

'They were caught through the acuity of a switched-on nun?' said Molly with approval, picking up her glass of Chablis from the table beside her.

'Yes, a very aged nun. Sister Mary Maud. She'd memorised the number of one of their motor-bikes – at the time, for nothing more heinous than what she regarded as the misuse of a tombstone.' The Bishop gave a grim smile before continuing. 'Appropriate really for a nun to be involved. Dr Picton was not only the church organist. He was also one of the convent beneficiaries.'

'Convent beneficiary? What's that mean? A licence for fun and games with the novices?' asked Treasure facetiously, moving to an armchair.

'It means there's a vacancy that I'd dearly like you to fill. Unfortunately, the appointment isn't exactly in my gift, though I have some influence in the matter.'

'I see,' said Treasure guardedly. 'Well, devoted as I am to you and the Church of England, John, I'm not sure I could justify the time to be a trustee, if that's what it is, of a bankrupt convent, even one near Hardy country. It *is* bankrupt, I suppose?'

'I said beneficiary not trustee, Mark, and I meant beneficiary, though there aren't any novices I'm afraid,' replied the Bishop, leaning forward. 'As for the convent being bankrupt, I'd assess the value of its assets at around eleven million pounds. Unfortunately there are only three nuns left, all in their late eighties. When they expire—'

'You did mean eleven *million*?' Treasure interrupted. 'How did that happen?'

'Not through the nuns keeping battery chickens, that's for sure,' said Molly. 'Perhaps they distil strong liquor?'

The Bishop smiled. 'Not a bad guess, Molly. Perhaps if I could explain?'

'I can't wait,' said Treasure.

'First, you need to remember that the Church of England reintroduced religious sisterhoods in the middle of the last century,' the Bishop began. 'There hadn't been any since the Reformation, of course. In the eighteen-forties a number of concerned High-Churchmen, as well as politicians, oh, and the estimable Florence Nightingale, all saw the need for Anglican nuns at around the same time. Frankly, for a mixture of social as well as religious reasons.'

'I suppose because in those days,' Molly put in thoughtfully, 'girls from pious middle-class families who didn't get married would have had nothing useful to do. And probably no chance of ever becoming independent.'

'They could become governesses, but that was about it, unless they converted to Roman Catholicism and joined one of their convents, which quite a few women were doing,' said Larpin with a nod. 'The first of our sisterhoods was started in Park Village, London, in 1845, followed by one in Devonport three years later. Dr Pusey, the Tractarian, was involved with both, strongly supported, incidentally, by William Ewart Gladstone. Well, despite very heavy opposition, claims of popery, that kind of thing, the movement survived, though only just in some areas. The sisters earned a lot of respect for the work they did during the cholera epidemics, and as Nightingale nurses in the Crimean War. In any event, by 1875 there were more than a thousand Church of England nuns.'

'In many different sisterhoods, with different names?' asked Molly.

'That's right. At the start, the convents were all single parish initiatives, and some have stayed that way. Individual houses, societies as they're called, supported by the contributions of local well-wishers.'

'You mean by endowments from early well-wishers long since dead,' said Treasure slowly, and beginning to understand where the eleven millions might come in.

'That's right, Mark. Which brings me to my point. The Society of Blessed Mary Magdalene was founded at Saint Timothy's Church, Chiversley, in 1850 by the then vicar. At first they were a small community living in a house in the High Street and ministering to the sick and poor of the town. Two years later, a convent was built for them on land next to the church and paid for out of public subscription, though the bulk of the money came from one source, the Utteridge family.'

'Utteridge, the Chiversley brewers?' said Treasure with a lift of one eyebrow.

'Yes. So, you see, Molly wasn't far out in her guess. Daniel Utteridge, the Chairman at the time, put up substantial money, for a substantial purpose. He wanted the convent to be a convalescent and rehabilitation home for young women driven to drink, or prostitution, or both.'

'An early exercise in public relations by Utteridge Ales.' This was Treasure again.

'That's one way of judging it I suppose.' The inflexion in the Bishop's voice implied it might even be his own judgement. 'Certainly local contemporary opinion suggested that it helped earn Daniel a peerage. A barony. He became Lord Chiversley. Gladstone was Prime Minister at the time.'

'Gladstone had a fixation about fallen women, of course,' Molly commented a touch dryly. 'And the enterprise flourished?'

'Indeed it did, unlike the Chiversley title. That hasn't been used since Daniel died in 1887. He had no male heir. Six daughters, but no male relative anywhere, not at the time or since, so far as anyone knows. Three of the daughters married. The other three became sisters at the convent.' Larpin paused. 'And that was something which had a profound effect on the way Daniel disposed of his estate. He owned all the shares in Utteridge Ales, which was a private company.'

'Still is,' said Treasure, informed and interested.

'Quite. Well, after providing for the married daughters, he left fifty-one per cent of the brewery shares in a discretionary trust to support the convent.'

'A controlling interest. But with strings? Conditions?' Treasure questioned, warming to the subject.

'That's right. Daniel was concerned about two things. First, the possibility that opposition to nunneries could resurface, forcing their closure. It was still a bit touch and go for them in those days. Protestant prejudice and pressure were very strong. Secondly, like a lot of High-Churchmen, Daniel was afraid the then Ecclesiastical Commissioners for England might eventually be authorised by Parliament to take over all local church endowments.'

'To set up a common central fund for paying the clergy,' Treasure nodded as he spoke.

'There was strong talk of such a measure the year before Daniel died.'

Treasure stroked his chin. 'So, in the first place, Daniel was determined to leave the Chiversley nunnery with much more than enough resources to survive, even if others were closed.'

'Exactly.'

'Of course, he was also looking after the future well-being of three of his daughters,' Treasure construed. 'Then, in the second place, he fixed up the trust fund in a legal way that made it safe from the predatory Ecclesiastical Commissioners.'

'Right again. Instead of having say three trustees, and the convent as the sole beneficiary, he had one professional trustee, who was his lawyer, and three honest gentlemen as beneficiaries. The convent didn't officially come into it at all by name.'

'All clever stuff,' commented the banker with an appreciative smile.

'I don't understand,' said Molly, pulling a face.

'Quite simple really,' said her husband. 'The three honest gents were the people who in the normal way would have been unpaid trustees. It would have been understood, of course, that as beneficiaries they'd employ the trust capital and income wholly for the benefit of the convent, not themselves. That way, if church endowments were taken over by the Commissioners, the assets in the Utteridge trust would be safe. That's because, on the face of it, it wasn't a church endowment at all.'

'Well done, Mark. That's exactly what Daniel arranged,' the Bishop agreed.

'The idea's been used again since,' the banker responded with a shrug. 'To protect church endowments for broadly the same reasons.'

'Let's be clear,' said Molly, because as yet she wasn't. 'You mean these three beneficiaries were exactly that? They owned all the assets of the trust, the income—'

'And the capital,' her husband put in, looking at the Bishop for confirmation. 'That's why it was a discretionary trust.'

'So what was to stop them taking everything for themselves?'

'Nothing, except their innate honesty,' said Larpin. 'And that's applied to the succession of beneficiaries who've followed the original ones over the years.'

Molly sighed. 'How very refreshing. To know there are enough honest people left to work such schemes.'

'It's not all that exceptional,' offered Treasure with some brusqueness. 'Thousands of lawyers and accountants have to apply the same degree of integrity. Daily. Handling clients' money. It's their way of life.'

'You forgot to mention bankers, darling,' said Molly archly. 'Anyway, a dishonest lawyer only gets away with cheating a client so long as he's not rumbled.' She touched the gold bracelet on her wrist. 'It seems to me the Utteridge beneficiaries could help themselves to the money quite openly if they chose. That's the difference. And can I have a little more wine, please?' She held up her glass.

'No one would ever forgive them if they did help themselves, of course,' said the Bishop. 'And they'd have to do it together, too. The trust deed prevents them from acting individually.'

'That's sensible,' said Treasure, while refilling Molly's glass. 'Anyway, Dr Picton was one of these honest beneficiaries, and you want me to take his place, John? Except you said the job isn't in your gift?'

'Quite. The beneficiaries appoint each other, but new ones have to be approved by the vicar of Saint Timothy's.'

'Over whom you have some influence, naturally.'

'And, as it happens, over one of the two existing beneficiaries. The other to a lesser degree,' the Bishop had finished on a less confident note.

'And you think the beneficiaries and the vicar would approve of me? But why choose me in the first place? A local man would be handier. Are the present beneficiaries local?'

'Broadly so, yes. One owns and runs the local prep school. The other's a woman.'

'Glad to hear it,' said Molly. 'What's she do?'

'She's a resident lecturer at Wessex University, but with a house in Chiversley.'

'So they're both academics?'

'Yes, as it happens. Like Picton, they've both made admirable stewards for the convent in recent years. In its declining years, I'm afraid.' The Bishop paused briefly, drawing the long fingers of one hand across his forehead. 'But sadly, the three beneficiaries hadn't been able to agree about what should happen to the trust assets when the nuns are no more. And up to now, the two remaining beneficiaries haven't been able to agree either on a suitable replacement for Dr Picton.'

'And I'm supposed—'

'Mark, it's vital we bring in a top money man. Someone the others will respect; who'll take practical measures, cutting out the wishy-washy thinking that's been going on about the future. I've told you, there are only three very old nuns left.'

'And with no fresh recruits – postulants are they called?' said Molly, 'the Society of Saint Mary Magdalene is really coming to an end?'

'I'm afraid its effective work stopped some years ago,' the Bishop replied. 'So the income or the assets have to be re-channelled. We need someone to give clear, sound guidance on that.'

Treasure sniffed. With so much at stake, he was irreverently glad they weren't leaving it entirely to prayer. 'I'll meet the two beneficiaries when I'm in Chiversley,' he offered. 'And the vicar. And the solicitor who runs the trust. Let's not make any decisions until after that.'

'Agreed, Mark. Thank you,' Larpin put in promptly and looking unduly satisfied.

'There's no firm promise, and I just hope it won't kill off too much of our fishing time,' Treasure added ruefully.

'I'm sure it won't do that,' replied the bishop, quite accurately as it later proved.

It was nothing so trivial as fishing time that was killed off during Treasure's visit to Chiversley.

Chapter Three

Chiversley stands on the edge of a high plateau with spectacular views to the south over the Vale of Wibble.

The High Street, not long since refurbished to picture post-card standard, is the spine of the place. Looking west to east, it emerges from beyond the already noted church, passes the islanded, lilac-stoned Town Hall halfway along, and disappears around a right-hand bend in front of the Feathers Hotel. This last, a pretty, authentic Elizabethan relic – whitewashed rubble walls bulging between exposed black beams – enjoys multi-star guide-book ratings. It has crooked gables to all aspects, upper storeys that jetty drunkenly over the lower one, a genuine inside coaching yard approached via a narrow, low and equally genuine coaching arch – and a 'No Coaches' sign outside that any resur-rected Elizabethan would thus find curious if not inexplicable.

About a third of the shops in the High Street sell antiques. All the others, including those that are branches of usually instantly identifiable national chains, have been made to adopt fascias that eschew brashness: even the McDonalds is sometimes mistaken for a Scottish tea shop. It was in the late 1960s that Tudor and Georgian Chiversley was rejuvenated (and in large part rebuilt), making up for a century or so of civic neglect. Since then it has enjoyed increasing popularity as an overnight or longer stop for mostly well-heeled tourists. The Feathers is merely the priciest of four superior hotels in the town.

Nothing much of note happens beyond the Feathers at the eastern end of the High Street, except for Flax's School and the brewery, both Victorian and of no particular architectural significance. At the other end, after the church car park, the street becomes Shaftsborne Road. To the north the ground falls away gradually, the old stone houses in the side streets giving way fairly soon to more modest brick villas and 'semis', with building development stopping in front of a narrow belt of preserved woodland. To the south the hillside dips sharply down to the banks of the clear and shallow River Wibble crossed below the town by a stone, low-parapeted bridge. The bridge, like the Town Hall, is hopefully attributed to the seemingly indefatigable Inigo Jones.

Steep Street, the most substantial thoroughfare to the south, climbs up from the bridge to join the High Street. Its right side is lined with little shops, while on the left is a grassy bank, with trees and footpaths reaching up to the retaining wall of the terraced churchyard, the whole area at the moment alive with late daffodils in bloom.

It was at the top of Steep Street that Mark Treasure, warm from exertion, paused to admire his first uninterrupted view of St Timothy's Church.

It was nine-thirty in the morning on Friday the third of May, with buds fairly popping in the brilliant sunshine after two days of rain. The banker had motored down very late on the previous evening, but a day earlier than he had been expected. Since Molly had been collected by a studio chauffeur just before dawn, the two had barely communicated since Treasure's arrival, except over the vexed question of the fishing. Molly had discovered that the fishing beat at the bottom of the garden was permanently leased to an outsider from Tuesdays to Fridays inclusive. Her disappointed husband had thought about golf, but Bishop John Larpin had not been expecting him, and was engaged for the whole day. So more through elimination than desire he had set off on foot to see the town, after making arrangements by telephone to meet three of its more prominent inhabitants.

Treasure's first appointment was with the vicar, Canon Miles Stonning, but not for another half an hour. Now he turned into the churchyard intending to inspect the church exterior more closely – only he very nearly fell over a black bundle after opening the lichgate. And then the bundle turned out to be a body – or more accurately the rear end of one.

'I beg your pardon,' said Treasure. 'Can I help?'

'So kind, yes. I seem to have mislaid a letter,' answered

Sister Mary Maud in a tiny voice and some distress, from a kneeling position behind the gate. She had screwed her neck round awkwardly to speak. Now she sat back on her heels with a sigh, brandishing her ancient pocket torch, a curious accoutrement for such a bright day. 'I'm certain I had it with me. Before I left the convent.'

'Let me help you up.'

'Oh, I can manage that. Plenty of practice.' She gave a brief, winsome smile and stayed where she was. The elderly face, though itself pale, still contrasted starkly with the white linen wimple that framed it under the black veil. The grey eyes blinked several times behind the old-fashioned glasses before Sister Mary Maud dived forward again, terrier like, to re-examine the recess behind the gatepost, her torch to the fore. 'I thought it might have dropped in there when I opened the catch,' came the muffled words. 'There's a gap. The catch was a little stiff. Difficult to open.'

'Then let me get in and have a look.'

This time the Sister took the proffered hand absently but without cavil. Crookedly she got to her feet, but the grip was released promptly with a shy look and backward movement as soon as she was upright. She was a diminutive figure against Treasure's six feet.

'Well, there's definitely nothing here,' said the banker shortly after looking on both sides of the gate. 'Did you come through the church?'

'No, round it. By the tower. The convent's on the other side. Sister Patricia will be upset at my losing her letter. It was so foolish of me.' The speaker seemed almost to be on the brink of tears and communing as much with herself as with the stranger.

'Then I'm sure we'll find it.'

'You see, the ground is so wet still. It could get very damp during the day.'

'The weather, you mean?' He looked at the cloudless blue sky. 'I rather gathered from the forecast—'

'The letter. Wherever it's fallen. Envelopes aren't one bit waterproof. They don't care for damp. Not at all.'

'Quite. Does your . . . your habit have a lot of pockets?'

He looked her up and down gravely, like a royal personage inspecting a very small guardsman.

'Not many pockets. I'm sure the letter's not in any of them. I've looked already.' She was pulling the outer garment about quite roughly and vigorously as she spoke, searching its folds, and twice exposing pale bare ankles above the sandals. She even shook herself and twice jumped up and down. Then a slightly ashamed expression suffused the elderly face, as if she were conscious of having gone too far in these overzealous and not wholly decorous demonstrations. The head was lowered modestly, the hands joined together in disciplined composure. The expression, what could be seen of it, was still miserable.

'Come on, Sister, let's retrace your steps,' said Treasure cheerfully.

A few minutes later the pair had reached the Gothic-style porch of the convent – a two-storey building with a half basement, and fashioned in a shallow U-shape. This main entrance was in the farthest of the two protruding end wings. Sister Mary Maud had led the way to it from a branch of the churchyard path and across the wide gravel driveway fronting the building. There was another, older building in a plain Georgian style to the right of the convent, nearer the main road, and served by the same driveway. Treasure assumed this to be the vicarage.

'Since we've had no luck so far, do you think you could have left the letter inside?' the banker asked, aware of his companion's increasing despair. She had hardly uttered a word since leaving the gate, while darting ahead to examine all likely and as many unlikely repositories for dropped envelopes.

'I'm sure I had it with me. I took it from the hall table,' Sister Mary Maud replied, with, for the first time, a hint of doubt in the tone.

Treasure levered open the heavy door with a twist of the wrought iron ring-handle. Inside it was much as he had expected – a wide hall with dark panelling, a heavy oak table in the centre, shining coloured floor tiles, a wall crucifix, and a melded scent of holiness and furniture polish. There was also a somewhat larger nun than the one he was with. She was standing before the table, fanning herself with an envelope in an overly deliberate manner.

'Ah, there you are Sister. We've been expecting your return,' said the new nun who was altogether a more formidable figure than her colleague, quite as old, but with a commanding, undulating voice, the upright bearing of a superannuated games mistress, and the kind of expression Queen Victoria probably used for putting subjects at their ease, but not too much at their ease. 'In your hurry to get to the post you forgot to take the letter.' She accompanied this richly tremoloed, near admonition with a frosty smile. The alert Sealyham terrier sitting beside her shuffled on its bottom and fixed Treasure with as stern a look as any Sealyham can manage, head inclined to the right.

'Oh dear. Thank you, Reverend Mother. I'm so sorry.' Sister Mary Maud had not questioned her mistake. She turned to Treasure. 'I'm so sorry Mr . . . er . . . to have wasted your time.'

'Not a bit. I'm only glad the mystery's solved.' He beamed at both nuns. 'What a fine building this is. Bishop Larpin told me it's by G. E. Street.'

'That's correct. He designed it in 1852. You know the Bishop well?' asked the Reverend Mother, regarding him steadily but not yet quite benignly. Treasure wondered idly if her evident caution was because Sister Mary Maud was in the habit of bringing in strange men.

The still interested dog bent its head to the left.

'The Bishop and I are old friends. I should have introduced myself. My name's Mark Treasure.'

Sister Mary Maud spontaneously clapped her hands together in delight, then, after a swift glance at her superior, just as quickly subsided into an overly demure pose, her cheeks reddening guiltily.

The Reverend Mother this time vouchsafed a nearly indulgent smile. She nodded slowly at the visitor: it was the gesture that dignitaries employ to avoid tiresome handshaking without giving offence. 'How do you do, Mr Treasure. Your charming wife took tea with us yesterday.'

The Sealyham marked the general relaxation by getting up and sniffing around the table end.

'It was such a treat,' put in Sister Mary Maud, confidence regained. 'It was raining, you see? They couldn't make the film in the rain. Whoops. Naughty Lazarus.' She had suddenly dived forward, scooping up the terrier that had lifted a rear paw prior to anointing the table leg. The offending but equally offended animal stared indignantly at Sister Mary Maud – eyes level with hers, neck drawn back – as she swept it past Treasure and unceremoniously bundled it out through the front door.

'Thank you Sister. My dog is not yet house trained,' said the Reverend Mother, wooden faced. Despite her comment, Lazarus looked fairly mature if not actually elderly.

'My wife didn't tell me she'd been here,' said Treasure. 'We've hardly had time to talk since I arrived last night. She wanted to go to bed almost at once,' he said, then wondered if the words might be begging a wrong interpretation. 'She needed to get to sleep early. Has to leave at the crack every morning. If they're filming. It was a fine day for filming today,' he ended lamely, and irritated with himself that this authoritative lady was prompting him to talk drivel.

'We sorely miss Dr Picton,' said the Reverend Mother, abruptly changing the subject, and allowing a pause for thought before continuing. 'There should be three beneficiaries of the Utteridge trust, of course. Would you care to see round the convent, Mr Treasure? We could begin upstairs.'

In those few short sentences the speaker had shown that she was aware of Treasure's interest and the reason for it, and in the probable need for him to assess the building and the people who lived in it – and all this without betraying any confidence placed in her that might or might not have been placed in him too. But just as clearly, her attitude implied, the business of character assessment was a focus for both sides. Molly had evidently passed muster. His gender apart, Treasure was not yet sure he would have qualified as a candidate for enrolment in the Society of Blessed Mary Magdalene.

He followed the Reverend Mother up the stone steps. Sister Mary Maud had already hurried ahead of them.

The upper floor, now uninhabited, had once been the dormitory for a great many residents, and was largely divided into individual cubicles. Each cubicle had its own dormer window and partitioning from shoulder down to ankle height with a door to match. To Treasure, traversing the broad corridors down the

30

centre, the arrangements were more reminiscent of stables than bedrooms.

While most of the cubicles were empty of furniture, from time to time the party came upon islanded stores of single iron bedsteads, narrow wardrobes, wooden washstands, enamelled basins and buckets, and, at one point, two lonely china chamber pots. The bathrooms and lavatories were not exhibited to the visitor, but it seemed that there could be very few of them.

'In the days when we were fully staffed there were forty sisters, a varying number of novitiates, and up to a hundred young women patients,' the Reverend Mother recounted as they went.

'Patients?' Treasure queried.

'Alcoholics, drug addicts and women possessed by evil spirits. All redeemable, as our dear Lord taught us,' the Reverend Mother replied earnestly. 'Mary Magdalene is our patron saint, of course,' she then offered in a nearly confidential tone, as though that most celebrated if sometimes misrepresented example of redeemed womanhood was an intimate who might be relied upon for an annual visit, as well as, possibly, for a sizeable donation.

The ground floor, visited next, offered a refectory, kitchens, a library and common rooms, and a chapel in the other end wing. None of these seemed to be much in current use except for the chapel, a corner of the immense kitchen, and an annexe to the refectory.

The chapel was smallish, and though it rose through two storeys, its size seemed the more diminished by heavy Victorian High Church embellishment – wood carving, statuary, gold and brass ornamentation, and a richly canopied altar.

The corridor leading to the chapel contained a number of doors at uniform close intervals. 'The rooms of the sisters who remain,' said the Reverend Mother with a slight indication of her hand as they passed these.

'This one's mine,' said Sister Mary Maud, throwing open the second door and standing beyond it meekly. Throughout the tour her manner had been as frenetic as her superior's had been sedate, her movements matching those of the worker ant she so much resembled in attitude as well as appearance. Usually

31

she had been ahead of her two companions, hooking back doors and clearing passageways. If she hadn't still been tidying away the remains of a broken washstand after the others had passed it, Treasure was quite sure she would never have allowed them next to come upon the chamber pots, an event that had clearly embarrassed Sister Mary Maud although it had failed to register at all with the Reverend Mother.

'How er . . . what a nice view through that window,' Treasure remarked about Sister Mary Maud's room but without moving beyond the threshold. Even from there it was evident that the Sister was gloriously untidy and a hoarder. The small easy chair just inside the door was a mélange of ancient, undiscarded extra cushions pressed tightly together but overflowing at back, front, arms and seat, the variety of worn fabrics melded possibly for years to trace the shape of their owner. Every wall and furniture surface in view was adorned with minor possessions, some religious (like crucifixes and Madonnas), some secular (like several worn copies of the Reader's Digest), some medical (like a bottle of Veno's cough syrup on the chest of drawers), and some edible (like the re-wrapped remains of a Mars bar on the book table by the chair). Only the perfectly made bed was entirely uncluttered, its pristine white sheets symbolically virginal, while the bookrest of the prie-dieu at its foot was overloaded with prayerful volumes, indexed and decorated with a profusion of frayed, bookmark ribbons in liturgical colours, medals dangling from their ends.

'The basement used to house classrooms and workshops,' the Reverend Mother provided later, as the three descended the steps. 'They're seldom used for any purpose now . . .'

'Except for Sister Patricia in the printing room,' put in Sister Mary Maud too quickly. She was only slightly ahead of the others this time.

'Except for Sister Patricia's work,' the Reverend Mother completed portentously.

'You had a printing school?' Treasure enquired.

'It was our earliest and most successful venture into vocational training. Our girls' – the Reverend Mother pronounced the word as 'gels' – 'were taught to do a variety of printing jobs, including the operating of typesetting machinery. Nowadays I believe printing is largely controlled by computers. No doubt many of our old girls will have adapted their skills to fit changing methods,' she continued as they entered a corridor which, whatever its basic dimensions, had been narrowed to allow only single-file progress due to the encroachment of perilously stacked, discarded impedimenta on both sides, including books, pictures, crockery, school desks, blackboards, kitchen utensils, candlesticks, old knitting machines, coal scuttles, a large Christmas crib, and a mounted poster of Elvis Presley. It was evident that whatever had ceased to be useful in most other parts of the convent had been relegated to the basement corridor, and this over a fairly long period.

'We seldom throw things away,' remarked the Reverend Mother unnecessarily as she led Treasure through a doorway on the left, which again had been held open in advance by Sister Mary Maud.

The quite large room they now entered was as neat as the corridor had been chaotic. A good deal of what was in it looked ancient but far from abandoned. Stocks of paper in varying sizes and colours were stored on the wall shelves in clear wrappings, as were quantities of printed sheets and leaflets. Trays of printing blocks were visible in slatted open cabinets. There was a silk screen printing press, a Monotype machine, a flat-bed printing press, and a steel-topped printer's table. More samples of finished print work were mounted on the walls – including parish magazine covers, posters, bookplates, bookmarkers, visiting cards and a range of private stationery.

And with her back to the middle one of three basement windows sat a studious nun, tall but stooping, wearing owlish glasses and working with a watercolour brush at an inclined draughtsman's desk. She had not been aware of the others' entry until Sister Mary Maud was standing beside her.

'Sister Patricia,' said the Reverend Mother, loud enough to suggest that the other was very deaf, 'this is Mr Treasure come to visit us.'

'His wife came yesterday,' said Sister Patricia, even before she looked up to greet Treasure with an unruffled stare. The voice was girlishly high but cracked, the long face dried and bloodless like parchment. When she removed her glasses Treasure thought he could detect pain in the eyes.

'You do the designing as well as the printing, Sister?' he asked, studying the biblical illustration she was doing.

'I used to. There's not much print work now,' she answered. 'This one won't be printed here. It's for a bookplate. To go in confirmation presents.'

'Sister Patricia's artwork is in great demand,' supplied Sister Mary Maud proudly.

'Because it costs nothing, I expect,' the other commented without emotion.

'Sister Patricia was in charge of our printing school. There was a studio next door,' said the Reverend Mother on full volume still, except Sister Patricia seemed to be registering well enough what the others had said in normal tones. 'I try to persuade her to abandon this room and work from the ground floor. It would be so much more . . . convenient for her.'

Treasure's eyes followed the speaker's to the unmatched pair of walking sticks leaning against Sister Patricia's desk.

Sister Patricia's gaze had done the same. 'Reverend Mother means that one day I'll get down here but won't be able to get back up again,' she commented. 'That'll be a sign to stop. Yes.' She paused reflectively, but without conceding anything to the autocratic Reverend Mother's undisguised view that she should vacate the place before then. 'I like working in this room. I've been doing it for seventy years,' she completed in an even higher register than before.

'Everything here is in such apple pie order,' remarked Treasure.

'It must all be kept dusted, and the machines in working order, you see?' said Sister Patricia solemnly. 'In case we ever have to sell any of it.'

'To make ends meet,' Sister Mary Maud added with a worried frown.

'It's why we throw nothing away,' completed the Reverend Mother, just as earnestly as the others. 'We never know when we may be sorely in need.'

Chapter Four

Nine miles to the west of Chiversley, the shirt-sleeved Detective Constable Steven Rawlins got up from his chair, smoothed down his hair, straightened his tie, and moved across the three feet that separated his desk from that of his immediate superior. He then coughed politely. He could just as well have spoken his piece from where he'd been sitting, in the CID outer office on the first floor of the Shaftsborne Police Station, except there was an essential difference in his mind between having a friendly conversation with Detective Sergeant Hardacre and reporting progress to him on an official assignment.

Rawlins, who was twenty-five, had not long been transferred from the uniformed branch. He wanted the switch to be permanent, which is why he did everything by the book – or by even a bit more than the book. A local West Countryman with a polytechnic degree in social sciences, he was looking for promotion and the commendations that would lead to it.

'I'm doing the follow-up on that fax from the Met Fraud Squad, Sergeant,' he said. 'I called them, like you said.'

'Oh yeah? Yeah, I heard you, yesterday. Sort of.' DS Hardacre, a fast-talking Yorkshireman married to a local girl, looked up from the typewriter he was using, then looked up a bit higher because Rawlins was quite tall and because the deeply preoccupied Sergeant had imagined the other man had still been sitting at his desk.

The plumpish, ginger-haired Hardacre, also in shirtsleeves but tieless, leaned back in his chair, yawned, stretched his arms above his head, wiggling the wrists and exercising the fingers, before diving forward eagerly to sift through the paper on his desk in search of his cigarette packet. For the previous half-hour he had been composing a summary report on a well-planned break-in at a large electrical store in the town. The burglary had happened two nights before. He was a conscientious detective, but he hated writing reports, especially ones about professionally executed felonies that were destined, like the events they recorded, to be shelved quite soon and to be forgotten entirely after a further decent interval. The chances of the store burglars ever being apprehended he considered as remote as those of the Shaftsborne Football Club winning the Cup Final, or even getting back into the Fourth Division come to that – which was one of the reasons why he still supported Leeds United.

'About stamps wasn't it?' Hardacre went on, his lighting of an untipped, high tar cigarette not at all affecting his low sense of guilt, despite the promises to his wife about his smoking. 'So did the Metropolitan Police give an excuse? Tell us why we got to waste time on bloody stamp collections? Earn public displeasure by interfering with a respected local trader? A widow at that? Did you tell 'em?' He inhaled deeply.

'Yes, Sergeant. The investigating officer I spoke to was a woman.'

'What's that got to do with it? No sense of feminine camaraderie you mean?' Hardacre exhaled and scratched his stomach, an expression of total contentment on his chubby face. For the next minute or so he could enjoy his cigarette, and a justified respite from a purposeless chore, while Rawlins unburdened on a topic that offered more nourishment than the list of camcorder serial numbers he'd been working on. 'Mark you, they got some good-looking birds in the Met,' he added. 'This one sound classy? Up your street? Up to your intellectual standards?' This last was a good-humoured reference to Rawlins' higher education. The Sergeant had left school at seventeen, and had never regretted it. Ten years older than the Constable, he was neither envious of others nor particularly ambitious.

'She sounded all right. Difficult to tell on the telephone.' Rawlins replied indulgently. 'They're following up on a list of addresses they got from a North London stamp dealer called Hechler. He's out on bail pending trial.'

36

'What's he done? Been passing counterfeit Green Shield Stamps?'

'Worse than that. Most of his business is through the mail. A lot of it with customers abroad. It's alleged he's been selling fakes. His defence is he mostly gets stamps on definite requests from customers. Accepts merchandise in good faith from other dealers.'

'Specialist dealers, of course?'

'That's right, Sergeant. With more knowledge than he's got, he says. So he's been going on their word.'

'He'll want luck and a following wind to get by on that for starters. Still.' Hardacre sniffed. 'Doesn't sound like the Met has a lot on its plate does it? Not if they're chasing after small fry like that. They've a nerve asking other forces to do the leg work, too.'

'There's more to it than that, though. Some of the stamps involved are pretty pricey.' Rawlins placed one of the typed sheets he'd had in his hand on the keyboard in front of Hardacre. 'It looks as though he's made more than two million quid passing off counterfeits. That's just in the last three years.'

'Two million? That's a tidy lot of brass.' Hardacre glanced down the list. 'I didn't think the stamp trade still generated money like that, did you? Supposed to have been on the rocks for the last decade, let alone the last three years.'

'I thought the same till now. And the two million only covers Hechler's crook transactions reported so far. There's more coming in since he's been arrested.'

'And they want to know if old Mrs Garnet's tied up with him in some way?'

Florence Garnet carried on her recently deceased husband's second-hand bookshop and philately business in a Shaftsborne side-street. The fax from London had mentioned her by name. Hardacre had noticed it when Detective Inspector Lodger had delegated it to him for action, and during the few seconds it had taken him to decide to pass it on to Rawlins. He knew the shop well enough because he was a science fiction addict and bought old paperbacks there.

'Her address is in his book, Sergeant.'

'I'll bet Stanley Gibbons Limited is too, but no one's suspecting them of anything.' For a moment he contemplated the sharp Gothic arch of the north-facing window, the only one in the room and the reason why Shaftsborne CID officers had to go out to see the sun – a fact their uniformed colleagues said was the best incentive they had for getting up off their bottoms. Even so, except for Hardacre and Rawlings, the floor was empty at the moment, and that included the Detective Inspector's office behind the half-glazed partition. DI Lodger was appearing in court this morning, and the other two DCs on the watch were in the town following up cases. 'And Mrs Garnet isn't much of a stamp specialist. So far as I can see she doesn't do much more than flog cheap assorted stamp packs for kids,' the Sergeant completed.

Rawlins nodded. 'That and a trade in what they call educational facsimiles. Reproductions of rare stamps marked somewhere to show what they are. Museums and schools buy them. Her husband was well known in the business for that. She's carried it on, but in a very small way.'

'So has someone reported Hechler for selling an expensive fake he's supposed to have got from Mrs Garnet?'

'Not an expensive fake. A private edition specimen, according to her. An 1853 Prince James Island twopenny blue. She told me when I went there this morning. The genuine article's very rare. Less than five thousand issued. It was to do with the island Governor turning down the design. Something like that. She wasn't too clear. Anyway, only a few hundred of the stamps are known to have survived. Hechler sold this one to an American customer who'd ordered it. For fifty-five thousand dollars.'

'And how much did Mrs Garnet get?'

'Ten pounds plus VAT and postage. She showed me her sales ledger. Very meticulous she is.'

'Ten quid? You're joking.'

'For a facsimile.'

'So how does Hechler explain the price he got?'

'He says Mrs Garnet doesn't know the value of her stock.'

'And he's never bothered telling her?'

'Something like that. He says philately's a cut-throat business these days. Like the art and antique markets. Everybody's looking for bargains.'

'And doesn't let on to the vendor if they get one.' With half-closed eyes, Hardacre was now inhaling from the butt of his cigarette, holding it between the tip of his thumb and his first two fingers, which prompted his little finger to poise genteelly in the air. 'That's credible enough, I suppose.'

'Accepted trade practice, he says.'

'And what about Mrs Garnet being one of his specialist suppliers? With more knowledge than him? That's a load of cobblers in her case. Has to be. You say she knows the stamp wasn't genuine 1853?'

Rawlins scratched the back of his neck, moving his balance to the other leg. 'She thought it wasn't. Not the real thing. When she sold it. Anyway, it had facsimile printed on it. She says if Hechler got à lot of money for it, his customer's bonkers. Or it's a different stamp.'

'Ah, well that's always possible.' He ground out the cigarette in the china ashtray. 'How did Mrs Garnet come by this stamp? If it's hers?'

'From her husband's stock. Hechler ordered it from her four months ago.'

'So he knew where to apply? Has she got more?' The Sergeant's watery eyes had a speculative look in them.

'Not in stock. It's the only Prince James Island she had. She remembers seeing others, when her husband was alive.'

'Does she know how much he got for them?'

The constable hesitated. 'She's not sure. Or she's not telling. Seems he didn't keep ledgers as carefully as she does.'

'Seems he may have been charging more too?' The sergeant tapped the side of his nose. 'So is she replenishing this stock?'

'She was cagey about that.'

'But you asked where she ordered from? One source was it?'

'Yes. The Prince James Island stamps and a lot of the other facsimiles come from Chiversley.'

'Oh aye?' Hardacre frowned. 'Come to think, there's a stamp dealer there in Steep Street. I've passed it.'

'Not from a stamp dealer, Sergeant. Mrs Garnet says from Saint Timothy's Convent.'

The Sergeant gave a tolerant smile. 'Go on. She was pulling your leg, lad.'

* * *

'There was a lady for you on the phone, Graham. While you were in the loo,' said Daphne Rode, the big girl who did copy-typing and supervised the semi-automatic switchboard at the Chiversley branch of the Southern Bank. Her tone, like her look, had been a touch severe, suggesting Graham Brown had been too long at his ablutions.

'I've been upstairs in Foreign Exchange,' he invented boldly and without breaking his stride as he crossed the bank's busy general office behind the line of tellers at their windows. In fact he had thought about going the further half flight up to the Foreign Exchange Department after he'd left the men's room which was between floors. That he hadn't actually done so was less important in his estimation than the need to stop Daphne from speaking out of turn. He made for his desk with its waist-high moveable partitioning on all sides except the front, which gave him more status than privacy.

'You never said,' called Daphne after him. 'Anyway, the lady couldn't wait. I said you'd ring back. I didn't know the caller. Church business is it?'

'You've put the number on my desk have you?' he responded stiffly, without answering the question. He tried ineffectively to pull on his beard which was neither long enough nor really strong enough for the purpose.

' 'Course I have.' Daphne went back to her word processing.

Brown frowned. He supposed it might have been Mrs Stonning, the Canon's wife, except Daphne knew Mrs Stonning and would have said.

As the recently promoted second Assistant Manager at the biggest bank in the town, Brown was overly anxious to underline his new position, especially with the less hierarchically conscious members of staff – such as Daphne: for instance, he had cautioned her twice already about not addressing him by his first name in office hours. Not that he ever saw Daphne out of office hours. As Honorary Treasurer of St Timothy's (and still its only regular male chorister), until recently he had commanded far more respect from members of the church congregation than he had from employees at the bank. That situation should now alter. There should be a levelling up. His mother was always saying as much – and she was right.

He looked at the name and number on the message slip. Then he looked sharply across at Daphne, who was affecting to be busy at her work. He wondered how she could possibly have known the call had been about church and not bank business. He studied the slip again. Of course, there was no way Daphne could have known. She was just stirring things up.

Some years back, a previous manager at the bank had admonished Brown several times in front of other employees for spending too much of the bank's time on church affairs, particularly as St Timothy's account was lodged at another bank. The manager had been a confessed atheist, something Brown (and his mother) had been sure had been behind the criticism. Since that time – and under the present, nominally Church of England manager – Brown had succeeded in having all St Timothy's financial business transferred to the Southern, including the convent's quite profitable current account. So nowadays there should have been no question of anyone begrudging him the small amount of office time he gave to church business – compared to the hours of his own time which in his private estimation he unselfishly applied in the same cause. Even so, Brown was still uncomfortable about what he was sure had been behind Daphne's snide question.

He began dialling the Shaftsborne number, but was still undetermined about doing it because he felt that perhaps he should make the call at lunchtime, from a pay-phone in the town. The matter was church business all right, except it wasn't really the sort of church business the bank was involved in. Not strictly. It was a long time before lunch, of course. The caller might ring back here herself if it was urgent, and he didn't want to risk having nosey Daphne intercept the call again. So after making the conscious decision to complete the dialling it irritated him to find that the line was engaged.

He replaced the phone. It rang almost immediately. He looked across the room at Daphne who nodded at him knowingly. She had been holding the incoming call for him.

'Hello. Graham Brown speaking.'

'Hello darling. You sound marvellously managerial,' purred a woman's voice. It had a hint of a foreign accent – like Ingrid

41

Bergman's. 'Am I interrupting anything important? Are you making huge financial decisions?'

'Oh . . . Oh, hello Christine,' he answered breathily, while fighting to remain articulate. He felt his face redden and covered it with a hand to his forehead because Daphne was almost sure to be looking. 'How . . . how nice of you to call. Yes.' He crossed and uncrossed his legs, kicking one of his ankles painfully in the process. Tortoise-like, his neck sank below his collar as he crouched over the telephone wishing he could crawl right into it. 'I'm not making decisions. No. Not at the moment. A-huh. A-huh.' The guffaws were inane, but he couldn't help that – nor the way his free hand was now clawing at his cheeks.

No other woman he had ever known (not even his mother) called him darling – he wasn't the darling type, although he wished he were. No other woman he had ever known was as startlingly beautiful as this one – and intelligent, and lusted after by every man who set eyes on her. To be seen with her was the most wonderful boost to his ego, even though it meant his being on edge the whole time. He still hadn't got over the fact that she cared for him at all, let alone deeply.

'You here for the week-end, then?' he asked, then bit his teeth together hard enough to break a filling.

'For more than the week-end, lover. And dying to see you. What about lunch today? Are you free?'

'Yes. I think so.' His hand was now furiously clenching and unclenching the beard. 'I could—'

'Good. Nothing fancy. At the Feathers. In the bar,' she interrupted.

'That's fine.' The Feathers was fancy enough – and pricey. They only ever met at her instigation, and usually at short notice to fit her plans, as now. Well, she wasn't in Chiversley that often, snatching time out of her busy, glamorous life he persuaded himself, though of course she hadn't been quite so busy these last two years. 'Could we meet early, at—'

'There'll be someone there we both want to meet,' she broke in again.

'Who?' He wished now he'd put on his other suit this morning.

'Your rival, darling.'

'My rival?' he exclaimed, too loudly. He swallowed, glancing around at the people working nearest him – and at big Daphne who might be listening in, or lip-reading. His nervous misgivings often generated bizarre hypotheses – Daphne could no more lip-read than speak Hindustani. 'A friend of yours, you mean?' he almost whispered into the phone.

'No, silly. Not that sort of rival. Not for my affections. A rival as a convent beneficiary. Mark Treasure. He's a banker too. The one Uncle Miles and the Bishop want to have elected. He's having lunch with Charles.'

'Oh.' He wasn't at all sure that this was anyone he wanted to meet – although he was very keen to be nominated himself as a beneficiary: his mother was keen for him too. It was Christine who had encouraged him, saying she'd get Sir Lucius Bittern to support him.

'See you in the bar at one-thirty, then. I can't do it before. Bye.' She rang off.

The nervous excitement of meeting Christine, and having to rearrange the time of his lunch break, led to his overlooking a lot of things during the rest of the morning – including ringing back Mrs Garnet in Shaftsborne.

Chapter Five

Treasure had still been pondering the nuns' touching concern for thrift as he let himself out of the convent. Lazarus, the terrier, had been waiting for the door to open and had made a sedate, unhurried progress back inside. While he was waiting for the dog before closing the door, the banker involuntarily glanced at the address on Sister Patricia's letter which it had now fallen to him to post. Then he strode off toward the church.

'Morning,' called a hearty male voice somewhere to his left. 'You Mark Treasure?'

'Yes, I am.' He stopped so that the mature clergyman, in cassock and biretta, and just appeared from the vicarage, could catch up with him. 'And you'll be Canon Stonning, I expect?'

'Well met, my-my-my dear fellow. Well met,' enthused the Canon as they shook hands. His long, thin V-shaped face was deeply dimpled and wreathed now in smiles, while the bushy eyebrows had risen toward a kind of corrugated forehead. He was rocking his body as he continued: 'Saw you cavorting with Sister Mary Maud earlier.' This remark prompted the speaker literally to half double up with mirth. 'Oh what-what-what a trio they are.' He clapped his hands, then rubbed them together vigorously as though to stop them freezing.

The Canon was a fraction shorter than Treasure, with a figure that, while it still had the foundations of wiriness, was running to a paunch in the middle – a tendency that the exercising gesticulations might well have been designed to counter.

'I just hope I can leap up staircases like Sister Mary Maud when I get to her age,' said Treasure, grinning.

'If you ever get to her age. D'you know she's eighty-eight? The other two are not far off. Offer you coffee, did they?'

'Yes. I refused.'

'That was diplomatic. I always do the same. Except after I've said mass in their chapel. That's on-on-on Saturdays. When I've missed coffee at home. The labourer being worthy of his hire, don't you know?' The clergyman's arms went upwards suddenly, only to come down folded together, elbows pulled well into the chest as their owner led off again briskly toward the church.

'Is the convent coffee that bad?'

'Not quite. But you see, the Reverend Mother disapproves of coffee breaks. Says it-it-it wastes time. Stops her getting on with her work. Hah! Her work, can you credit?'

'She probably spends a lot of time praying.'

'No doubt,' the Canon sounded dubious all the same, while staring at his middle. 'She spends the deuce of a lot of time mending things. Those-those-those habits they wear, for instance. Forever darning and patching them. New ones haven't been bought for donkey's years. I keep telling the Reverend Mother the convent's rolling in money. Plenty on call at the bank. Millions invested. Doesn't register at all. They still use candles for reading. To save electricity. Creates a fire hazard, of course.' He moved a hand to scrape at an egg stain he had spied on the front of his cassock.

'Are the nuns under a vow of poverty, perhaps?'

'Yes. But you-you-you can take that sort of thing too far.' The Canon followed this surprising theological adjudication with a loud sniff. 'I mean their habits are so threadbare they could fall apart any day. And having a bunch of nuns running about in their undies wouldn't be very-very-very seemly would it? Or elevating? Not at their age, anyway. Or-or-or fitting with their vow of purity?' A triumphant nod followed the last comment because the speaker considered it had cancelled out the debatable one on the vow of poverty.

'I said I'd post this.' Treasure waved the envelope.

'That's Sister Mary Maud's job.' The Canon had gone back to swaying his trunk backwards and forwards from the waist as the two moved along, but at a tempo a touch slower than their pacing, like a metronome that needed a wind. He was also still scratching at the egg stain. 'Didn't she object at all?' He wet a finger and studiously applied that to the stain.

'It was Sister Mary Maud who asked me to do it. I think I saw a postbox by the church gate.'

'Mmm, I'll show you before we go inside. Let me see.' He studied the envelope. 'Second class stamp, of course. Typical. Lucky if it gets to . . . Shaftsborne, is it? Yes . . . by tomorrow. Later probably. Still.' He made a punctuating noise with his lips. 'Glad you rang this morning.' They had arranged to meet in the church at ten. It was nearly that now. The Canon had offered a conducted tour. 'John, our Bishop, wanted us to meet as soon as possible. I don't think he knew you'd be here this morning though.'

'I didn't myself till yesterday afternoon. A meeting in Manchester was postponed, so I got a day free unexpectedly.'

'You must be a fearfully busy chap.' The speaker shook his head, then glanced up sharply. 'So, will you be our-our-our third beneficiary?'

'I rather thought that was as much up to you and the present beneficiaries as it is to me.'

The Canon's now re-folded arms hugged his chest while the shoulders rose and fell dramatically. 'Oh, you're the chap we need all right. I'm sure Jill Wader will think so. Met her, have you?'

'No. She's one of the existing beneficiaries? University lecturer?'

'That's right. She says the local candidates are non-starters. Well, of course they are. Even Charles Utteridge-Flax should accept you'd be-be-be heaven sent. If the trust's to continue as it is. Except of course he wants to wind it up.'

'He being the other beneficiary. I'm meeting him later this morning.'

'And we'll all be together tomorrow, of course.'

'Tomorrow?'

'At dinner. At Sir Lucius Bittern's. Chiversley Hall. On the Shaftsborne road. Know it already do you?'

'No. And we aren't dining tomorrow as far as I know.'

46

'Invitation not-not-not reached you yet? It will do. Ours came just now.'

'There was no post—'

'By hand, with apologies for the short notice. No doubt yours will be waiting when you get back. Telephone would have been more practical, but Sheila, that's Lady Bittern, she's a stickler for form. Well, in some ways.' He blew his nose in a red silk handkerchief, then continued. 'All the same, my wife just rang her to say we were on. Only fair to the cook to know the right numbers as soon as possible, don't you agree? Anyhow, that's how I know who else is coming. Hope you and your-your-your famous lady wife can make it.' There was another heave of the shoulders. 'No secret the occasion's in your honour, of course. Better to post that letter now, before I show you the church. Otherwise it might not get to Shaftsborne till after the holiday. The box is out there.'

'Place was originally a Benedictine monastery,' Canon Stonning was elucidating a few minutes later as he and Treasure stood in the nave of St Timothy's. 'Founded by Edgar the Peaceable, King of the Angles, in the year 971. Not much of that church left, I'm afraid, and nothing of the monastery. The site of that was used for the convent though. Quite appropriate really. The original church was dedicated to Saint Mary the Virgin. It was changed to Saint Timothy after the Reformation. Don't know what-what-what good they thought that'd do, I'm sure.'

'And the present church was finished in 1460?'

'Most of it. Nave, tower, north aisle, and Lady Chapel in Ham Hill stone. Golden sort of colour, as you can see. Nice. The fan vaulting is famous, of course. The south aisle and the chapel beyond came later than the rest, in 1544. They're in Portland stone. Same as Saint Paul's Cathedral, but that was more than a century later.'

'And the stone was probably more difficult to bring here inland than it was to take by sea to London,' mused Treasure.

'Quite. But no-no-no expense would have been spared, my dear sir. The south chapel here was more to the glorification of the Bittern family than it was to God. I'll show you.' The

Canon was already off up the centre aisle. He threw out short descriptions of the Elizabethan lectern, the Jacobean pulpit, and the stone rood screen as they went, and with much gesticulation.

'That's the door to the organ loft,' he said, pointing to the right after the two steps into the chancel. 'It was on the spiral staircase behind it that poor Ambrose Picton met his death.'

'I noticed the two youths involved got very light sentences last week.'

'Couple of years each. Rather less than that in one case. Absolute scandal. Deserved to hang. And they say there was a third scoundrel they never found. They-they-they should have been flogged at least.' After delivering this robust, uncompromising conclusion, the Canon genuflected piously before the altar and tabernacle, tipping his biretta. The last action revealed that the hair sprouting below the rim was not matched by any at all on the scalp above it, suggesting that the biretta was used to serve vanity as well as liturgical tradition. The wearer next led Treasure past the choir stalls, then right into the south chapel.

'The reclining effigy is of Sir Principle Bittern, with his four wives and six children kneeling at his feet,' said the Canon, stopping before an elaborate, canopied tomb in stone and Purbeck marble. 'He attended at the court of Queen Elizabeth. All the-the-the wives are supposed to have died in childbirth, though accounts differ.' He paused with a shrug before moving on. 'This next tomb is Sir Edward Bittern's, Sir Principle's grandson. He fell at-at-at Edgehill in 1643, fighting for the king.'

'Wasn't Edgehill in 1642?' asked Treasure.

The Canon stooped beside the tomb, eyes squinting to read the lettering. 'The inscription says forty-three. Perhaps he took a long time to fall.'

'So the Bitterns are well established hereabouts?'

'Yes. A touch less exalted now than they were in the old days, though.' The volume of the Canon's voice dropped to a confidential level. 'Most of the land has been sold. They still have the title, of course. Lucius, the present baronet, is Chairman of Utteridge Ales. It's what I believe you call a non-executive job. He spends most-most-most of his time being a partner in a London stockbroking firm. Know him at all, do you?'

'No, we've never met. I know the firm.' He'd also heard that it had been looking to merge or to be taken over. Times were hard for the smaller independent stockbroker.

'Would you suppose he's Chairman of Utteridge Ales because his wife Sheila is a great grand-daughter of the founder? And a shareholder?' enquired the Canon again conspiratorially.

'Your guess is as good as mine.' The banker hedged. 'It seems quite possible. It's a private company so she may be a substantial shareholder. I gather the Utteridge ladies don't produce male offspring,' he added.

'Not for four generations they haven't. But there's always the possibility.' The clergyman had turned to contemplate the effigies of Sir Principle's supplicant brood of wives. 'Sheila is with-with-with child at the moment. It'll be their first.'

'Have they been married long? I'd imagined he was in his middle fifties?'

'He is. She's much younger. Early thirties, as I recall. It's his second marriage.' The Canon made a pained face. 'Divorced the first time. Well, that's the way these days. Oh, and I think Sheila's the second largest Utteridge shareholder.'

'The largest being the beneficiaries of the Utteridge trust?'

'That's right. Jill Wader and Charles Utteridge-Flax. Well, you know that.' He made his lip-smacking noise again.

'Why aren't they electing Sir Lucius Bittern to be the third? He seems to be better placed than I am. Handier too.'

'Ah, there's-there's-there's a complicated reason for that.'

'The reason Sir Lucius couldn't be made the third beneficiary is that one of the existing beneficiaries is deemed to be a member of the family,' said Terence Natt, addressing Treasure later that morning from behind an antique partner's desk in the generally antique offices of Natt & Sampole, Solicitors.

The offices were at 1, Abbot's Way, part of a Georgian terrace in this narrow, cobbled opening off the Chiversley High Street, nearly opposite the top of Steep Street. Treasure had arrived there by appointment at eleven.

As sole trustee, Natt was professionally responsible for the administration of the Utteridge trust. He was a small, compact, serious man, fiftyish, with thinning grey hair, tiny, dark, and penetrating eyes, and scarcely any eyelashes or eyebrows which helped to give the moon-shaped face an enigmatic dimension. He spoke distinctly, the tone high-pitched, with every aspirate prolonged by the whistle that emerged through a gap between his two front teeth. The whistle was particularly marked at the end of 'beneficiaries' and all the way through 'Sir Lucius', titles he had been using a good deal. Treasure wondered why Natt didn't have his dentist do something about the whistle – except the lawyer seemed more to cultivate it than suppress it.

'I assume it's Utteridge-Flax who's deemed to be a member of the Utteridge family. And that stops any other Utteridge serving as a beneficiary?' said the banker.

'Under the terms of the trust deed, only one Utteridge, or spouse of an Utteridge, may serve as a beneficiary.' Natt took off his rimless spectacles and began polishing them with his handkerchief.

'Which excludes Sir Lucius, since Utteridge-Flax is one already. Why is Utteridge–Flax only "deemed" to be an Utteridge?'

'Although it was assumed he could be counted a bona fide member of the family in the context I've just mentioned, he is not so accepted in others. There are special circumstances.' The lawyer licked his lips. 'I was obliged to take counsel's opinion in the whole matter. London counsel.'

'Indeed?' Treasure guessed that a visit to the chambers of learned counsel at one of the Inns of Court had been an event to savour in the life of this West Country solicitor.

'I should explain, Mr Treasure, that Mr Utteridge-Flax was adopted as a baby by Mr and Mrs Edwin Flax. Mrs Flax was a grand-daughter of Daniel Utteridge.'

'Like Sheila Bittern?'

'Lady Bittern is a great grand-daughter,' Natt corrected, putting on his glasses again. 'She and Charles Utteridge-Flax are in that sense of the same generation, though he is some-what older than she.' All this came with a hail of orchestrated aspirates. 'He formally appended Utteridge to his surname ten years ago.'

'With the idea of promoting himself as a genuine male Utteridge?'

'One might construe that he had some legitimate aim of that kind in his mind,' the solicitor said, as carefully as a solicitor would – especially one who had already taken higher legal opinion in the matter.

'Did it help him to become a beneficiary?'

'No. He was that already. Before he changed his name. As I've already implied, counsel did later confirm, *inter alia*, that he was sufficiently an Utteridge to prevent any other family member serving as a beneficiary with him.' Natt nodded benignly while this was digested, then sat tight-lipped as if to indicate that he was not going to divulge more tit-bits without prompting.

The banker frowned. 'I believe there's a Chiversley title in disuse? And Bishop Larpin understands there's a benefit for the Utteridge family if the trust is ever wound up.'

'Ah, there could be no revival of the Chiversley barony by any but a legitimate male heir. Even then the possibility of revival would be remote.' Natt leaned back in his chair, elbows on the arms, the fingers of both hands just touching across a gold watch-chain. 'Mr Utteridge-Flax would have known that before he added to his surname.'

'And if the Trust were ever wound up, is there a benefit for him personally?'

'The benefit the Bishop alluded to relates to the disposal of the trust's controlling shares in Utteridge Ales Limited. Under the terms of the trust deed, the trust may be wound up in certain circumstances, at the discretion of the beneficiaries, but not less than a hundred years after the death of Daniel Utteridge.'

'And he's been dead more than that already?'

'Indeed, Mr Treasure.'

'So in what circumstances could the trust be wound up?'

'If its original purpose ceases to exist.'

'The purpose being the maintenance of the convent?'

'Yes. But that could not have been explicitly stated in the trust deed. Legal reasons precluded that, you understand?'

'Because the trust was not supposed to be set up as a church endowment?'

'Precisely. But the point was spelled out clearly enough in

51

an accompanying witnessed directive from Daniel Utteridge, the First Lord Chiversley, to the beneficiaries. That states that if the convent closes, and if the trust income cannot usefully be employed for similar work, then, provided all the beneficiaries agree, the assets may be sold and the proceeds donated to another cause or causes consonant with the Anglo-Catholic faith.'

'Wow!' said Treasure, 'that could cover a lot of things. I'm not surprised you've taken counsel's opinion.'

The lawyer's brow had creased at the other's exclamation. 'It's not that part of the directive on which we've taken learned advice. Not yet,' he added slowly, and with the relish of a man who has already consumed the oysters and now looks forward to the suckling pig. 'You see, if the beneficiaries agree to sell the trust's controlling shares in Utteridge Ales, then in accordance with the trust deed as well as the directive, the shares have to be offered first to Daniel's oldest surviving male descendant, if there is one.'

'At what price?'

'At the net asset value in the balance sheet.'

'And if there isn't a male descendant?' Treasure leaned forward in his chair.

'Then they should be offered to Daniel's oldest married female descendant.'

'*Married* female descendant?'

'Yes. The resulting estate to be managed in trust by the lady's husband.'

'That's a curious arrangement.'

'Not if you accept that Daniel was a quintessential Victorian. Although he had six daughters, he was never persuaded that a woman could look after wealth or property without the guidance of a spouse. Three of his daughters were married – contentedly so, we understand – but to men it's known he chose for them.'

'And the other three daughters became nuns, meaning they had no wealth or property.' Treasure shrugged. 'I see now why it was important to find out where Utteridge-Flax stood. I mean in terms of qualifying as Daniel's oldest male descendant, though I'd still have guessed he stood nowhere.'

'Precisely, Mr Treasure. And despite a romantic embellishment by Mr Utteridge-Flax concerning his entitlement, that was counsel's opinion also. It may yet have to be tested, of course.'

'You mean Utteridge-Flax doesn't accept it?'

'Let's say the circumstances for our finding out haven't yet arisen. The late Ambrose Picton and Dr Jill Wader have been content to leave things as they are, even beyond the point where there will be no reason to maintain the convent. A good deal of the trust income is already given toward the upkeep of other convents, mostly in what used to be called the mission fields overseas.'

'And with two out of three beneficiaries taking that view, there was nothing the third could have done about it? But things have altered with the death of Picton?' Treasure questioned.

'Not substantially. But they may do so with the election of a new beneficiary. One who might bring the others to a fresh and unanimous viewpoint.'

'I see. But you believe Utteridge-Flax wants the trust wound up so he can demand to be offered those shares?'

'He has never said so precisely,' the lawyer replied cautiously.

'What has he said?'

'Only that the trust assets should be given to a cause which Dr Jill Wader does not believe to be sufficiently consonant with the Anglo-Catholic faith. That is, in the sense that Daniel intended.'

'What's the cause?'

The lawyer shuffled in his seat and looked out of the window. His office was on the first floor and offered a particularly fine, angled view of St Timothy's across the main street. 'I fear I am professionally obliged not to disclose that to you, Mr Treasure,' he said, returning his gaze to the room. 'It has not been mentioned outside formal meetings of the beneficiaries. Since you are seeing Mr Utteridge-Flax shortly, may I suggest that you put the same question to him?'

'Very well.' Treasure looked at the time. 'Tell me, as sole trustee of this somewhat unusual trust, how much part do you play in decision making?'

'To date, the trustee has never promoted his view over that of the beneficiaries. A century of record in the minute book demonstrates as much. This is clearly as Daniel Utteridge intended. Legally, however, any trustee has basic statutory powers which, if it came to it, it would seem the courts would have to uphold. In the case of this trust the point has never been tested. We must pray it will never need to be.' But the last observation came with more speculation than conviction in the tone.

'And it'd be handy if a new beneficiary could be appointed. To put the balance back into things?' said Treasure. 'But he or she can only be appointed with Utteridge-Flax's approval.'

'That is certainly the case.'

'Yes, well I'd like a little time to think about what you've told me. To talk to the Bishop, too. But now I'd better be off.' The banker rose from his chair. 'One last thing, the market price for fifty-one per cent of the ordinary shares in Utteridge Ales Limited would be a hell of a lot higher than their net asset value, of course?'

'I believe so, Mr Treasure.'

Treasure stuck his hands in the outside pockets of the light-weight blazer. 'Have you ever quantified that belief?'

'I fear not. It's never occurred to me to do so.' The lawyer also rose, blinking disarmingly.

'But the Canon told me you also act for Lady Bittern. You must have speculated on the likely value of the holding she could be offered in Utteridge Ales if the trust were dissolved? That's in addition to her present holding. As Chairman, I assume Sir Lucius has some shares in the company too.'

'I am Lady Bittern's legal adviser, not her husband's. He retains London solicitors.' Natt cleared his throat softly. 'I can only repeat that I'm not given to idle speculation about the notional future value of my clients' real or prospective possessions, Mr Treasure.'

'How interesting,' the banker replied flatly, astonished at the other's glibness and irritated by his obduracy. In truth, he already had an answer to his main question, and had merely been fishing to have Natt confirm it.

Using the figures from the brewery's last filed balance sheet and accounts, Treasure had calculated that to an interested outside buyer the difference between the asset and the market value of fifty-one per cent of the Utteridge shares would certainly be over four million pounds. And given the right degree of outside interest, the difference could be a lot more.

So, whatever his motives, Utteridge-Flax was in a big numbers game for a prep school headmaster.

It was incredible also that Natt should want to pretend ignorance of the size of those numbers.

Chapter Six

When Treasure re-emerged into the High Street it was noon, still sunny and a good deal hotter. He crossed over to the shaded, southern side of the street, heading for an antique gallery he had noticed earlier. There had been no really pressing need for him to have left the lawyer when he did. He was meeting Utteridge-Flax for lunch at the Feathers, but not until twelve forty-five. Simply, he had found Terence Natt a self-important pedant. The man's refusal on ethical grounds to say what Utteridge-Flax wanted to do with the trust assets had been particularly exasperating: the confidence invoked had been more technical than real.

In truth, if the lawyer had been less than forthcoming, so had Treasure in at least one important respect – and he had to admit to himself now that this was the real cause of his enduring vexation. For as Chief Executive of Grenwood, Phipps he was developing a distinctly commercial and far from dispassionate interest in the effect of Daniel Utteridge's instructions for winding up the trust. Those instructions provided a sound reason why it might be profitable for the bank to have Treasure officially involved in the future of the convent.

In addition to an analysis of the brewery's balance sheet, Treasure had brought with him from London a report on the company's past performance and its future prospects. The report had been completed the day before by the bank's research department. Utteridge Ales was profitable, but far less so than formerly. It was too small to be cost-efficient on its own when measured by current operating standards, and was ripe for amalgamation with a larger entity – ideally a bigger brewer in the south of England. It happened that Grenwood, Phipps were bankers and financial advisers to just such a company, and one that was under-represented in Utteridge's strongest area. The last point was something that the Monopolies Commission could be expected to look upon sympathetically if a takeover were ever put in prospect.

Treasure had intended to mention all this to Natt, and it was Natt's fault that he hadn't done so – except an objective observer might have construed that Natt's pompous attitude was being used by the banker as an excuse for being devious himself. As he was crossing the road, he decided he should kill any criticism of that sort now by telling John Larpin about the possible conflict of interests.

'Sir? Like to buy some rare stamps. They're by Peter Raffite. For collectors they are. We haven't got many left.'

Treasure, now in affable mood again, glanced down amiably enough at the unlikely source of this address – a small boy with curly red hair, innocent wide eyes and an expression that could have been described as earnest or plausible, depending on the extent of one's charitable instinct. The boy was accompanied by a girl whose hair colour and other characteristics suggested that she was probably his younger sister. Both children were well-nourished and well-clothed, though the boy was a touch dishevelled. The girl looked embarrassed while she held open a plastic folder displaying several rows of stamps, each one in a transparent cover.

'They're made from itchins,' the boy embellished, while with the air of a practised salesman he adjusted the angle at which his assistant was holding the folder.

'I think you mean etchings, don't you?' said Treasure. 'And why aren't you two in school?'

'It's the dinner break,' the boy supplied, stuffing his shirt back into his dark blue shorts. 'Till half-past one.'

'We're going home. In the next street,' added the girl in a half whisper, and sounding as if she wished they were there already.

'Are you at Flax's School?'

'No. Chiversley Church School. Flax's is private.'

'They're mostly boarders.' The girl came in after the boy again.

'And does your mother know you're selling things in the street?'

'It's for the church choir fund,' answered the boy defensively, and with a meaningful glower at his companion who had been about to utter, but whose face now went a deeper shade of pink instead.

'I see.' The banker took the folder from the girl. There was probably no point in administering a homily on the dangers of small children accosting strangers – and possibly there weren't any dangers in broad daylight in the middle of the Chiversley High Street.

'Peter Raffite they are, sir,' said the boy, noting the prospect's kindling interest in the merchandise. 'Ever so old.'

The stamps were twice the size of normal postage stamps. Each was reproduced on white paper in two colours – black plus sepia, blue, or red. There were four designs and some of the examples in front of Treasure had miniscule differences suggesting that they might have been hand blocked. The illustrations were attractive and familiar: they were miniature engravings of mostly biblical figures taken from some of the best known works of William Holman Hunt. That they were instantly recognisable for what they were was a tribute to the etcher.

'There's no artist called Raffite,' said Treasure. 'The pictures are copies of Pre-Raphaelite work. Can you remember that? They're etchings of figures in paintings done by a famous artist between about 1850 and 1870. His name was Holman Hunt.' He wasn't very expert in communicating with children, and the fact was apparent in the faces of these two. The boy showed impatience. The girl was watching the traffic go by. 'They aren't postage stamps, either,' Treasure completed.

'They're Sunday school stamps. From the olden days. They gave 'em for attendance,' said the boy promptly, but in a tone that suggested he found the practice surprising.

'Did you get them from the convent? From Sister Patricia, perhaps?'

'No,' said the boy warily.

'But they could have come from there originally?'

The boy shrugged. 'I dunno. They're old though.'

'We haven't got a Sunday school,' offered the girl, hopping on the spot from foot to foot. 'Not now. We go to the big service. We're in the choir.'

'So what are your names?' the banker asked.

'I'm Peter, she's Esme.'

'Peter and Esme what?'

'Edicomb. She's my sister. Aren't you a tourist then?' There was disappointment in the question. The speaker had his eye on the folder still in Treasure's hands.

'No, I'm not a tourist. I'm a visitor though, and I know your vicar, Canon Stonning. It is Saint Timothy's choir you're in?'

'Yes,' said Peter. 'You can have the stamps half price if you like.'

Treasure debated whether this offer was made out of despair or because of his acquaintance with the vicar – he decided it was probably the former. 'Tell me first where you got them,' he said.

'They're our Mum's. From when she used to be a Sunday school teacher.'

'When she was little,' provided Esme, removing a slide from her hair then putting it back again.

'Don't be soft. You can't be a teacher when you're little, can you?' her brother admonished, looking to Treasure for confirmation.

'And your mother knows you're selling her stamps?'

'She gave 'em to us.'

'For playing post offices,' added Esme, absently adjusting the leg elastic of the matching knickers under her dress.

'And how much do you usually sell them for?'

Peter's head jerked up. 'Ten pee each.' It was still more a question than an offer.

'And how much of that goes to the choir fund?'

'All of it, I expect,' the admission came in a resigned voice, prompted this time almost certainly by the fact that the prospective buyer knew the vicar and the names of the vendors.

'All right. I'd like sets of four in each of the three colours. How much is that?'

'One pound twenty,' said Peter promptly, his arithmetic proving to be on an altogether higher level than his artistic knowledge. 'There's sets on the last page.'

'So there are.' Treasure helped himself to the three packets of stamps, examining the contents in turn. Then he handed back the folder with two pounds and forty pence he had sorted from the coins in his pocket. 'Half of that's for you two, for being honest. The rest is for the choir fund.'

'Thank you.'

' 'Cue.' Esme offered a dazzling smile with her attenuated thanks.

The children hurried away, leaving Treasure with the vague feeling that he had done a good deed, and the less ennobling one that he might have got a bargain.

'Pint of bitter, thanks. Never drink anything stronger midday.' Charles Utteridge-Flax was a big man in his mid-forties, with heavy features, a bristling black moustache, and coarse, tightly waved hair of the same colour, brushed straight back from his face. He had on grey flannels, a crumpled pink shirt, a badly knotted tie, and a worn, fawn-coloured cotton jacket of a type often favoured by schoolmasters and clergymen for summer wear.

Treasure recognised the tie as belonging to a Cambridge college, but he couldn't remember which one. 'Are you pushed for time?' he asked after ordering beer for both of them.

'Not unduly. I've a lesson at two. Better get the food soon though. And a table. Place gets crowded after one.'

The two men were in the King Edgar bar of the Feathers where they had just met. The barmaid had identified Utteridge-Flax for Treasure as the other had entered. The bar was low-ceilinged, with thick oak beams, and red tiled flooring. There were alcoves around the sides fitted with polished wooden tables and cushioned benches, with more tables and high-backed chairs in the centre. The walls were hung with hunting prints, brass horns and foxes heads with identical deeply accusing, glass-eyed stares. The place was cosy, was what passed for traditional, and thankfully, in Treasure's estimation, had no piped music or fruit machines. Only the price of the beer served to remind that the Feathers was an expensive hotel and not a country pub – that and the cold buffet at the far end of the bar where the provender looked on a par with what is offered at the cold counters at Harrods' Food Hall.

Utteridge-Flax had commended the food here when he had

spoken to Treasure on the telephone earlier, after he had dismissed the suggestion that he should lunch as Treasure's guest in the hotel's main restaurant.

'Have you owned Flax's school for long?' asked the banker when the two were settled with pewter tankards and plates of cold meat and salad in a windowed alcove.

'Took it over from my father. He retired twenty years ago. Died shortly after. My mother died eight years later. Prep schools don't make fortunes, but I enjoy the work.' Utteridge-Flax communicated in short phrases, and with clipped, military decisiveness. 'My mother put up the money. Started the place before the war. Just after she married my father. The old Utteridge family house was empty. It was perfect for a school. Extended it a bit since. We've seventy-two boys this term.'

'All boarders?'

'A dozen day-boys. Started that as an experiment last year. Not sure it's working. The tradition is to board. It's right too. Fellows get more out of boarding. My father wouldn't have countenanced day-boys. My mother was quite keen though. There's a shortage of private day schools in the area. We're filling a need there.'

'Do the boarders go home at week-ends?' Treasure asked. 'That seems close to being the rule these days.'

'More's the pity,' the other replied sharply. 'We're resisting it at Flax's. Wrecks Saturday sport. And Sunday churchgoing. This week-end's different. Because of the bank holiday on Monday. Most chaps are going home.' He took a long swallow of beer.

'And your mother was an Utteridge?'

'My . . . my mother was one of Daniel's grand-daughters, yes. We carry on his brand of churchmanship. Always have.'

'At the school?'

'That's it. You don't need to keep a redundant convent going to do it either.' Utteridge-Flax broke open a bread roll with some ferocity.

Treasure noticed how huge the man's hands were. 'I'm interested about what you think should happen to the convent,' he said.

'Naturally you are. As front runner for third beneficiary,' the other remarked without looking up.

'I haven't decided yet whether I want to be that. Assuming I'm asked. I thought Sir Lucius Bittern would be a better bet all round.' Treasure took a forkful of chicken and chewed on it, while he waited for a reaction.

'Out of the question. I'm an Utteridge, you see. Can't have more than one Utteridge as a beneficiary.'

'A male Utteridge is something of a rarity.'

The schoolmaster stopped buttering his roll. 'They've told you I was adopted by the Flaxes?'

'And that Daniel Utteridge's descendants have never borne sons since—'

'One did. My natural mother.' The interruption had been both abrupt and definite.

'I'm sorry?'

'My natural mother. She was the cousin of my adopted mother. If my natural mother had been married I might have been Lord Chiversley. That's if we'd got the title reinstated. And I think we would have. Anyway, my mother wasn't married, so I'm plain Mister.'

'I see.' Although what had just been explained was something neither Terence Natt nor anyone else had mentioned to Treasure directly, it was clearly the 'romantic embellishment' the lawyer had referred to so dismissively when they had been discussing the grounds for Utteridge-Flax's inheritance claim. 'I must say I hadn't realised that you were born an Utteridge,' Treasure completed.

'Unfortunately, those who do realise it don't recognise it. Because it can't be proved. My natural mother was a renegade. A drop-out in today's terms, disowned by her parents. She had a baby. In London, at the end of the war. Three days after the birth she came to Chiversley. That was the day I was found abandoned in the school porch. She was killed the day after. By a rocket bomb in Maida Vale. That's where she lived. V2s the bombs were called. This one demolished a whole block of flats, and everyone in it. That included my mother and, they assumed, her baby. Except I know better. When I first learned about her death the coincidence of the dates seemed too great to ignore. That was before I started collecting supporting facts. I was the baby all right. That should explain why I take Utteridge family affairs seriously. I happen to be the rightful head of that family.'

The speaker had eaten and drunk nothing during this account. And instead of looking at Treasure his eyes had been fixed on the huge clenched fists which he had kept knocking together hard as visual punctuation to his narrative.

'You say you can't prove this? Wasn't there some kind of birth certificate?' the banker enquired.

'No. There should have been. It was a home confinement. There was no doctor involved. The midwife was unregistered. That wasn't uncommon. There was a war on remember? Given time, my natural mother would have regularised things. There'd have been no option.' His jaw tightened. 'She was twenty-four. One-parent families weren't countenanced then. I'd say her immediate concern was to hush up the birth. To make sure her baby would be cared for. She succeeded on both counts. The Flaxes were childless. She guessed they'd adopt me.' He hit the upper knuckles of his fists together. 'Or knew they would.'

'Knew? You mean they knew whose baby you were?'

'I've come to believe so, yes. It was the simplest way out of a scandalous situation. For a respectable family. People were narrow-minded about bastard children then.'

'So you think the Flaxes could have been acting in collusion with your real mother?'

'Possibly. Perhaps agreeing to look after me till she found a husband. So her death offered some consolations. It saved the need for disclosure – and her memory from being disgraced further.'

'You don't know who your father was?'

'An American serviceman. Killed in Normandy six months before the birth. That's according to the midwife. Yes, I traced her. To an old people's home. That was after my mother died twelve years ago. My adopted mother, I mean. I was utterly devoted to her. It would have been disloyal to dig for information while she was alive. I was her . . . her only child, you see?'

'I understand. What else did the midwife remember?'

'Nothing really. She knew my natural mother had died a few days after the birth. She'd supposed the baby had died with her.'

'A supposition you knew about already?'

'Yes. It's the verifiable dates that matter. Like the date on my natural mother's death certificate. I've a copy of that.'

'And she died the day after the baby was left at Flax's school?'

'Also verifiable.' Utteridge-Flax took up his knife and fork and addressed himself to the food.

'And none of this has made any difference to your status as an Utteridge?'

'It's made some. Morally, it's made plenty. Legally, even if I could prove my real identity, there's no chance I could claim the Chiversley title. Try to have it revived, I mean. Not since I was illegitimate. But the courts will accept I've the best claim to other family privileges. I'm sure of that.'

'A better claim than your cousin Lady Bittern?'

'If there's any justice at all.'

'As I understand it, Lady Bittern has first claim to be offered the trust shares in the brewery if the trust is ever wound up.'

'That's something I *might* require her to prove before a judge. But that's not to say I would.' He smiled. 'The possibility's got Terence Natt running around in circles though.'

'The trust would have to be wound up first?'

'Which it ought to be. Without delay. Too much capital tied up there doing too little good. I hope you'll take the same view. If you become a beneficiary.'

Treasure smiled. 'You mean that's the basis on which you'd sanction my becoming one?'

'I didn't say that.'

'But no one can be made a beneficiary without your approval all the same.' Treasure drank some beer before continuing. 'So you'd like to wind up the trust and give the assets to . . . causes consonant with the Anglo-Catholic faith? I think those were Daniel Utteridge's words.'

'I'd donate the assets to one deserving cause, yes.'

'The cause being?'

The other man turned the base of his tankard on the table. 'The Anglo-Afro Hospices Society. For terminal HIV patients. You know it?'

'Afraid I don't. I—'

'That's not surprising. You will soon. Or you'll hear about

the reason for it. Why Anglo-Afro Hospices was formed.' He looked up from his tankard. 'One in four people in the sub-Sahara population will be HIV positive within ten years. That's an official World Health Organization statistic. The scream for help is going to be the loudest ever made. For anything. But it's the one affluent societies are least tuned to hear.'

'But a cure for Aids—'

'Is one thing,' Utteridge-Flax interrupted again. 'We're praying for that. So are the drug companies. But I'm talking about giving help to the nearly dying in countries who can only afford to be concerned with the healthy living.'

Treasure's eyebrows lifted a fraction. 'Your motive is laudable, of course. But is the specific cause something especially related to Anglo-Catholicism I wonder?'

'Have you ever witnessed an Aids death?'

'No.'

'We lost a boy from the school last year. Ten years old. A Kenyan. He got Aids from a contaminated blood transfusion years before.'

'In Africa?'

'Yes. He died in a nursing home here. I was with him. It was ghastly, but at least he had every comfort. Hundreds of thousands, maybe millions of his fellow Africans are condemned to die uncared for in abject misery.' The speaker straightened his substantial frame. 'Building hospices for Aids victims in Africa is totally in line with my religious convictions,' he announced solemnly, as if he was making a formal profession of faith.

'And with mine, I assure you. But just now you suggested proving a point before a judge. What view d'you suppose a judge would take if one Utteridge beneficiary tried to wind up the trust so that all the assets could be given away for medical relief? Or medical work of any kind? If it were challenged legally, would you think the beneficiary would get a judgement? That the conditions of Daniel Utteridge's directive were being fulfilled? Incidentally, it's more the principles of the directive than the trust deed that you'd be challenging.'

'How much status in law does the directive have?' Utteridge-Flax asked flatly.

'Probably not a lot. But if it comes to a legal action, it

would be because the beneficiaries couldn't agree, and the trust deed specifies firmly that they must act together. That being the case, the directive becomes important because it illuminates the founder's intention. And that's something a judge could find very helpful.'

'There are any number of Church of England medical charities.'

'I agree. And I imagine the beneficiaries can donate trust income to virtually any of them with impunity. But I question whether as one beneficiary you could petition to have the trust wound up, and the assets given to an organisation that no matter how worthy, couldn't be equated with advancing the cause of Anglo-Catholicism within the church. Not as a primary aim. I accept it's difficult to define the Anglo-Catholic cause accurately, but—'

'Hello Charles, darling. Can we join you? There isn't an empty table anywhere.'

The woman putting the question had spoken from behind Treasure. When he turned to look at her, her appearance more than matched the promise of the sensuous, husky voice. He had half expected Utteridge-Flax to show something less than un-alloyed pleasure at the intrusion, but the man was quickly on his feet, a little confused but smiling ingratiatingly – almost to the point of overdoing it.

'Christine, how very nice to see you,' he offered. 'Mark, this is Christine Stonning, Canon Stonning's niece. Christine, this is Mark Treasure.'

'Yes,' said the rivetingly attractive blonde. 'Delighted, Mr Treasure.' She shook his hand, holding it tightly and for a fraction longer than was necessary, though he found the effect entirely agreeable. The same also applied to the very direct and gravely appraising look in the astonishingly clear blue eyes.

'I met your uncle this morning,' the banker responded. 'Charming man.'

'We're supposed to look alike.'

'But you're much prettier.'

'Thank you.' A wry grin exposed at once perfect teeth, and pleasure at the facetious compliment.

Her accent, colouring, the high cheek-bones, and the sharpness of the rest of her facial features spelled Scandinavian origins. Treasure put her age at around twenty-three. It was not till some moments later that he noticed her beauty was blemished.

Chapter Seven

'And this is Graham Brown, my bank manager,' said Miss Stonning, moving her long, lissom figure a fraction to one side. She was wearing a tight, sleeveless, white linen dress with a short hem and a low, rounded neckline: the dress accentuated the deep tan of the parts of her body it was not covering – which was quite a lot of it.

'Pleased to meet you, Mr Treasure,' said Brown. He had been dithering behind the young woman, holding both their laden plates, a clutch of cutlery and paper napkins, as well as his own drink. He gave an uncertain grin. 'I'm not really the bank manager. One of the assistant managers, that's all. We have two.' He cleared his throat. 'Mr Utteridge-Flax knows, I expect.'

The schoolmaster acknowledged that he did know with a curt nod.

'Only a matter of time before you move up, I'm sure,' Treasure said affably, but wondering on consideration if it would be. He felt that the owner of a beard as palpably failed as Brown's should have made the decision long since to abandon it – a thought that then coloured his view of the man's likely capacity to manage anything more important than his whiskers. The banker wasn't much enamoured with grey suede shoes either. 'Look, we shall have to go soon,' he went on. 'Mr Utteridge-Flax has a lesson to take. Why don't you two sit in the middle?' He moved out to let Miss Stonning slide along the semi-circular alcove bench which offered room for four to sit and drink, but table space for only two conveniently to eat. He noticed for the second time how unusually graceful the woman's movements were – just before he caught sight of the savage scar on the right side of her forehead. The disfigurement was only partially concealed by the arrangement of her long, straight, golden hair which she wore parted in the middle and covering part of her face.

'I'll get a chair, shall I?' Brown volunteered unnecessarily, but since nobody told him not to, he deposited everything he was carrying on the table and darted back into the now crowded centre of the bar. He reappeared a moment later with a chair which he pulled up to the table, then sat on it himself. This set him at the furthest point from Miss Stonning, with Utteridge-Flax reseated at some distance to her left, and Treasure very close to her on her other side.

After a moment Brown's face clouded. He looked about him, again with uncertainty, made as though to say something, thought better of it, and instead arranged his cutlery around his plate as meticulously as a trainee waitress.

'Are you staying at the vicarage, Miss Stonning?' Treasure asked.

'Won't you call me Christine, please?' she replied, and as though his compliance in this really mattered to her. 'And the vicarage is my English family home. I come here a good deal. I have a flat in London. In Eaton Terrace. My mother lives in Copenhagen. That's where I was born and grew up.'

'And your father?'

'Was very British. Like my Uncle Miles. He taught English at the university. He died. Some years ago.'

'I'm sorry. And you choose to live in England?'

'Yes. I used to travel a lot. In my work.'

'Christine is an international model,' Utteridge-Flax provided quickly.

'Was,' she corrected.

'Still is,' said Utteridge-Flax gallantly, jerking forwards and fiddling with his tankard like a grizzly bear with a pot of honey.

Graham Brown gave an earnest nod and a sort of choking noise in support, his mouth being full of turkey and ham pie. This intervention was hardly noted by the others, except it drew a despairing glare from Utteridge-Flax.

'Then that's perhaps why I thought I knew you, Christine?' said Treasure.

'Because you're an avid reader of *Vogue* and *Harper's*, Mr Treasure?' Her smile was more good humoured than cynical.

'*Country Life*, regularly. Fashion article always comes just before the events diary. And please call me Mark, which makes the score deuce, I think,' he completed, grinning back.

'Thank you. Yes, I've worked for *Country Life*. Quite often. But not lately. Nor for anyone else either. I was in a car smash two years ago. In California. They're still patching my face.' She pushed the hair back from the scar with a sudden harsh movement, her eyes holding his to read the reaction.

'And they're doing a very good job,' he replied. 'I hadn't noticed until a moment ago.' He could now see there was also a nearly melded patch of grafted skin below the scar which the hair had been covering completely.

'I keep telling Christine she worries too much about it. That nobody'd know any more. I mean you don't see anything, stitch marks or anything, do you?' said Brown with forced conviction. But it was clear that the others, including Miss Stonning, thought his comments both extravagant and superfluous.

'Easy thing to say, of course,' countered Utteridge-Flax, which was as good as indicating that he took Brown for a fool.

'At this stage, Christine, I'm sure it's more noticeable to you than to anyone else,' Treasure offered easily, then changed the subject with: 'Tell me, any of you ever seen anything like these before?' He had taken the plastic envelopes from his pocket and had spread the four stamps from one of them on the table.

'Yes, I have. They were produced in the convent,' said Utteridge-Flax.

'In the convent?' Miss Stonning caught her breath, glancing at Brown. 'Why they're beautiful. May I take one to see? I'll be careful with it.' She drew the stamp very close to her eyes, holding it at the edges between thumb and forefinger.

Brown hadn't uttered, but his cheeks and normally pale, protruding ears were showing patches of pink, Treasure thought because of the snub from Utteridge-Flax.

'I bought them from two children called Edicomb, in aid of the choir fund,' Treasure said.

'Hope they didn't steal them,' blurted the still blotching Brown.

'Why should you think that?' demanded Utteridge-Flax.

The younger man shrugged. 'Were these all you were offered, Mr Treasure?'

'These four designs, in two other colours. They told me they're Sunday school attendance stamps owned by their mother. She was a Sunday school teacher,' Treasure explained.

'Moira Edicomb. She taught me,' Brown admitted.

Treasure wondered if the grunt that came from Utteridge-Flax indicated he thought the lessons had been a bit low on Christian charity.

'They still have no authority to be collecting for the choir fund,' Brown continued sourly, hand on beard.

'The work is so fine,' Miss Stonning murmured, taking another stamp to study.

'Taken from a composite wood engraving of the four designs. I haven't seen any for years,' said Utteridge-Flax. 'A product of the convent printing school, any time after 1853. They and similar stamps were much in demand until quite recently. Well, up to twenty years ago, I'd say.'

'Sophisticated work for a convent,' remarked Treasure.

'The engraving was done somewhere else in the early days,' rejoined Brown.

'Not at all,' corrected the schoolmaster. He had contrived to disagree with the younger man's every utterance so far. 'I thought you'd have known the printing school was quite large and surprisingly comprehensive from the start. They trained girls as illustrators, engravers, compositors, printers, the lot.'

'Weren't those curious trades to teach women?'

'Shame on you, Mark.' Christine Stonning laughed and touched his hand. 'You think they'd have done better to teach them to be parlour maids?' She gave him back the stamps.

'I wasn't being chauvinistic. I simply wondered if they could have got jobs in the last century as, say, compositors?'

'I was told some did,' Utteridge-Flax replied. 'Sadly, Christine was closer to the truth. Most of the girls went into domestic service afterwards.'

'But they would all have been better off than before? Morally at least?' This was Christine. 'Weren't they mostly prostitutes?'

The schoolmaster gave a sharp, embarrassed cough. 'Not all.

A good many, yes,' he said. 'And some of course were brought here for medical treatment.'

'For contagious diseases, I expect,' supplied Brown darkly, and making the sort of face that confirmed he hadn't meant measles.

'Sexually-transmitted diseases you mean,' said Christine. She had picked up a large gherkin from her plate. Her gaze turning to Treasure, she delicately bit the end off it. 'The treatment till the nineteen-forties must have been fairly primitive,' she added, then ran the tip of her tongue across her upper lip.

'Involving mostly rest and careful nursing. Tribute to the nuns. Also to the enlightenment of Daniel Utteridge. He made it all possible, after all,' said Utteridge-Flax, now less uncomfortable with the subject than he had been earlier when strangely the presence of the young woman had inhibited him.

'So I suppose they were running a sort of early VD clinic?' asked Christine, crossing her long and well-turned legs, and bringing them close to Treasure's. 'Interesting to think that was probably the basic purpose of the convent.'

'The nursing part of the Society of Saint Mary Magdalene was quite the largest,' Utteridge-Flax confirmed, a finger brushing one side of his moustache. 'Set up to care for sufferers from diseases of the type we've mentioned. A purpose the sponsor felt impelled to pursue as a Christian. Indeed, if Daniel Utteridge were alive today—'

'You wouldn't say that's overgilding the lily?' Treasure interrupted seriously. 'Surely the Society was a religious order dedicated to a number of—'

'It's a shame the convent has run out of nuns,' Christine interrupted in turn. 'Are you going to show everybody what they should do with all the money that's left, Mark?'

'Graham Brown is deliciously gauche, don't you think?' It was Christine again who put this question half an hour later. She and Treasure were walking together along the High Street. 'It's a shame he's only allowed forty minutes for lunch, but it's so . . . so diminishing of him to admit it. He should have said he had to leave me to call America or something. I would have, wouldn't you?'

'Perhaps.'

'Meaning not really. Oh God, that makes me out to be insecure or something, doesn't it?'

'Not at all. Protecting one's status is an understandable ploy, but not Brown's style. He was just being honest,' said Treasure.

'Hum. He is supposed to be an assistant manager, poor lamb. His honesty is splendid of course, but wouldn't it take more than that to make him a good convent beneficiary?' Her tone made it sound as if she really needed an answer.

'Is that what he wants to be?'

'It's been his ambition for years.'

They were heading toward St Timothy's. Utteridge-Flax had left them outside the Feathers to make off in the opposite direction. Brown had accompanied them the few steps to the bank, before darting inside. It had been his peremptory announcement about having to go back to work that had ended his lunch with Christine at the same time as Treasure and his guest were parting. Christine was returning to the vicarage.

'He told me he's church treasurer, so I suppose—' the banker began.

'But that has very little to do with becoming a beneficiary, surely?'

'I expect he thinks differently, and he could be right.'

'You're very wise. Also tolerant.' She touched his sleeve. 'I thought you would be. From what Uncle Miles said about you. The Bishop thinks you have one of the best financial brains in the City.'

'Where, so far as I know, the Bishop has seldom if ever been.' Treasure gave a deprecating smile.

'Anyway, that's why I brought Graham to meet you. So he'd understand the calibre of mind needed in a beneficiary.'

'That was a bit hard, as well as misleading,' he said, quite sternly. She evidently manipulated the hapless Brown, and Treasure preferred to do without compliments made at the man's expense. He nodded to their right. 'That town hall really is a gem. Similar to the one in Windsor. About the same period too.'

They stopped to admire the late Restoration building which stood on an island in the centre of the road. Its ground floor was open and stone-flagged, its upper one supported from below by rusticated stone pilasters at the corners, joined through elegant rounded arches on Ionic pillars. The upper storey had long windows above the arches, separated by Corinthian half columns.

'It had become pretty dilapidated before they decided to smarten up the town. I've seen pictures of it then,' said Christine. 'Can you imagine a community letting something like that fall apart? But people down here do live rather sheltered lives. Self-interest is about the only thing to shake them up. Graham is typical, I'm afraid.'

'So you didn't run into us at the Feathers by chance?' Treasure enquired as they moved along the street, stopping now and again to glance at the shop windows.

'No. Uncle told me you'd said that you and Charles would be lunching there, so I got Graham to take me. Rather short notice, but he's quite fond of me. It was risky. He and Charles don't get on.'

'That was plain enough.'

'It's the other reason why it'd be difficult for Graham if he was a beneficiary. He and Charles would take opposite views about everything as a matter of principle.'

'Except about you?'

'Perhaps so.' She laughed, and linked her arm with his, then joined her two hands together in an involuntary way which brought her still closer to him. 'It's a pity they don't care for each other. Graham isn't against the Utteridge trust being ended and the money given to Aids relief.' She frowned. 'If it came to it, probably he and Charles could agree on that. Only if Graham were a beneficiary, and if the idea was challenged, legally I mean, his support wouldn't count for very much. He's such a lightweight.'

'Such a move could only be challenged by the other beneficiary, Dr Wader. Hardly by anyone else, except I suppose Natt, as trustee. Do you know Dr Wader?'

'Jill? Yes. Quite well. She's . . . she's nice, but very conservative.'

They waited for the traffic to clear at the top of Steep Street, then crossed over, her arm in his still.

'But you knew about Charles's plan before today then?' he asked as they drew abreast of the church.

'Of course. I thought everyone here did.'

'Natt seemed to think it was a secret.'

'Terence Natt means well.'

'I'm sure,' said Treasure without meaning it. 'You're quite involved in what happens to the convent?'

'For an outsider? I suppose I am. Not involved. Interested though. If they decide to wind up the trust, Uncle Miles hopes Saint Timothy's will get some of the money for repairs and maintenance. As a sort of endowment.'

'I see. That's fair. If the beneficiaries have been supporting the church with trust money in the past.'

'Oh, they have. That was only right, don't you think? The convent relies on the church for lots of things. For daily services, for instance. And as vicar, Uncle is automatically the convent warden. He hopes the church would get half a million or so following a wind-up. You'd agree to something like that?'

Treasure hesitated. 'Very possibly, but I'm not a beneficiary, remember?' He chuckled. 'Only, it seems, being interviewed as a suitable candidate for the fourth time today.'

'I wouldn't presume to do any such thing.' She squeezed his arm, then let it go.

'I'm not so sure. I think you want to know where I stand on a wind-up of the trust. Your uncle didn't raise the issue, by the way.'

'Uncle isn't pushy. He's quite keen on the Aids idea. Provided the church gets the endowment, like I said.'

They turned to go into the churchyard. Treasure held the lichgate open. 'On balance, I think Charles Utteridge-Flax's proposal has merit,' he said.

'You'd vote for it if you were a beneficiary?'

'I'd need to know more about this Anglo-Afro Hospices outfit Charles proposes—'

'Oh Christine. Mr Treasure. Such dramas we've had since luncheon.' An agitated Sister Mary Maud had materialised on the path beyond the gate. The reluctant Lazarus was connected to her by a leather lead, though the Sealyham was several paces behind, rooted to the area around a drain cover and which was taking up his total attention. For this reason the lead was taut like the little nun's left arm, both being extended behind her and accounting for the backward tilt of her whole body. With her other arm outstretched in front as a balancer, she looked a little like a lopsided medieval scarecrow.

'What's the problem, Sister? Can we help?' asked Treasure.

'Well first Mr Brown telephoned Reverend Mother. That was about the Sunday school stamps. Well that was nothing really, I suppose. Only to know if Sister Patricia was still printing them. Reverend Mother didn't know, and we haven't been able to find out yet. Because it's Sister Patricia you see?' She paused indecisively, and was then suddenly tugged a little backwards as Lazarus altered his position at the drain. 'But then the policeman came,' she continued. 'Not from the Chiversley Police Station. The police there all wear proper uniforms. He was from Shaftsborne. In ordinary clothes. He'd been to the vicarage. And that was about stamps too. He quite demanded to see everything in the printing room. But the Canon said he couldn't. That was after they had spoken to Reverend Mother. It was gone two o'clock, you see?' She paused to take a breath after what she clearly judged to be a self-evident vindication of the Reverend Mother's decision. This was just as Lazarus finally lost interest in the drain and moved onward, for a moment reducing the tension on the lead but then, because he had changed direction, abruptly spinning Sister Mary Maud about as he hurried behind her, emerging on her right side, and gathering speed.

'Woe-up, Lazarus,' commanded Treasure, snatching the lead from the Sister. 'Did the policeman come about Sunday school attendance stamps?' he asked.

Sister Mary Maud looked surprised as well as disoriented. 'Oh nothing as trivial as that, Mr Treasure. He was in his twenties. He'd have been too old to attend . . .' Her hand went to her mouth. 'I'm so sorry. I didn't understand. No, no. This was official business. About *postage* stamps. The ones Sister Patricia does sometimes. Copies of old stamps. They're for schools, I think.'

'The policeman wanted to see those?' asked Christine.

'And Sister Patricia. After he'd spoken to your uncle. But

Reverend Mother wouldn't hear of it. Sister Patricia can't be disturbed in the printing school between two and four in the afternoons. That's understood.' Using both hands, Sister Mary Maud straightened her spectacles on her nose in an almost ceremonial manner, as though this added veracity to the information.

'That's her special work time, is it?' asked Treasure.

Sister Mary Maud gave him another bewildered look, as though he hadn't been paying attention. 'Oh, no, Mr Treasure. That's when she sleeps there. It saves her having to go upstairs to her room. Reverend Mother said the policeman would have to come back later today. Or tomorrow morning.'

'And did he agree?' This was Christine.

'Yes. He didn't seem to mind very much. Said he had other calls to make. I saw him leave in his motor-car a few minutes ago. That was after Canon Stonning took him back to the vicarage. To sponge his trousers.' She looked down at the Sealyham still tethered to Treasure. 'Naughty Lazarus,' she added.

Chapter Eight

'At which exact point the wretched animal was about to start piddling on my trousers as well,' said Treasure to his wife, some hours later.

'It's a matter of marking territorial boundaries,' Molly replied vaguely, while sipping her after-dinner coffee.

'You mean, it's a matter of inadequate training.'

Molly leaned forward slightly, focusing her gaze. 'D'you think those two beautiful swans need feeding?'

'No. Nor encouraging. They disturb the fish.'

'That's like saying rabbits only eat the lettuces.'

'They do.'

'Well, we've got some rabbits here and I think they're adorable.'

'They still eat the lettuces.'

'They're not our lettuces.'

'That's hardly the right attitude.'

Molly responded by wrinkling her nose.

The two were sitting side by side in long garden chairs on the paved terrace of their rented house. They were watching the sunlight fade over the lusciously green lawn, the healthiness of which, Treasure had observed, probably showed that garden and possibly house were flooded regularly every winter. The grass swept down to the willow-lined riverbank that was currently adorned by the swans and some other less commanding wild fowl.

The house was a substantial but low-lying building in mellowed brick, with a thatched roof. It wasn't particularly old, but its pleasing, hybrid farmhouse style suggested antiquity. Inside it was all old-fashioned chintz covers and drapes, but with efficient plumbing and a recently modernised kitchen. The owners, a Royal Navy Captain and his wife, were in Washington where the Captain was Naval Attaché at the British Embassy. Dinner had been prepared and served by the permanent and competent cook–housekeeper who lived close by. Her name was Ivy Cass, and she was also paid for by the television company.

'Anyway, the Reverend Mother admits Lazarus was never house trained,' said Treasure returning to the previous subject. 'Heaven knows why. Unspeakable creature.'

'You used to be so fond of dumb animals,' Molly drawled.

'I still am.'

'Except for swans, rabbits, and dogs, which narrows the field a bit.'

'Lazarus is far from dumb. He has a penetrating yap.'

'Poor little thing was a present from a devout member of the Saint Timothy's congregation,' Molly protested. 'Reverend Mother didn't feel she could refuse him, even though she hadn't the first idea about how to bring him up. He was the last of a large litter. Got his name because he was thought to be stillborn, then surprised everybody by showing he was very much alive.'

'In his favourite and inimitable way, no doubt.'

'He behaved perfectly well when I was there to tea yesterday. He obviously doesn't care for men. I'm not wild about two of them myself at the moment. Not you, darling.' Molly adjusted the thick cushion behind her back. She had suffered a long day on the set while an exacting director had shot the same longish take ten times because he and the male lead had never quite agreed on how it should be interpreted. 'I wonder what that policeman really wants?' she mused, but not at all keenly.

'I asked Canon Stonning that later. He doesn't much care for policemen, for some reason. It seems the chap was checking on possible sources of counterfeit stamps.'

'In a nunnery?'

'That in its day was the official printer for the stamps of a British Crown Colony.'

'You're not serious?'

'Absolutely serious. It was Prince James Island in the Caribbean. One of the Lesser Antilles. Considerably lesser,' he added in view of Molly's frown. 'Two down from Barbados. You'll find it in the large-scale atlas.'

'No, I'll take your word for it, darling. So go on.'

'Well in 1853 the Governor there asked the Agent-General for Crown Colonies in London to supply the island with its first postage stamps. Twenty pounds worth in two colours, denoting values of a penny and twopence. The stamps sent were similar to those in use by Mauritius and Trinidad. They'd both just started postal services. All the printers had to do was substitute Prince James Island for Mauritius or Trinidad on the second printing die.'

'Saving themselves a lot of money?'

'That's exactly what the Governor thought, apparently. On top of which, the basic design of the stamp wasn't at all to his taste because it didn't have the Queen's head on it.'

'Whose head did it have?'

'Nobody's really. Only the figure of Brittania. The Governor, who knew about such things, complained that this was an effigy of the pagan goddess Athena copied from an ancient Greek coin. He found it offensive both as a Christian and a dedicated monarchist. So he sent the stamps back.'

'And did the Agent-General have them redone?'

'No. He just sent the Governor the printers' bill.'

'For twenty pounds? Shouldn't have thought you'd have got many for that, in any case.'

'However many he got, it made the Governor so angry that he commissioned his own stamps through a merchant friend in Weymouth. The friend gave the order to the nuns of Chiversley who'd already provided stamps for a South American trading company. For Prince James Island they knocked up something very close to the then current English postage stamps. The Governor was delighted.'

'Was what he'd done legal?'

'No it wasn't. The whole thing became a minor cause célèbre at the time. Questions in the House, and so on. The stamps were banned by the British Postmaster-General on letters to England or to other colonies. Even so, they were used for a short time, mostly for local mail within the island. But the Governor had made his point. Soon afterwards the Britannia stamps were replaced throughout the colonies.'

'With ones with the Queen's head on?'

'That's what Canon Stonning told me.'

'So what happened to the Chiversley stamps?'

'Officially those left were destroyed, but some survived. They became collectors items, along with the used ones. Both are very rare now.'

'So d'you suppose the nuns have been sort of . . . running up a few extra, now and again?'

'Stonning doesn't think so.'

'But what a delicious idea. And if they've still got the printing blocks, the dies or whatever they're called? I mean what's to stop them?'

'They have more than that. Always have had. Stocks of the right paper. Etching equipment. Gumming and perforating machines. Everything needed for making stamps, on a cottage industry basis. I saw a lot of it this morning. It seems Daniel Utteridge was keen from the start and coughed up for the gear. From then on the printing school made a speciality out of stamps. Not just postage stamps, and never again on a grand scale. As works of art rather.'

'Like those Holman Hunt stamps you bought from the children today?'

Treasure nodded. 'Those were for a church purpose, of course. But after the First World War, and right up to the fifties, the nuns also turned out specimen facsimile postage stamps of the rarer types. That may have started through their having the dies for the Prince James Island stamps. I didn't ask.'

'Who were these specimens for?'

'Schools and libraries, the Canon said. They were all clearly marked in some way, so no one could take them for the real thing.'

'Except someone has now, perhaps? Which is why the cops are on to them.'

'The Canon is certainly bothered about it. So is his niece.'

'Ah, the lovely Christine? You say she's a well-known model? International?'

'That's how Utteridge-Flax described her.' He looked up over his coffee cup. 'Why, d'you think she isn't?'

Molly shrugged. 'I've no idea. I didn't recognise the face from her photo. There's one in the convent sitting-room where we had tea. Sister Mary Maud showed it to me. International models aren't all that common.' She paused and gave a little sniff. 'The title tends to be, of course. Like some of the girls who use it.'

'Christine certainly isn't common.'

'I'm sure not, darling. Not from the detailed way you've described her.' Molly's smile was a touch less generous than her tone. 'Is she here to get over her accident?'

'Partly, I suppose. And doing under-cover work for the Canon.' He grinned. 'I had the impression she was checking me out for him as a beneficiary. As one who'd be sympathetic to the enduring needs of Saint Timothy's. She could also have had a watching brief from Utteridge-Flax. To gauge my attitude to the hospices idea. He seemed delighted when she joined us.'

'Maybe he just fancies her. And what about the boyfriend who took her to lunch? The bank manager?'

'Assistant bank manager. He's loosely a fall-back candidate for beneficiary if I don't accept. Or match up. He's already treasurer of the church and the convent. Very concerned with the convent's well-being too.' He was thinking of Brown's prompt call to the Reverend Mother about the Sunday school stamps made so quickly after lunch.

'And Miss Stonning will be at the Bitterns' dinner tomorrow?' Molly had telephoned the acceptance of their own invitation earlier.

'Invited with her aunt and uncle out of courtesy, I expect. You'll find the Canon amusing.'

Molly poured herself more coffee. 'I must say you covered a lot of ground today.'

'I met a lot of people, as I promised John Larpin I would.'

'And has it made you keener about being a beneficiary?'

'Yes. But if I do become one I doubt it will be for very long.'

'Because everyone wants to wind up the trust?'

'Very nearly everyone, yes. For different reasons. And anyway, those in favour of a wind-up could make it difficult for anyone against it to become a beneficiary.'

'What about Dr Wader?'

'Ah, it's she who's the single strong supporter for leaving things as they are. And as an existing beneficiary she could keep them that way too. I haven't met her yet, of course. She'll also be there tomorrow night.'

'D'you think Charles Utteridge-Flax expects to be offered these brewery shares if the trust should be wound up?'

'In accordance with Daniel Utteridge's instructions? At their asset value? It could happen if Charles can persuade everyone that he's a genuine illegitimate Utteridge with the most legitimate claim. I don't think he'll succeed. As I told you at dinner, it's difficult to know if he really expects to. He may just be angling for a chance to establish what he claims is his true parentage.'

'But wouldn't he need millions in any case to buy the shares from the trust?'

'A bit over eleven million pounds, yes. But he could borrow it very easily.'

'A prep school headmaster could borrow eleven million pounds, just like that?' Molly asked in a surprised voice.

'Certainly. Because his collateral would be impeccable. The controlling shares in Utteridge Ales. Their market value would be a lot higher than their asset value. We'd lend him the money like a shot.' The banker smiled. 'For the minute or so he'd need it. Before he sold the shares on to someone else.'

'Would that be another brewer who'd be taking over Utteridge Ales?'

'Not necessarily another brewer, but quite likely.'

'Because you have one in mind?'

'Possibly. But that's all a long way off.'

Molly's tone hardened. 'But is this whole scenario really about a take-over and not about what happens to the convent or the trust?'

'Only if the trust is wound up. If it stays as it is, nobody can take over anything.'

'Golly, no wonder John Larpin said the situation was delicate. So do you believe Mr Utteridge-Flax's dedication to the Anglo-Afro Hospices thing is genuine?'

'Yes. And the more I think about it, the more I warm to the idea myself.'

'Because it's the sort of cause Daniel Utteridge would have approved?'

Treasure nodded. 'And very possibly have supported if he were alive now. Certainly the assets he gave to the convent could do more good for a dynamic charity than lying dormant in the coffers of a country church trust. As things are, the trust is only going to provide fees for lawyers and accountants, and headaches for the beneficiaries every year over how to distribute the income. And in the way of these things, they often won't distribute anything like all the income.'

'So the fund will get bigger and bigger?'

'Precisely, and to no purpose. It happens with moribund charitable trusts all over the country.'

Molly's hand reached for his across the narrow table between their chairs. 'And you don't approve of undynamic charitable trusts.'

'No, I don't. Especially not those whose initial purposes have disappeared, as the purpose of this one has. Or nearly. When that happens trusts tend to stagnate. And usually nobody can do anything about it. That's because the deeds of too many of the older charitable trusts have blinkering clauses that prevent radical changes. They rarely allow the opportunity to give away funds to causes other than the ones originally nominated. But it happens Daniel Utteridge provided the formula for doing just that. And on a very large scale, too.'

'But if the trust is providing income for lawyers and accountants, wouldn't this Mr Natt oppose its being closed?'

Treasure pondered for a moment. 'Hardly for that reason. Not overtly anyway. It's difficult to say if his opposition would mean anything if, for instance, all three beneficiaries were in favour. My impression is he's committed to supporting the person he judges to be the legal head of the Utteridge family.'

'That's Lady Bittern? Or, in terms of Daniel Utteridge's male chauvinist regulations, her husband.'

'Hm, I believe you were right the first time. It's Sheila Bittern. Who's pregnant, and who may be about to produce the first male Utteridge descendant for a century. Natt handles her legal affairs, which could be very big business if she gives birth to a son.'

'Is he her husband's lawyer too?'

'No. And his services are not the only things the couple don't have in common. That's according to the Canon.'

Molly's eyebrows lifted in surprise. 'He told you they don't get on?'

'He wouldn't have been so indiscreet. Not quite so indiscreet, anyway. He gave me the impression it'd been a marriage of convenience. Sir Lucius, the Chairman of Utteridge Ales, to the lady who happens to be the largest shareholder, except for the trust.'

'Mmm. I've known successful marriages with less going for them at the outset. And perhaps the baby will bring them closer together,' Molly concluded brightly.

'How early in a pregnancy can one find out the sex of the unborn child?' her husband asked.

'Very early if the mother wants. Many don't want, of course.'

'I imagine Lucius Bittern could want very much indeed. If the trust is wound up, and the child is a girl, the brewery shares would end up in an entailed trust under his control.'

'As Lady Bittern's lord and master?'

'Yes. As Daniel specified. Whereas if its a boy, they'd have to be put in a temporary trust on the child's behalf.'

'Another trust?' Molly sighed.

'Family not charitable, and only until the boy comes of age. Lucius Bittern would probably have himself made a trustee, but it wouldn't give him quite the same sort of control as the other.'

'And if Utteridge Ales is taken over or merged, the shares are bound to increase in value?'

'Certainly.'

'So will it make such a difference whether the shares go to Sir Lucius or to a son? I mean, it's all in the family.'

Treasure pouted: 'It makes the difference to Lucius Bittern of being a pretty free agent over what he does with the shares. Or with the proceeds from selling them. Of course, if the Utteridge trust is wound up and the shares are offered before the baby's born, he'd be in that position too.'

'Do you know when the baby's due?'

'November the Canon said. He also has an axe to grind, of course.'

'Because if the trust is dissolved he wants the beneficiaries to settle a substantial sum on the church?'

'Yes. For its upkeep.'

Molly smiled. 'And you think John Larpin knew the Utteridge trust situation was as complicated as this? I mean when he asked you to become involved?'

'I'm sure he did. I also think he knows all about Utteridge-Flax's hospice plan.'

'So why didn't he mention it?'

Treasure stroked his neck. 'Misplaced ethical considerations, I should think. Didn't want to colour my view in advance. Come to think of it, Natt may have been motivated in the same way. He downright refused to tell me what Utteridge-Flax had in mind. Irritating at the time, and I may have misjudged him for it.'

'And you think he and John want you to be the arbiter over doing the right thing? I must say, the Utteridge-Flax plan sounds convincing to me.'

'Assuming that if a wind-up happens he doesn't show feet of clay by suddenly mounting a legal action to prove he's the rightful Lord Chiversley. Apart from anything else, that could hold up the whole shooting match for years.'

Molly pulled the woollen wrap she was wearing closer around her neck. 'It's getting cold, darling. Let's go in.' Then before she got up she added: 'You know, in the circumstances I'd be surprised if the Bitterns don't already know the sex of their child.'

'In that case, I'd say Natt probably knows it too. From Lady Bittern.' Pensively, he studied the outlines that the trees along the river bank made against the night sky. 'That would also partly explain his attitude this morning,' he said.

Chapter Nine

'You'm as good a right as any London banker, Graham. More if truth be told. That enough carrots then?'

There was a strong West Country lift to her final word as the widowed Mrs Bertha Brown placed the hot and laden plate in front of her son. She straightened with a self-satisfied look, then darted forward again, dipping to wipe the plate rim expertly with her tea-cloth where she had noticed the gravy had spilled.

Now she stood back properly, admiring the results of her creativity, which included not only the home-made steak and kidney pie, but also the only child she had borne, nurtured at her breast, and brought to manhood – single-handedly in all contexts, except for the moment of Graham's conception. And the way Mrs Brown sometimes put it, she scarcely credited the boy's father with a full half share even in that last important exercise, though appearances suggested otherwise. Her gaze lingered lovingly on her son. He was the light of her life, despite the fact that he resembled her hardly at all.

'Mr Treasure's a merchant banker, mother.'

'What're you then, I'd like to know?' she questioned with vehemence and an undeniable, simple logic from over her shoulder, as she moved to the cooker to fill her own plate.

Mother and son were having their supper later than intended because, as Graham had explained, he had been kept working at the bank, clearing up bank and church business ahead of the extended week-end.

They were in the kitchen of Mrs Brown's semi-detached bungalow in Jubilee Avenue, a turning off the north side of the High Street, opposite the town hall. The long straight avenue

87

had been part of a property development in the mid 1930s. It had involved the demolition (now deeply deplored) of the best large Georgian house and garden in the town.

Mrs Brown's late husband had been a wages clerk at Utteridge Ales. He had paid off very little of the mortgage on the bungalow before his precipitate, early demise over twenty-five years before this. He had died of peritonitis while on holiday in Weston-super-Mare. A stubborn man, he had insisted that he was suffering only a stomach upset brought on by the boarding house rhubarb he had consumed against his better judgement. The protest had been vain and, since he had repeated it with his dying breath, cruelly inaccurate.

Happily, Mr Brown had covered the loan on the bungalow with life insurance. So with the roof over her head at least secured, Mrs Brown had provided everything else for herself and her son out of her modest wages. Now sixty-three, until her retirement, two years ago, she had worked in the bottling department at the brewery. Short, strong, and naturally buxom she had sensibly not anticipated remarriage, had quickly ceased to trouble with her appearance, and had let her figure go, spending next to nothing on herself, her clothes, or on new things for the home. But with her support and encouragement, Graham had been able to stay at school till he was eighteen. He had gone straight from there to work in the bank.

In Bertha Brown's estimation, her son had more than justified the sacrifices she had made for him. She couldn't have been more proud of him if he'd been Governor of the Bank of England – an office she had no doubt he'd fill one day if he chose to. She had mixed feelings about his still being a bachelor, though none about his choosing to go on living at home. She would have liked grandchildren, but she had yet to meet any girl remotely qualified to be her Graham's consort.

'The Southern is a clearing bank, mother. That's different from a merchant bank,' he said, tackling a dish of pie for the second time that day.

'But you'm the assistant manager.' Mrs Brown had never recognised that there was more than one of those.

'Mr Treasure's the head of his whole bank.'

88

'Still no reason why he can come down 'ere struttin' and puffin'.' She sat down opposite him at the table.

Graham reached for the salt cellar.

'Potatoes not salty enough for you? I'm positive I put in the usual.' She shook her head. She prided herself that she knew his tastes exactly.

'The Bishop was at college with Mr Treasure. Oxford. Makes a difference, that sort of thing.'

'Bein' at Oxford College may be all very well, but it don' make you the best one to look after the Chiversley convent, now do it? Not necessarily. Not better'n the local man who knows the place and the sisters. Like your tea now or wait till pudding? It's apricot crumble. Your favourite.' She blinked emphatically behind her spectacles as she poised the spout of the pot over her own cup. It would be her second cup of tea since she sat down. All those years bottling cold beer had only served to increase her endless craving for hot tea.

'I'll wait, thanks, mother. It's not the convent they're worried about. It's the money. What to do with it. When the nuns are gone.'

'But you'm been lookin' after their money all this time.'

'As treasurer of their maintenance account, not . . . not as a beneficiary of the trust.' He hoped she wouldn't ask again what that meant because he wasn't in the mood for complicated explanations.

'Ar, you told me about that before.' She paused, then gathered some carrots on her fork. 'I don't understand such things a'course, 'cept it seems to me they think very highly of you. The sisters. Reverend Mother told me again on Easter Sunday, remember?'

'I don't have to do very much.'

'Yes you do. What about tonight and such? Working late for the convent.' She stemmed his protest by speaking louder. 'Or for the church. In your own time. Anyway, Sister Patricia says you do a lot. Make her very happy you do, keepin' her hand in doin' them stamps. She do love doin' them.' Mrs Brown slurped some tea. 'Which ones have you got her on now?'

Graham had reddened at the mention of the subject. 'She's working on book plates. That's what she meant. Not stamps.'

'She said stamps. An' she don't waste words that one, an' that's a fact.'

'She forgets. She's very old.'

'Lovely. Lovely them stamps used to be.' She ran her tongue around her lips, then her eyes narrowed as she changed the subject. 'I expect they got too many for dinner tomorrow. At Chiversley 'all. Too many visitors over this benediction business.'

'Beneficiaries, mother.'

'That's what I said, warn't it? You was asked there before Christmas, all said and done.' She had watched the look of disappointment return to his face. Probably she shouldn't have brought the matter up again, but she was keen to know more. He'd said the Canon had asked in the bank this morning if Lady Bittern had invited him with the nobs, which meant the Canon thought she was going to.

'Christmas was only a wine and mince-pie party, mother. For honorary church officers.'

'It was plenty according to most people. Moira Edicomb didn't get asked.'

'Mrs Edicomb isn't an officer. She's only in the choir.'

'Goes on enough about it though.' She reached across for his empty plate. 'And you met Lady Bittern again the other day. You said.'

'That was only in the convent. By chance. She's often there.'

Mrs Brown picked a sliver of meat from between two of her back teeth. 'They could still ask you tomorrow. Now her ladyship knows the Canon's niece is going. Now they've accepted for her. They probably waited for that, like the Canon said. So you can escort her.'

'The Canon didn't say that, mother. Not exactly,' Brown explained accurately, wishing he hadn't mentioned it in the first place.

'Good as. It's not as though you aren't good enough to take her. Other way round really. She bein' half foreign. Pretty thing, of course,' Mrs Brown added grudgingly, putting her own plate on top of his. 'No doubt she'm after you. Asking to have lunch like that. You could have brought her here. There was plenty as it happens.' She sniffed. 'And if there hadn't been, I could have done without easy. Wouldn't have been the first time.' She sniffed again, then got up and put the plates in the washing-up basin in the sink.

He normally came home for lunch. It was only a three-minute walk from the bank. He had telephoned his mother at the last minute today to say he couldn't make it, and why.

Mrs Brown had mixed feelings about Christine Stonning. She was pleased because such an attractive, classy girl, a clergyman's niece, had fallen for her son, but she was worried because she was sure that, given time, Graham could do a lot better for himself. It bothered her too that if they married, Christine didn't seem the kind to want to live in Chiversley. And while these were Mrs Brown's surface concerns, deeper down she also had the suspicion that the relationship between Graham and the girl was too one-sided, that Christine might just be using him to suit her own ends. She wondered, for instance, why Christine had never come to Jubilee Avenue when Graham was always at the vicarage. Mrs Brown had only ever spoken to the girl twice, both times after church.

In truth, Mrs Brown was grossly over-estimating the seriousness of the liaison between Christine Stonning and her son. Nor was this entirely her fault. Graham had exaggerated the extent of the friendship to her, though not to anyone else. This was mostly because no one except his mother was ready to believe that Christine cared for him at all.

'Here's your crumble then.' She held out the plate for him to take. 'Your crumble love,' she repeated more loudly.

He started. 'Sorry, mother.'

His thoughts had been elsewhere, though not still on the dinner at Chiversley Hall to which he now hardly expected to be invited. He had told his mother what the Canon had said because he was always trying to build his social success in her eyes. He was much more concerned about the stamps. If Sister Patricia had been telling all and sundry that he put her up to printing . . .

'Don' you want no cream Graham?'

'Oh, thanks.'

Of course, he should have called Mrs Garnet back before lunch – sensed that there were problems since she had never rung him at the bank before. He had called her as soon as he had returned. If he had known earlier that the police were already involved in Shaftsborne he might have been able to put them off coming here, disturbing people in Chiversley. He could even have been late for lunch with Christine. It was that important. Not to upset the nuns.

As it was, he could have done with another word with Christine except she hadn't been at the vicarage when he had telephoned there later. Driven off in her car, the Canon had said, but he hadn't known where.

Graham was agonising over whether he had done the right thing.

'You look hot, love. Why don't you take off that waistcoat? Scorcher today it was.' Mrs Brown quenched matters with another cup of tea.

But it was apprehension not the heat that was making Graham Brown sweat.

With the motor only ticking over and the headlight switched off, Sean Ribble steered his Honda 350 cc off the Shaftsborne Road across the unlit, entirely empty carpark behind St Timothy's. He drew up in the far corner against the hedge, and under the overhang of a tree from the vicarage garden, before he cut the engine. The church clock showed four minutes after midnight. He had been careful with his speed on the ride from Tidmouth – at the time of night when the police were watching for drunk drivers. Sean had been careful to stay off alcohol all evening.

Being careful was what had kept him out of jail the last time.

After what had happened here in March, he'd had doubts about coming back at all – except the doubts had been outweighed by the size of the payment, in favours as well as cash. He'd received both in advance, too, this afternoon – in a deserted barn between here and Tidmouth. He had hidden the cash in his room, taped under a drawer where the old tart wouldn't find it: his pulse increased even now at the memory of what he'd got on top of the money – 'a bit of the other, like last time,' was how his patron had described the bonus when they had met.

He took off his helmet and donned a woollen balaclava. Despite the moonlight, he was a shadowy figure dressed now entirely in black. He left his gauntlets on the bike with the helmet, putting on soft leather gloves instead. He always wore gloves. It was fingerprints that had shopped Joss and Knuckles before – plus that witness remembering the number of Joss's bike. Neither of them had grassed. Sean hadn't believed they would. There'd been no point. The sentences had been light, considering the old geezer had croaked to order – not that Joss and Knuckles had known it was to order. But they did know their share of the money for the job was safe till they got out. Of course, they only got cash: the favours were exclusive.

He vaulted the stile that led into the field behind the vic-arage. Crouching from this point, he followed the dilapidated, bramble-covered iron fence that marked the back boundaries of the vicarage and then the convent grounds. Close to the boundary, on the other side, he passed what he realised was a burial ground, but not an ordinary one. In a rectangle confined by low clipped hedges, there were regular rows of small, identical metal crosses, and a big cross in the middle with a Jesus figure on it. He thought at first it must be a dog cemetery because the spaces between the little crosses were so small; then he figured it was for the nuns. He reckoned there were two or three hundred crosses, then looked away because graveyards gave him the creeps, especially this one. He stopped when he had covered almost the width of the convent building and counted off the windows in the half-basement. The garden frontage was seventy yards from where he was standing, and the whole place was in darkness.

When he was ready, he stepped over the bars of the fence in a place where it had entirely collapsed. After filling his lungs, he sprinted across the grassed open space, heading for the sixth basement window from the end.

He felt safer once he was within the shadow of the building, and safer still when he dropped down into the open basement area. He moved his feet carefully so as not to rustle the dead leaves that must have been there since the autumn.

The window sash went up to his touch and with very little noise, just as he'd been told it would. So far the job was a piece of cake.

He was wary as he got inside, switching on his torch while

he was still balanced on the window ledge, and before letting his feet touch the floor. It was a small room with upright pianos against three walls, a stack of chairs in the middle, and piles of music on the pianos and in the corners. It was tempting to do the job here without going further, but he was under orders.

After closing the window and the latch, he crossed to the door and slowly turned the knob. The door yielded with the same ease as the window and with even less noise. He listened for a moment, then stepped out into the corridor. The risks here were obvious. Unless he took care he could bring down what looked like a lifetime's hoard of junk.

He moved forward gingerly, making for the second door on the left. It slipped open at a touch like the other one, but with a loud creak, or so it seemed to the intruder, now overacclimatised to the dead silence.

It was the printing room he was entering. Once inside he moved more easily. He purposely left the door open behind him.

The briefing had been spot-on again. The stuff in the room was perfect for what he'd come to do. He threw the catch on the centre window and opened it wide ready for his exit. He had to remember to partially close it again from the outside when he left – to within a foot of the bottom. That's how it would have been if the usual occupant had forgotten to close it when she had left an hour or so before this.

The night breeze wafting in from the outside seemed brisker to Sean than it had been before – and better for the purpose. It was strong enough even to have worked the corridor door open by itself. The catch was very worn.

He picked up the small brass candlestick on the desk. With the penknife from his pocket he carefully cut off half the candle in the stick without disturbing its base. Then he took out his lighter and lit what was left of the candle in the stick. Next he systematically set light to a dozen stacks of paper on the shelves, beginning close to the desk, working toward the door and then just into the corridor where he lit the brown paper wrapping around a burst parcel of old curtains. Quickly retracing his steps, he put the flame to the papers on the desk, tipped the candle onto them, had a last satisfied look round at what he had done, then left through the window.

'Do behave, Lazarus,' whispered Sister Mary Maud. 'No, we're not going that way. Not to make messes on gravestones.' She tugged at the lead.

Lazarus responded with a determined pull in the direction he wanted to go, but for once it was not nearly determined enough, not with Sister Mary Maud in her present mood. While being partially dragged along in her wake, Lazarus glared his protest and made expiring noises in his throat. But both these last demonstrations went for nothing. Sister Mary Maud wasn't looking and her hearing wasn't up to registering subtle canine emissions below barking level – something Lazarus should have learned by now.

The Sister was far from ready to indulge Lazarus whom she had caught sniffing with serious intent in the corridor outside her room on the ground floor near the chapel. This had been on her return from the bathroom. It was lucky she had still been fully dressed. In fact she had earlier fallen asleep in her chair and been woken up in the darkness by the church clock striking midnight. She had not put any lights on. Using electricity or even candles was wasteful in such strong moonlight.

Sister Mary Maud had no idea why Lazarus had been in the corridor. He normally spent the night in Reverend Mother's room which was next to her own. There had been no purpose in letting him in there now either, risking waking up Reverend Mother, and worse, at the very point where Lazarus was about to have a bowel motion. Sister Mary Maud knew the signs well enough. That kind of sniffing meant only one thing, and where the untutored Lazarus found himself at such a time was immaterial to him.

The two had emerged not through the main door of the convent, but by the smaller one near the chapel which the nuns used if they were en route to the vicarage. The thing now was to keep the dog moving till they reached what Sister Mary Maud considered a seemly spot for his operations. Neither the front of the convent nor the front of the vicarage qualified in her estimation, and neither did the churchyard – especially not the churchyard. She simply couldn't countenance his again desecrating his favourite tombstone there. She hurried her charge onwards into the carpark and then for the first time slackened the lead and allowed him to sniff again on his own account. Except perversely he now seemed to have lost the urge.

It wasn't until they got to the end of the vicarage hedge that Lazarus applied his nose to the ground in front of him with the same business-like intent that he'd been showing earlier in the corridor.

Sister Mary Maud gave a little sigh of relief. 'Hurry up, Lazarus. Do get on with it,' she pressed. Then, as always, her better nature took hold of her. She was ashamed at being so unfeeling – at issuing so indelicate a directive on so intimate a subject, even to an animal. But really, Lazarus was a fearful nuisance. There, she was being unfeeling again, in her heart at least.

Penitently, she followed her charge under the boughs of the overhanging tree only to discover him with one leg cocked against the front wheel of a motor-cycle. He fixed her with the reproachful look he levelled at anyone who stared at him at all such moments, then moving forward a little, he settled on his haunches and at last began to make serious straining movements. He also intensified the reproachful look.

Almost as relieved as Lazarus was going to be, Sister Mary Maud averted her gaze toward the motor-cycle. It was after she had done so that she became vaguely aware that there might be something familiar about it. She memorised the licence number partly for this reason, but mostly because it continued to give her something to concentrate on, aside from the quivering animal.

It did not immediately occur to the Sister that the owner of the machine had parked it where it was for any illicit purpose. It was a public carpark after all, and putting the machine under a tree would protect it from the damp – a strategy with which Sister Mary Maud was wholly in sympathy. Certainly she had misgivings about that same owner stepping in what Lazarus would leave behind. But she really couldn't risk interrupting *that* operation at this stage.

It was some moments later that Sister Mary Maud and Lazarus started their quite slow return to the front of the convent – just as Sean was leaving quite quickly at the back.

Chapter Ten

'If it hadn't been for-for-for Sister Mary Maud they might all three of them have been-been-been burned in their beds,' said the cassocked Canon Stonning accelerating the delivery of his words, and finishing on a crescendo. The exaggerated swaying of his trunk lent extra gravity to the judgement.

The Bishop of Shaftsborne considered the matter more coolly. He was looking rather less than half episcopal because although the golf shirt he had on was reddish, his slacks were a distinctly non-liturgical yellow. 'But the chapel and the nuns' bedrooms have survived,' he said. 'That's about all that has of course.' He gazed in the direction of the chapel

'With a bit of the main entrance,' said Treasure, also dressed for golf, but more conservatively than the Bishop.

'Well, I think they owe their lives to that little dog,' offered Molly Treasure with spirit.

'Indirectly,' her husband agreed grudgingly. It went against the grain to credit the anti-social Lazarus with good works.

'Well, if the fire took hold that quickly, another few minutes before the alarm was raised might have done for the sisters,' Molly insisted.

It was 7.30 on Saturday morning. A few minutes before this, the Bishop had been collecting Treasure for golf when the Canon had telephoned the news that a fire in the night had virtually destroyed the convent. The golfers had postponed their plans, and Molly, who wasn't filming, had insisted on joining them to drive up in the Bishop's Rover to view the damage.

The Canon had been waiting to greet them at the vicarage door, the jaunty angle of his biretta indicating haste not intention. His manner was nervous, it seemed to Treasure, less because of

97

the fire than the presence of a Bishop, even a dishabille bishop, and to whom the lesser cleric was being almost penitentially obsequious.

The Canon had explained that on returning from airing Lazarus in the carpark, Sister Mary Maud had found the convent ablaze in the middle, the flames already licking up from the basement to the upper floor. She had gone straight into the burning building and roused the others, both of whom had been asleep still. After she and the Reverend Mother had brought out Sister Patricia, Sister Mary Maud had then hurried to the vicarage and woken the Stonnings.

Once the fire brigade had arrived, the Canon continued, it had fought the blaze for more than an hour before getting it under control, partly because of the amount of highly combustible materials on all floors, particularly the basement. It had been a further two hours before the flames and smoke were completely extinguished.

Now the area in front of the convent resembled the aftermath of a battle as much as a fire. All except one of the fire appliances had left the scene already. Firemen were homing on the remaining appliance, rolling in hoses, and stowing equipment and protective clothing. Other vehicles looked more abandoned than parked because the earlier departure of fire engines and two ambulances had left them isolated at what now seemed unaccountably odd angles. They belonged to the police, the fire and rescue services, the council, local builders and volunteers. There were numerous gangs working on the clearing up operation, some in uniform or overalls, others in ordinary clothes. It seemed to Treasure that there was too little left now for so many to do, and that people were getting in each other's way.

Knots of mostly elderly sightseers, restricted by rope barriers and a diminutive policewoman, were contemplating the scene, exchanging sad glances and probably equally sad words.

Graham Brown was supervising what was evidently an authorised band of parishioners. They were transporting furniture, pictures and other impedimenta from the surviving part of the building to supplement a scattered collection of larger items rescued earlier by the firemen, and now lying on the grass between the convent and the vicarage.

As for the convent itself, most of what had been the long main section had been reduced to a roofless, floorless, blackened shell – a gaunt, bare pair of uneven charred walls with holes for windows. In the very centre even the walls had collapsed, or were being pushed over by the flexing giant arm of an orange coloured tracked vehicle that was poking about like a scavenging dinosaur. The protruding chapel and a short section of the adjoining part of the building had certainly survived, but on the other side, only the façade of the balancing entrance wing was still standing.

As the Canon and his party warily stepped past the temporary obstacles, trying to avoid large pools of water and muddy ruts in the churned-up grass, another builder's lorry arrived carrying metal scaffolding and shoring materials.

'Our builder, Mr Molyneux, is over there. He says he can make the chapel wing functional and-and-and habitable again quite quickly,' said the Canon, but shaking his head and sounding doubtful.

'Where are the nuns now?' asked Molly, stepping round a short wooden pew, an exercise bicycle, a galvanised wash-tub, and a large china statue of Sir Winston Churchill clustered together like some surrealist's invention, and abandoned on the grass.

'Sister Patricia and Sister Mary Maud are both in Shaftsborne General Hospital,' the Canon announced mournfully. 'Sister Patricia broke her ankle attempting to go back for something when Reverend Mother wasn't looking. Or when Reverend Mother was doing the same herself as like as not. Sister Mary Maud actually did go back before that without anyone knowing. To fetch her armchair and the statue of the Virgin from the chapel. When she re-emerged she was bowled over by a water jet. Sent flying like-like-like a prison rioter. They didn't know she was there, d'you see? Not till it was too late.' He paused, wiping a hand over an anguished face. 'The chair disintegrated. The Virgin she saved, but Sister Mary Maud fell against something. It knocked her unconscious for a bit. She came to quite quickly but she wasn't making any sense. That's why they shipped her off with Sister Patricia. Good thing too. They're all incorrigible, of course.' The Canon extended his arms outwards then drew them behind him, clasping his hands together as he led the way in the direction of the chapel. 'Reverend Mother is asleep in the vicarage. Lazarus is there too. D'you know Reverend Mother was out here till nearly dawn, fetching and carrying? And praying?' He stopped abruptly after making the last point, his eyes and bits of his face moving about in an anticipatory kind of way. He seemed also to be slowly collapsing one leg.

It went through Treasure's mind that the Canon was about to follow the Reverend Mother's example by leading the group in prayer. This might have been appropriate enough – even an example to the firemen – but not if Stonning intended everybody to follow his pious urge from a kneeling position on the sopping wet ground. It was also questionable whether with a bishop present the Canon should be taking the initiative with unscheduled importuning of the Almighty.

It was then that the Canon straightened up again, revealing that, with some difficulty, he had merely been extricating a large handkerchief from a trouser pocket under his cassock. He blew his nose loudly.

'So you were here too, Canon,' said Molly in a sympathetic tone.

'Most of the time, yes. So was my wife. And Christine, my niece. Towers of strength, both of them. Made tea for everyone amongst other things. Oh, and Charles Utteridge-Flax was here too. We've all had forty winks since then.' It seemed the others were having them still. 'And there's the very chap we want. Divisional Fire Officer. Well, Mr Arridge, any-any-any clue yet about how it started?' he called, hands now thrust behind his back, body lunging forward from the waist.

Arridge was a jolly looking heavyweight with a Kitchener-style moustache and enormous eyebrows. He was wearing yellow fire-fighting gear that squeaked loudly as he walked, and a white fireman's helmet with two black bands around it. He had emerged from the chapel doorway with as purposeful a step as his clothing allowed and was being followed by another man, yellow-coated, head covered by an ordinary safety helmet, and who was moving less quickly. The second man was carrying a Polaroid camera and a clipboard with papers secured at the top.

The Divisional Fire Officer changed direction, halted in front of the group, and smacked his lips. 'Definitely started in the printing room, Canon. Lighted candle knocked over by the wind probably. This one,' he said, holding up a stubby, blackened brass candlestick protected inside a clear plastic bag. 'What's left of the centre window frame there was definitely wedged half open.'

'But Sister Patricia is sure the window was shut when she left the room. And she said she blew out the candle,' the Canon offered in a troubled voice.

'That's the one who broke her ankle or the one we washed away, sir?'

'Broken ankle. She's—'

'She also said there was three or four inches of candle left in the candlestick,' Arridge interrupted. 'There wasn't. Only about an inch when the fire started. Memory plays tricks on the elderly, of course,' he ended tactfully.

'How can you tell anything from a candle, Mr Arridge? Wasn't what was left of it burned away in the fire?' asked the Bishop, challenging as much as questioning.

'This is the Bishop of Shaftsborne, Mr Arridge,' the Canon explained quickly. 'The Bishop,' he repeated pointedly, implying his superior's appearance might be making the identification hard to credit.

'I know that, sir. The Bishop and I have met before. Spoiled the golf this morning, and no mistake, Bishop,' Arridge responded with a cheerful salute to the prelate. 'And this is Miss Molly Forbes, of course.' He gave Molly a warm smile from behind his moustache, an object that Treasure concluded might constitute a fire hazard in itself. 'My wife heard you were filming locally. Great admirers of yours we are.' He turned back to John Larpin after a nod at the banker, evidently meant to indicate he had worked out his identity too. 'Condition of the wick, you see, Bishop?' he continued. 'Burns differently if it's in a fire. Mr Curslake here's got what's left of that. The wick. He's the area inspector for the Home Office.'

Curslake, who seemed old for the job – almost any job – had a downcast air, possibly because he was out of breath. He lifted his eyes after the introduction and treated each member of the group to a gimlet gaze, head moving slowly up and down as well as along, like an undertaker checking heights for future reference. 'We have the tests to go through. But Mr Arridge is right enough . . . I'm afraid.' He added the final phrase after everyone had assumed he had finished speaking. 'The centre of the conflagration was the candle on the desk.' He began again slowly, his eyes now reappraising everybody's feet. Because all present waited for an expected further utterance there was stony silence as Curslake's stomach next gave a highly audible rumble – and one that went on for some time. 'No doubt of that,' he ended, looking up at Arridge with a surprised expression as though it had been the other's stomach that had rumbled.

'It must have been blowing a gale to topple a candlestick of that weight,' said Treasure, regarding the object in the bag again.

'Those sort go over easier than you think . . . It's not weighted,' Curslake replied. 'It was on its side.' He wet his lips. 'On the desk.'

'Couldn't it have been knocked over during the fire? By falling debris from above?' asked the Bishop.

'Possible. Or it could have been knocked over accidentally by the Sister as she left the room,' said Arridge guardedly.

'That seems very—'

'I'm not saying it was, mark you,' the fireman cut off the Canon's burgeoning protest. 'But it could have been. With those big sleeves they have.' With a wide movement of one arm he brought a hand to undo the top of his own voluminous suit. 'If the candlestick started the fire before it went over, loose papers from the desk must have blown against it. Got caught by the flame. That could have done it, easy. It was this candle that started things off. No question. The fire began in that room, and there's nothing else there that could have been the cause. No electrical shorts, no burnt plugs, nothing. Forensic tests will prove that all right.' He looked over his shoulder. 'That reminds me, there's a policeman over there wanting an urgent word. Will you all excuse us?' He smiled broadly at Molly again, then moved off with Curslake in tow.

'That's the same policeman who was here yesterday,' said the Canon watching them.

'Mr Treasure told me about that,' the Bishop remarked. 'They weren't printing stamps in the convent were they?'

'I don't believe so,' the Canon replied in a worried voice, as though he'd been asked if they'd been distilling gin.

'Well they certainly won't be any more,' said Treasure.

'The building was insured, of course?' Molly asked.

'Not for what it'll cost to rebuild,' replied the Canon, this time almost as sadly as Curslake.

'If rebuilding's the answer,' said the Bishop, looking at Treasure.

'Ah, morning Terence. Morning Jill,' said the Canon suddenly, turning to address two newcomers, 'Know Mr and Mrs Treasure do you? The Bishop you do know, of course. Mrs Treasure, this is Dr Jill Wader, one of the beneficiaries.'

'With rather fewer benefits to indulge this morning,' said Dr Wader dryly, in a husky, bronchitic voice. She had marched briskly up to the group with a golden retriever dog following obediently at her heels. The dog was not on a leash, but Dr Wader had a chain lead clasped in her hand. Terence Natt was with the Doctor. Her height – which was nearly six feet – made him seem even shorter than he was.

Dr Wader was thin as well as tall, with fair wavy hair, and a tan to the parched skin of her face. Attractive in an outdoor way, she had on a white open-necked blouse, a light wool cardigan, a pleated blue skirt, ankle socks, and stout walking shoes that were practical if less than flattering to her lean but well-proportioned legs. She wore neither make-up nor ornaments, only a man's gold wrist watch on a leather strap.

Treasure had looked up the lady in an academic directory. She was a senior lecturer in modern languages, single, and aged thirty-seven – but she looked younger. 'Dr Wader, delighted to meet you, despite the circumstances,' he said as he and Molly shook hands with the lecturer. 'Good morning Mr Natt,' he added, before introducing the lawyer to his wife.

'Dreadful business. A blessing no one was killed,' said the sober-suited Natt, whistling through the 'blessing'. 'Though I understand both Sisters Patricia and Mary Maud were injured?'

'Broken ankle and concussion,' said the Canon, sounding like an automatic recording.

'The fire was an accident, of course. But do we know how it started?' asked Dr Wader. 'Sit,' she added quietly to the dog, which did so promptly, much to Treasure's satisfaction: it made such a sharp contrast to the conduct of the unruly Lazarus. 'Sorry to be so out-of-date everyone,' the Doctor continued before her previous question had been answered, 'I've only just driven over to my house here from campus. Started early to avoid the traffic. The news has been an awful shock.'

The Canon bent forwards then back again. 'The Divisional Fire Officer believes the fire was caused by a candle Sister Patricia left burning. After she left the printing room.'

'Nonsense,' rejoined the Doctor, and choking back a cough.

'Why do you say that, Jill?' the Bishop asked, hands in his pockets.

'Because Sister Patricia is a meticulous woman. She just wouldn't leave a candle alight in . . .' the rest of what she was about to say was lost in a heavy outburst of painful coughing. 'Sorry,' she cawed breathlessly some moments later from behind her handkerchief. 'Giving up smoking is supposed to have . . .' the coughing broke out again, '. . . supposed to have cured this.'

'Just look at that,' said a fresh voice from behind the Canon. 'Fate seems to have caught up with evolution. With a terrible vengeance too.' It was Utteridge-Flax who had appeared during the Doctor's coughing fit. 'How do you do Mrs Treasure,' he went on, giving Molly his name and glancing round his acknowledgements to the others.

'I gather you did sterling work here in the night, Charles,' said the Bishop. 'We're all very grateful.'

'We all did what we could, Bishop. Couldn't have saved the building, of course. But it must have been ordained you know? A sign.'

'Is that what you meant about fate catching up, Charles?' asked Jill Wader woodenly.

'Well hasn't it?' he answered. 'The useful life of this building, it's purposeful life, well its been over for some time. Don't you agree Bishop?'

'I can't accept the fire was ordained. No.'

'All right. But it didn't happen fifty, a hundred years ago when the place was a power-house of good works. It happened when three spent old ladies were seeing out their days.'

'If you mean we shouldn't rebuild, I don't agree,' Dr Wader interrupted.

'The problem might be what to rebuild,' said Natt, eyeing the Bishop and trying to sound profound.

'I should have thought that was obvious,' replied the lecturer, though judging by the looks of some it wasn't as obvious as all that.

'The site will be quite valuable,' observed Utteridge-Flax.

'As though the trust isn't rich enough already,' Dr Wader came back sharply before her coughing started again.

'Won't the insurance company insist that we rebuild? I mean if-if-if they give us the money?' asked the Canon with a perplexed expression.

'No,' supplied Treasure, who was non-executive chairman of a large insurance company. 'And depending on whether you do or you don't, there may be benefits or penalties. Better read the policy.'

'The convent is insured for two hundred thousand pounds,' said the voice of Graham Brown. He had come across from the working party and joined the group quietly at the back. He was dirty and dishevelled and was holding a processional cross.

'Graham, you look like a latter-day John the Baptist emerging from a wilderness,' said Dr Wader.

'The cross belongs to the church not the convent. It was borrowed over Easter,' Brown offered in the direction of the Canon. 'I thought I might as well put it back now.'

'We'd better go and see if we can help with anything,' Dr Wader announced. 'Excuse us, will you?' She moved off with the retriever and Natt both at her heels.

'Where's the other stuff going?' the Bishop asked Brown.

'Back in the convent chapel, Bishop, when everything's dried out. That's when we can make the place secure.'

'How secure was it before?' asked Molly. 'I mean if Sister Patricia didn't leave that candle lit or the window open, could someone else—'

'Are you Mr Graham Brown, sir?' Molly was interrupted by the quiet but insistent voice of Detective Constable Rawlins, not deliberately so because he hadn't heard her speaking as he approached with Arridge.

'That's me, yes,' Brown responded, his grip tightening on the processional cross.

'And you're the treasurer for the convent, sir?'

Curslake now appeared behind Arridge, clipboard under one arm. He held his Polaroid camera up to one eye as though about to take a picture of the group, then brought it down again to his side.

'I'm the Honorary Treasurer, yes.' Brown had watched Curslake's performance with evident apprehension.

Rawlins brushed his hair back with his hand. 'Could we have a word, Mr Brown?'

Brown glanced from side to side as if he was looking for an escape route, but he stayed rooted to the spot. Only his arms began to tremble, just perceptibly shaking the cross in his grasp. 'A word?' he repeated, blinking furiously.

'In private, sir. Just routine.' Brown, still carrying the cross, moved toward the policeman who continued in a confidential tone. 'It's about a Mrs Garnet of Shaftsborne. I believe you know her?'

Chapter Eleven

'You were the first to suggest it could be arson,' said Treasure to his wife. They were driving in the Rolls along the three miles of the Shaftsborne Road that separated Chiversley from Chiversley Hall, seat of the Bittern family. It was nearly eight o'clock. They were summoned for dinner at the Hall on the hour.

'But how was I to know they were just about to arrest Mr . . . er . . . Mr Smith was it?'

'Brown, actually. Graham Brown,' he corrected, adding, 'He's not very memorable. They didn't arrest him, by the way. I thought I'd told you. John Larpin rang the Canon about it when we got back from golf. You were still out shopping.'

'So Mr Brown hasn't been running a counterfeiting operation in cahoots with Sister Patricia? How disappointing. But he is treasurer at the convent?'

'Yes. And the Canon says he's as tight-fisted with the nuns' money as they are with it themselves. More concerned with hoarding it than spending it.'

'Isn't that a good thing?'

'Not if it keeps them dressed in rags and undernourished.'

'Is it as bad as that?'

'Nearly. That's again according to the Canon, and I'm inclined to believe him. The trust is worth millions. Well you know that. Incidentally, I'm sure now that Brown would have been a bad choice for third beneficiary.'

'Even if John Larpin hadn't conjured you up for the job? Because Mr Brown is parsimonious? But the police weren't after him for that surely?'

Treasure slowed the car to read a signpost, then accelerated again. 'No. It seems, without telling anyone, he did put Sister

Patricia up to printing the odd block of facsimile stamps—'

'Forgeries,' Molly interrupted expectantly.

'With the word "facsimile" overprinted on the front,' he completed. 'No question of duping anyone.'

'Prince James Island stamps? For educational purposes?'

He shifted in the driving seat. 'And a few other sorts too.'

'Still sounds fishy to me. Anyway, why put Sister Patricia to work at all at her age? Even to fill an educational need?'

'For money. For the convent house account. As I told you, all the materials were available. Brown arranged for a dealer in Shaftsborne to distribute the stamps.'

'To schools and museums.'

'And a few other dealers. That letter I told you I posted yesterday for Sister Patricia, the one Sister Mary Maud thought she'd lost. That was addressed to the Shaftsborne dealer, Mrs Garnet.'

'And it only had facsimile stamps in it?'

'No idea. I mentioned it to the Canon. I expect he told the police.'

'But a lot of money's been involved?' Molly still sounded sceptical.

'No. Quite nominal amounts. And it was all above board. The total income was shown in the convent accounts that Brown produces every year. The income from stamps came to about two hundred pounds last year, that's all. It was included in the accounts under the composite heading of "sundry print work". That was the sticking point though. He could have been more specific.'

'Like listing them separately as "sundry forged stamps"?' Molly smoothed the skirt of her colourful designer dress. 'And no one else knew anything about it?'

'Seems not. Sister Patricia knew of course, but she's pretty uncommunicative. Well, most nuns are, I suppose.'

'Only the ones in contemplative orders. Where they're not allowed to talk. Sister Mary Maud is quite a chatterbox, and the Reverend Mother does her bit too. Now I think about it, Sister Patricia didn't say much when I had tea with them. But if the stamps had facsimile printed all over them, why were the police so interested?'

'Because they're after the source of a forged Prince James Island stamp. They just wanted to see an example of Sister Patricia's work. Except . . .' he paused while eyeing an arched stone gateway several hundred yards ahead on the left.

'Except this morning there conveniently aren't any examples to see. Because they've all been burned to a cinder. Hard cheese for the police,' Molly completed for him. 'Is this it?' she added.

'Must be.' He slowed the car, then swung it through the opening.

'That was less a gate than a triumphal arch,' said Molly. 'Except it's seen better days. The lodge looked empty.'

'And the house needs attention, by the look of it,' her husband commented. 'But it's getting some though. Unless that scaffolding at the back is just to hold the place together.'

The building he was talking about was fleetingly visible through clumps of trees on rising ground. It lay beyond about a half mile of sweeping drive that was also in need of repair. A square, stone, three-storey edifice, it was a stately home of the kind common enough in the West Country though of more modest proportions than some. On first sight it was difficult to date. The east and the north fronts, now clearly visible from the car, were under a dormered mansard-roof, heavily balustraded, and with a cupola behind in the centre. There were nine sets of windows to both façades, the centre three under plain pediments. The northern façade also incorporated the main entrance in the middle, but this was hidden from view behind a *porte-cochère*.

'Architect or architects?' asked Molly, assuming her husband would have looked the house up somewhere.

'Yes, various. There's been a house here, seat of the Bittern family, since Elizabethan times. This one was originally designed by the illustrious Roger Pratt in 1666. It was substantially altered by Robert Furze Brettingham a century later. Bathrooms, flushing loos and other civilising appurtenances were put in by Charles Barry who did the place over in 1839.'

'Well let's be thankful for that because it doesn't look as if they've done much since. Mind that sheep.'

Dilapidated iron fencing was enclosing the pastureland on either side of the drive, but in a desultory way. The car was just passing the only livestock in sight, about ten Dorset Horns which, in the perverse way of sheep, were nibbling the grass on the wrong side of what was left of the fencing.

'The place is rather magnificent though,' said Treasure who had brought the car down to a crawl as they neared the house. 'Pity the stone facing is flaking quite so badly. I imagine it'll be the very devil to make good. That's probably what the scaffolding is about on the garden front.'

'Expensive job?'

'Mmm. And the Canon told me Lucius Bittern is hard-up. So's his stockbroking business in the City.'

'But he's still Chairman of Utteridge Ales?'

'Non-executive Chairman. All he gets for that is a quite nominal director's fee.'

'But Lady Bittern is the second largest shareholder. Perhaps she's paying for the repairs. Did he become Chairman after they married?'

'Yes. I hadn't appreciated that before. Not till John mentioned it during golf this morning.'

'So that could be why he married her?'

'Bit too obvious wouldn't you say? Difficult to guess, of course, without knowing either of them. We'll have a better idea in a minute or two. I imagine her as a timid violet.'

'A rich timid violet, who goes for older men and married one. No, that doesn't sound right. I'll bet she's gorgeous and a raver, and he's an impecunious but well-preserved and . . . and dashing aristocrat. Of course, if they don't get on that well—'

'Who said that?'

'You did. The Canon told you.'

'I'd forgotten. Anyway, I never postulate on gossip.'

'Hardly ever,' Molly answered promptly. 'Only in the company of bishops and canons.'

'We're not the first to arrive,' he said, changing the subject. He drew the car up beside four others parked in the drive which opened out into a semi-circle opposite the entrance.

'So there couldn't have been a future for the convent—'

'More coffee, Mark? My husband looking after you is he? Absolutely delighted you came. Both of you. Weren't we Lucius?' bellowed the immense and entirely unpredicted Sheila

110

Bittern, interrupting her husband in mid-sentence. She had sailed across the room to offer hostess attentions, with a serving maid trailing behind her. 'You happy with that glass of port still?' she went on. 'Marlene here can get you anything else.'

Dinner had ended. The guests had left the dining-room, a draughty area in need of redecoration, and had moved to the drawing-room, where the carpets were even more threadbare, and where the singular lack of furniture befitting the age of the house and the status of the family occupying it was even more marked. Treasure was standing with Lucius Bittern and others before the only item of enduring quality in the room, a painting of Daniel Utteridge, First Baron Chiversley, painted by John Lavery in 1886. It was hanging on the otherwise empty wall space between two long windows overlooking the garden front.

The banker had regretted accepting what had been advertised as a Buck's Fizz at the start of the evening, and which he was sure had contained neither genuine champagne nor freshly pressed orange juice. The wines at dinner had been unremarkable, a lack of distinction that they had shared with the food, while the port, brought now from the dining table at the host's suggestion, was as subtle on the palate as an acid drop.

'D'you know, I'd quite enjoy a whisky and soda,' said Treasure, cleaving to the axiom that there is no such thing as bad Scotch. He debated whether he ought to consume the rest of the port, but decided against. He put the far from empty glass on the coffee tray held at a careless and precipitous angle by Marlene, an overpainted teenager who, while dressed in the part of the maid this evening, at first sight he believed had been the cashier at the Chiversley petrol station he had used earlier in the day. The girl had confirmed this by leering at him in an embarrassingly familiar way at every opportunity all evening, including this one. 'That's a very fine portrait,' he continued to Lady Bittern, and avoiding Marlene's lustful gaze.

'Good looking old bugger, wasn't he? Sorry Bishop,' the hostess replied cheerfully, nodding at Bishop Larpin who was on the other side of Treasure with Dr Jill Wader. 'One of the few half decent pictures we've got in the house. All of them my family's, I may tell you. You'd have thought there'd

111

have been a few Bitterns on the wall of the ancestral pile still, wouldn't you? But Lucius's father flogged 'em all off, decades back. To pay his gambling debts. All the Bittern portraits went, along with the good furniture, and quite a few old masters they used to have here. That included a Munnings, chap who painted horses, you know? Bloody shame we lost that.'

Since her interruption, the lady's husband had suffered the subsequent soliloquy with the outward appearance of equanimity. His face showed the wooden tolerance of someone waiting for an overdue train who has just been reliably informed it will be arriving shortly. He had not truly reacted to anything she said. It was almost as though her torrent of words, and Treasure's polite few in response, had never been voiced, except he had given the vacillating Marlene a terse nod to indicate she should get on with taking the coffee tray away and bringing back what the guest had asked for.

When his wife fell silent momentarily – while lighting a cigarette – Lucius Bittern continued with what he was saying exactly where he had stopped earlier. 'So there couldn't have been a future for the convent in any case,' he insisted. 'Waste of time and money to rebuild it, I'd say. Not like this house. The three surviving nuns ought to be institutionalised,' he finished, stolidly unaware of any incongruity in the last sentence.

Bittern had proved nearer to Molly's expectation than his wife had done. Of medium height and sparish build, there was no hint of flabbiness about him, and he carried himself like a soldier. His straight, still light brown hair was neatly brushed across a pock-marked forehead. The nose was sharp, the mouth thin, and the out-thrust chin very square. There was a boyish suppleness to him, which a cynic might have said was a good match for the immaturity of most of his statements. He had also demonstrated that he was quite lacking in humour.

Lady Bittern was an inch taller than her husband, and of a much more formidable build. If he looked to be in less than what the Canon had described as his mid-fifties, she looked to be well into her early thirties. That she was pregnant might have begun to show in her figure, though this was difficult to determine with certainty. She was wearing a sleeveless sack dress made from a coarse black material. This was adorned by a brooch crookedly attached to the shoulder of the dress and depicting a horse, inset with jewels. The lady's straight dark hair, cut short but hardly dressed, was parted on the left and held in place with a schoolgirl's gilt slide in the shape of a miniature hunting crop. The podgy cheeks and button nose had a ruddy outdoor glow to them like the rest of the face. But it was Lady Bittern's impish dark eyes that Treasure had remarked at first encounter, and which he later decided just might denote a capacity for something more malign.

'You might not think it from what he says, but Lucius is quite religious really, aren't you, Lucius?' the hostess next asserted, blowing smoke at the group, which also included Terence Natt and Christine Stonning. 'He's gone off nuns a bit, that's all. Can't see the point of keeping the Chiversley convent open. Especially not now,' she went on, without giving her husband the chance to confirm his spiritual predilections, enduring or declining. 'Of course there's only one building Lucius cares passionately about. The one we're in.'

The hostess had moved to one side as she had been speaking and grasped the drawer cord to the heavy curtains. 'Should have closed these earlier,' she said, giving the cord an energetic tug. In response, the left-hand curtain gave a little tremble down its whole length but otherwise stayed as it was. In contrast, the right-hand curtain gave a cracking noise at the top, then collapsed dramatically and entirely, scattering the guests. Amid cries of alarm and nervous laughter it crumpled in a heap on the carpet in a cloud of dust.

'Oh well, another job for the morning,' observed Lady Bittern as though nothing unusual or surprising had happened – a view not shared by those who had removed themselves just ahead of being buried under a now dormant pile of damask. 'Better leave the others open, I suppose,' she concluded, puffing at her cigarette while tentatively pushing back the heap with her foot and disturbing more dust.

There was an awkward pause while the others regrouped.

'Sorry about that everyone,' said Lucius Bittern gruffly. 'We don't use the main reception rooms much.'

'Could happen in the best regulated house,' Natt provided inanely, while looking even greyer than usual.

'Sheila was saying you'd gone off nuns, Lucius,' said Christine, tactfully getting the conversation back to where it had been. 'Did you know they all dote on you? It's partly the title. Reverend Mother's a terrible snob.'

'There are plenty of thriving Anglican convents elsewhere in Britain,' Dr Wader offered seriously in her throaty voice, and stepped back to avoid the smoke as well as the dust the hostess was continuing to generate.

'Oh, there's no fear of nuns becoming extinct in the Church of England. There are nearly a thousand still in England alone. Religious communities are going through a period of rationalisation, that's all,' observed the Bishop, showing the against-the-odds optimism he considered appropriate to the company.

'It's an absolute tragedy we'd not quite reached the stage of sorting out the bits and pieces at the convent before the fire,' Dr Wader went on. 'There was so much there that should have been preserved. Showing the sort of work that's gone on through a century and a half.'

'At the print school for instance?' said Treasure.

'Absolutely. I'd imagine that was unique. I spent an hour chatting about it with Sister Patricia only last Sunday.'

'Chatting with Sister Patricia is a pretty unique experience all by itself,' said Christine, a hint of enquiry in her tone.

'I always feel guilty when I talk to her. As if I'm making her break a vow of silence,' offered Sheila Bittern, though most of her hearers thought that the Sister's opportunity for breaking that particular vow in Lady Bittern's company would have been fairly slight.

'I've felt the same at other times,' the Doctor replied. 'But something had been bothering her. About her work.'

The speaker was not the only one of the group to look concerned at the disclosure.

'To do with postage stamps, was it?' asked Treasure.

'Yes, it was. Why?'

'Has no one told you the police are interested in that too?'

114

'The police? No.' She looked a lot more surprised than her hearers. 'I'm afraid I haven't talked to anyone since I left you this morning. Been working in the garden all day.'

'What was it Sister Patricia was saying?' asked the Bishop.

'If you'll forgive me, Bishop, I believe Jill should tell the police that before telling anyone else,' Natt interrupted. 'There are serious enquiries going on. They concern at least one member of the Saint Timothy's congregation whom I am advising. I wouldn't have mentioned it, but since the matter has now arisen . . .' He looked at Dr Wader. 'I'm sorry, Jill. If you'd told me earlier about your conversation with Sister Patricia I'd—'

'Aren't we being a trifle overdramatic?' Treasure questioned dismissively.

'I think not. One wouldn't want to prejudice anyone's relations with the authorities,' the lawyer replied.

There was a slightly embarrassed silence at the end of this exchange, so that most of those present were glad to affect rapt interest in Marlene's return with Treasure's whisky – on the tray that still contained not only the coffee things, but also his half-consumed glass of port, an object, he felt, which was doomed to survive as a public affront to his conscience and wasteful habits.

'If you think it's that important, Terence, of course I'll tell the police, though she said nothing exactly shattering,' said Dr Wader eventually. 'D'you want me to do it tonight?'

'No, no. The morning will be soon enough. A call to the detective in charge at Shaftsborne Police Station. I'll give you his name.'

'Well, I'd like to hear more of your views on something much more wholesome,' said the Bishop in an ebullient tone. 'On whether or not the convent at Chiversley should be rebuilt. It's a problem the beneficiaries will need to face seriously quite soon.'

'Is there really a problem?' asked Christine. 'I don't believe my uncle thinks so. He was saying so earlier.'

Canon Stonning and his wife had left before the end of dinner because Mrs Stonning had been unwell.

'He doesn't think we should rebuild. You feel the same don't you Mark? That so far as Chiversley is concerned, the convent's finished?' asked Dr Wader carefully. She and Treasure had been seated together at dinner.

'I think so. One might think of building something else on the site.' He looked up again at the painting. 'But of course a decision not to rebuild the convent wouldn't mean that Daniel Utteridge's work had ended.'

'Simply closed in Chiversley, with the funding still available to continue it elsewhere,' the Doctor completed for him.

'Can we know where you stand regarding the central question, Mr Treasure?' Natt asked. 'On how or if Daniel Utteridge's work should be usefully continued?'

Treasure frowned, but more because he had just tasted his new drink than because he had any difficulty formulating a reply. 'If I were a beneficiary, I'd want to give that question the very closest examination,' he said blandly.

'In the light of both the suggested alternatives, Mark?' This had come from Utteridge-Flax who had joined the group a minute before with Molly Treasure, but in time to have heard the previous exchanges.

'Naturally. And any other viable looking ones that presented themselves,' the banker replied.

Dr Wader began: 'The obvious course being to carry on as we are, supporting Anglican convents in this country and abroad with the income from the trust—'

'Or to wind up the trust and put the capital to far better use.' Utteridge-Flax had interrupted his fellow beneficiary.

'Except you know perfectly well where I stand on that, Charles,' she countered.

'You mean you're immovably against my plan? Mind closed? Decision made?' he countered in turn, sudden anger flaring in his voice, his face and neck reddening.

'Not immovably. But I could only be convinced by better arguments than you've offered so far. A lot better.'

'I wish I could believe that, but I can't. So there's really no point in further discussion is there?' He made to turn away.

Natt cleared his throat loudly. 'A moment, Charles. Isn't the more pressing question whether you both accept Mr Treasure as the third beneficiary? The man to balance your deliberations and help bring them to a conclusion?'

It was Jill Wader who replied first. 'I'd accept that. If you're willing, Charles? And Mark, of course.'

There was silence for several seconds, with everyone looking to Utteridge-Flax who now appeared to be even more furious than before.

'Come on Charles. You'll go along with that won't you?' said Christine. 'Do say yes straight away, because I must go to the loo and I can't bear to miss anything.'

The angry man turned his face to her. His mouth opened as if he was about to say something, then it closed again. He breathed in and out several times, and his expression softened a little before he finally uttered. 'Very well. I'd accept Mark as a beneficiary, but without any other commitment.'

'Then since Canon Stonning has told me he's very much in favour of your becoming a beneficiary, Mark,' the Bishop said promptly, 'it seems the decision is now up to you.'

Treasure nodded. 'I'll be honoured to accept.'

'Splendid,' said the Bishop above the murmur of approval from the others.

How much this resolution was the climax of the evening – as the hope for its achievement had for some present been the purpose of the dinner – was clear from the way the company quickly dispersed after the banker's acceptance.

Natt and Utteridge-Flax both said their good-nights almost immediately and left in separate cars – Natt to his home a mile down the road towards Chiversley, Utteridge-Flax to the school on the other side of town.

Since Christine Stonning had come in her uncle's car, now long since departed, the much mollified Utteridge-Flax had offered to drive her home to the vicarage – except he had been too slow going about it. When he asked her, after she rejoined the others just before they all left, it transpired that she had already accepted a lift from Jill Wader.

The Bishop drove off to Shaftsborne just ahead of the Treasures. They waved their final farewells to the two women guests in the drive, as Lucius Bittern was seeing them into Dr Wader's Ford Escort.

Sheila Bittern had been roaring adieus from under the outer archway of the *porte-cochère*, waving her arms, and blowing kisses with one hand like a prima donna taking curtain calls. Clasped in her other hand was the doorknob to the hall cloakroom. It had just come away in her vigorous grasp and she had had nowhere to put it.

At the time it was all a conventional enough departure scene. Only the banker was to speculate later whether the tragedy might have been averted if he and Molly had delayed their leaving by a minute.

Chapter Twelve

'I've eaten worse dinners,' said Molly as the car moved away.

'When?' her husband questioned grimly.

'Well, not recently. You didn't finish your whisky.'

'It wasn't whisky.'

'It was the right colour.'

'So's syrup of figs, I remember. I swear what Marlene put in that glass was cooking brandy. For a brewer, Lucius Bittern keeps a very poor cellar. And an incompetent barmaid.'

'Non-executive brewer, you said. Perhaps you should have asked for beer.'

'It crossed my mind, too late. I think they're just very hard up. Or possibly just keen to give everyone that impression.'

'Why?'

'For a variety of possible reasons. As a long shot, they could have been trying to soften up the beneficiaries.'

'To do what?'

'To fold up the Utteridge trust.'

'What, just to make life easier for the Bitterns?'

'That being a clear if incidental effect. And incidentals are important in marginal situations.'

'Would their situation sway the decision for you? Now you're going to be a beneficiary?'

'Certainly not, but they weren't to know that.'

Molly frowned. 'And Charles wants to wind up the trust anyway. So they could only have influenced Jill with their show of genteel penury. But surely Sheila can't expect anyone to credit she's that poor. After all she's—'

'The second largest shareholder in Utteridge Ales. I now suspect that's all she is.'

'You mean that's her total wealth? Wouldn't it be enough for her to—'

'She owns precisely three per cent of the company. That's just under three hundred thousand shares. Current notional value about £650,000.' Treasure paused as he swung the car to the right, out of the drive, and in the direction of Chiversley. 'But it's a private company and there's a very restricted market in the shares, so it's possible she couldn't sell them even if she wanted. Meantime she'll be getting dividends of around £16,000 a year. A modest return which would hardly pay for the upkeep of that stately pile.'

'But you said if it was taken over the company would be worth a lot more than it is now.'

'If it was taken over. At the moment it can't be. Because the trust holds a majority of the shares.'

'Someone must be paying for the building work. The scaffolding.'

'The minimum work I should think. Really to stop the place falling down. I mean there's plenty else they should be doing. The furnishings are in an appalling state. My dining chair had lost half its stuffing.'

'Mine too. And the curtain episode was a riot. Of course, that could have been staged, I suppose? No, surely not? Anyway, Lucius is crazy about the house. He talked of very little else at dinner.'

'Perhaps because he knows about very little else. He and Sheila don't seem to communicate much.'

'They just about tolerate each other.'

'Curious in a newly married couple. Especially since they're expecting a baby.'

'A baby conceived within wedlock, yes.'

'Possibly they have a good physical relationship and a remote mental one.'

Molly looked doubtful. 'No, it seemed to me their relationship is a business one. Quite unemotional.'

He blew his lips into a pout. 'That could be right. With each providing what the other needs.'

'Her money. His title.'

'As the Canon implied. But I imagine it's more subtle than

that. And he's a better catch for her than some run-of-the-mill gold digger. Utteridge-Flax told me yesterday there'd been a few of those about.'

'Besides himself?' She smoothed an eyebrow with her middle finger.

'Ah, sour grapes, you think? Could be. But there probably were a few locals after her fortune, despite her being so . . . so formidable.'

'Formidable? Big you mean. Lots of men find big women irresistible,' Molly observed with spirit, while absently crossing her slim and shapely legs.

'I meant more the penetrating, non-stop voice, and the bois-terous ways. I'd find all that very exhausting to live with.'

'Lucius may enjoy that bit. Having Sheila exhaust him,' said Molly, a touch archly.

'Possibly. Wasn't she a bit long in the tooth for an eligible spinster when they married?'

'Thirty-two she told me. That's no age these days for a first-time bride. They may well have had an affair first. Lucius was getting on. Even for second time round.' Molly patted the side of her hair. 'Would a title mean a lot to a woman like Sheila?'

'It might to one who knows she might have been Lord Chiversley if she'd been born a man. That could be something that's festered in her mind for years.'

'In which case she could probably have afforded something better than a mere and ageing baronet.' Molly paused. 'No, that's not fair. Lucius is really quite attractive. Christine Stonning obviously thinks so.' She turned to look at her husband. 'She goes for you too, incidentally. The way she was hanging on your every word at dinner. When you were going on about the futures market, for instance. I don't believe she understood a word you were saying. I certainly didn't.'

'Our Miss Stonning is better informed than—'

'Than me, I suppose?'

'No. I wouldn't think so. I was going to say, better informed than one might guess. She's obviously having a hard time building her confidence after that accident.'

Molly gave a nearly charitable smile. 'Oh, I think she's

managing pretty well. She certainly tamed Charles Utteridge-Flax out of that tantrum. He adores her, don't you think? In an awed kind of way.'

'Yes. That was clear enough at lunch yesterday with young Brown, who significantly wasn't invited tonight. Come to think of it, it's pretty surprising that Charles gets on the Bitterns' dinner list.'

'Because he may be challenging Sheila's right as the senior legitimate Utteridge? Could all that be an academic kind of wrangle?'

'No. The money at stake is too substantial.' He paused. 'I wonder if Charles and the Bitterns have reached some kind of arrangement? Over his main priority.'

'He's an odd man.'

'Mmm. Basically shy and retiring. But a fanatic about helping Aids victims.'

'That being his main priority?'

'Yes. The only other thing that seems to get him worked up is the possibility of his being the rightful Lord Chiversley.'

'But you think he'd abandon that in exchange for getting his way over the hospices?'

'That could be the deal with the Bitterns. So they'd use their influence with others.'

'With Jill Wader?'

'Chiefly, yes. I'm pretty sure that Charles isn't after money for himself, or status for that matter. I could be wrong. As you say, though, he's putty in the hands of Christine.'

'So d'you suppose he would have agreed to your becoming a beneficiary if Christine hadn't intervened to encourage it?'

'Ah, that's difficult to say. I think he must have decided beforehand that I'm a better proposition than others on offer.'

'To resolve things the way he wants?'

'More to persuade Jill Wader that there are two points of view.'

'With the ultimate hope that you and she will support his hospice plan. Is that really a runner with you?'

He shrugged. 'As I said, I need to examine the detail. If I eventually side with Charles, Jill might come round. Of course, a decision to wind up the trust would have to be unanimous.'

He shifted in the driving seat. 'Jill's a very intelligent woman with a highly developed intellect.'

Molly sighed. 'That sounds worse than being formidable. Or is it about the same? And if you don't side with Charles?'

'He's no worse off than he is now. The two of them have created a stalemate. That's since the death of Picton, the organist. Neither would have accepted a third beneficiary nominated by the other.'

'And as John Larpin's nominee they both regard you as neutral?'

'Seems so. Both must imagine there's now a fifty-fifty chance of formally getting his or her own way.'

'Why formally?'

'As opposed to getting it by default, which Jill is doing at the moment. She doesn't want fundamental change. Charles actually wants the trust wound up.'

'So it's more to Jill's credit that she's accepted a new beneficiary? I mean, she could have kept things as they were for ever.'

Treasure looked doubtful. 'For some time, anyway. Eventually I think they'd have had to bring the numbers up to strength.'

'To three?'

'Mmm. I think there's something in the trust deed about there being a time limit on having fewer than that.'

'And when will you actually become a beneficiary?'

'There has to be a formal meeting with Natt, the trustee, and the existing beneficiaries, convened at a week's notice. That's to approve my nomination. Then there'll be exchanges in writing with Natt. Should take about a fortnight.'

'Can't all that be taken as done?'

'No. Natt's a stickler for doing everything by the book.' Treasure sniffed. 'Now his was the really surprising turn of the evening.'

'His more or less scolding the other two into accepting you like that?'

'Absolutely. I was staggered. At our only other meeting I was almost rude to him.'

'To such a harmless man? How unkind of you.'

'Not at all, he was being impossibly pompous. He was again

tonight. That business of not allowing Jill to tell us what Sister Patricia had said was bothering her. Anyway, I really didn't expect him to be pushing me for beneficiary. I'm sure someone else had twisted his arm.'

'His wife perhaps? Had you met her?'

'No. Didn't know he had a wife. Why wasn't she there tonight?'

'He gave me the impression you met her yesterday. At his office. She left for Bognor Regis this morning. To look after an invalid sister, while the normal carer's on holiday. He was telling me at dinner. And about their bird-watching.'

'That must have been enthralling.'

'It was quite. I got the impression he didn't care much for Charles.'

'He doesn't. He describes himself as Sheila Bittern's man of business.'

'Watch out for the turning. It's just here.'

'Thanks. I see it.' He slowed the car, then turned right onto a narrow side-road a mile before Chiversley. This was a quicker route to their house, crossing the River Wibble by a modern steel bridge of no aesthetic attraction but probably capable of supporting heavier loads than the historic stone one at the end of Steep Street.

'So was it for Sheila's sake that Natt wanted you as beneficiary? Because you may agree to wind up the trust so she gets offered the control of the brewery?'

'She and her husband. Or her child, if it's a boy.'

'With her husband as trustee you said? That makes it sound as if it was Lucius who wanted you nominated. But Natt isn't his man of business?'

'No he isn't.'

'Natt seemed to be very thick with Jill this morning. At the convent.'

'I think that may have been because they both felt so badly about the fire.' He stroked his chin. 'If there are any other alliances at work, I'm expecting they'll come to light when I've been a beneficiary for a bit.'

'Roy,' whispered Moira Edicomb urgently to her husband a bit over an hour later. She was sitting bolt upright in their double

124

bed, one ear cocked toward the window which was half open behind the curtain. 'Roy, are you awake?'

'Well I am now,' he answered from his pillow, staring at her back silhouetted in the half-light. He was a small, bald-headed man, a jolly sort with a tolerant disposition – the last being a fairly essential attribute in anyone married to Moira. 'What's the time?' he asked, blinking at the illuminated dial of the alarm clock.

'Never mind the time. Why's Thackeray barking like that?' Thackeray was Dr Wader's retriever. 'It's not normal. He's outside, but the Doctor keeps him indoors at night. Always. Listen.'

So far Edicomb had had no opportunity to do anything else but listen. But now his wife had stopped speaking he could hear the dog for the first time. He recognised the bark all right, though it was difficult to be sure exactly where it was coming from. 'I expect she's let him out for a jimmy riddle,' he said, but the words lacked conviction.

'Never. You know as well as I do, she always goes with him. He's been barking for ages.'

'Perhaps it isn't Thackeray?' he offered without conviction.

'Of course it's Thackeray. And Dr Wader's here for the week-end. I saw her in the garden tea-time. Something's wrong Roy, I know it. You'd better see. Don't wake the children.'

The Edicomb children, Peter and Esme, had bedrooms on the street side of the semi-detached house, number 17, Jubilee Avenue. This was nearer the High Street than the bungalow – number 21 – where Bertha Brown lived with her son Graham.

All the houses this far down the western side of the Avenue had gardens that backed onto Keeper's Wood – a large, squarish copse of mature oak and ash. There was a dirt path between the gardens and the wood leading south along the wood's eastern boundary and finishing in Salt Lane. The Lane was one of the town's oldest thoroughfares. Like newer Jubilee Avenue next to it, it ran down from the High Street.

'Appledram', the name of Dr Wader's Georgian cottage, was in Salt Lane, across the road from where the path finished. It was at 'Appledram' that Salt Lane curved to run along the wood's southern and then its western boundaries before ending in a T-junction with Shepton Way, a main road that bordered

Keeper's Wood to the north. Jubilee Avenue also ran into Shepton Way but on the near side of the wood.

A few minutes after his wife's injunction to him, and as St Timothy's clock was chiming midnight, Roy Edicomb was letting himself out onto the path through the back gate of number 17. He had pulled on trousers and a raincoat over his pyjamas, and had brought his big 'Community Watch' rubber-covered torch, for protection not illumination, while putting on his cap for roughly the same reason. Thackeray was barking still, but the closer Edicomb got to 'Appledram' the more obvious it was that the dog was in the wood not at the cottage.

There were no lights in the cottage when Edicomb got there. He crossed the road and went into the garden, then checked through the window of the wooden garage at the side to see if Dr Wader's car was there, but the garage was empty. Perhaps the Doctor had gone back to the university, but that would be unusual on a Saturday night.

The path through the wood directly opposite 'Appledram' was the one Dr Wader used when she took the dog out first thing in the morning and last thing at night: Edicomb also used it sometimes for the same purpose, and it was the one he took now. The Edicomb family usually looked after Thackeray when its owner needed to go away without her dog. This happened quite often in the vacations. The Doctor never cared to put Thackeray into kennels. The Edicombs' liked dogs, though they didn't keep one themselves, and were glad of the boarding fee Thackeray's owner insisted on paying.

'Where are you, Thack? Good old boy. Here then,' Edicomb cried, beaming the flashlight ahead of him along the path. It was dark in the wood, and a touch eerie. 'Come on, Thack. Good old boy,' he repeated, in a bolder, sterner voice intended to steady his nerve and to give pause to anyone lurking in the undergrowth.

At the sound of a familiar voice the dog briefly stopped barking but started again almost immediately, and this time in a much more frenzied way, the barks shorter, shriller, and nonstop.

'Come on, Thack. Here then,' the man called again, wondering why the animal hadn't scampered down the path to him by this time. The barking seemed to be nearly dead ahead of him, but

126

on the far north side of the wood, close to Shepton Way. 'Dr Wader, are you up there? Are you OK?' He didn't really expect a human response, but he stopped to listen in case, before moving forward again.

It took Edicomb another fifteen seconds to reach the nearly demented dog which was tugging to escape only a yard or so in from the path. Despite his evident efforts to get free, the animal was firmly secured to the chain lead attached to his collar and looped through itself around the trunk of a stout oak sapling. He stopped barking and started moaning on his rescuer's arrival, tail lowered, head dipping and rising, body quivering, muzzle thrusting into the open hand as soon as the man stooped beside him.

'It's all right, Thack. All right old Thackeray. Calm down. What you doing out here, then? Mistress deserted you, has she?' he crooned, trying to pacify the dog and to unravel the lead at the same time.

It was then that the wobbling beam of his torch lit first on a bare foot half covered by fern a pace away.

'Oh dear. Oh my God. Oh no. No. Don't let it be,' Edicomb mumbled tensely to himself, releasing the dog and scrambling forward still on his haunches. 'Oh, my God. Oh, dear God,' he breathed as he drew back the foliage. For what he had revealed was the nearly naked body of the dead Dr Wader, a length of thick cord wrapped around her neck.

Chapter Thirteen

'Do come in, Inspector. Is it about Dr Wader? We heard about her murder in church this morning. Dreadful. Dreadful.' Molly Treasure was ushering the caller through the hall into the sitting-room.

'That was Saint Timothy's Church, Mrs Treasure?' asked Detective Inspector Ian Lodger, stooping as he entered the room – a reflex precaution for one of his height.

'Yes. We were at the eight o'clock communion. Canon Stonning gave the news to everyone from the altar. And about the death of one of the nuns. Sister Patricia. In the hospital.'

'That was a heart attack, madam.'

'Yes. The Canon said. It's very sad all the same. She was a dear old lady. Very talented. Now, do sit down, Inspector. I expect you want to see my husband.'

'Both of you. If it's convenient?'

'I'll call him. He's fishing. At the bottom of the garden.'

'In that case I wouldn't—'

'No, he was coming up at noon. It's nearly that now. There's a handbell somewhere, specially for summoning fishermen. Ah, here it is. I've been dying to use it. Won't be a jiff.' She grasped the brass bell by its wooden handle and went out through the open french windows.

Lodger, still standing, watched her carefully. The tall police-man was in his middle thirties, well spoken, overly thin and dark, with small, very alert eyes. He was dressed in a summer-weight, light grey suit, neat white shirt and a dark blue tie. He was noted for being well turned out, but what people most remembered about him was his being six feet five inches tall.

Molly re-entered after pealing the bell with some abandon.

128

'That should bring the cows in as well, don't you think?' She smiled.

The Inspector returned the smile uncertainly. What he was not noted for was a capacity for mirth.

Molly seated herself in a chintz-covered armchair, indicating to Lodger that he should do the same in the chair opposite. 'My husband will be here soon. He was already on his way up. I expect you know we were with Dr Wader last evening.'

'Yes, madam. That's partly why I'm here. Could you tell me where you last saw her? And at what time?' He had removed a small black notebook from a side pocket.

'It was in the drive of Chiversley Hall. When we were all leaving. It was just after eleven. About five past. Dr Wader was getting into her car with Christine Stonning. She was giving Miss Stonning a lift. Except I gather, after we left, the Doctor's car wouldn't start.'

'That's right, madam. In the end Sir Lucius drove them both back to Chiversley in his Jaguar. He dropped the Doctor at her cottage, then took the other lady to the vicarage.'

'And the Doctor was raped and strangled while walking her dog later?' Molly shook her head. 'Miss Stonning gave us the details after church. Have you any idea—'

'We know now she wasn't raped, madam.'

'Oh? I see. Well, I suppose that's some small consolation.'

'It usually is to the relatives.'

'You say Dr Wader wasn't raped?' questioned Treasure who had just come in from the terrace. He was wearing an open-necked shirt and corduroy trousers. His waders and the rest of his fishing things he had discarded outside, except for the wooden box of flies in his hand.

The Detective Inspector stood up and Molly introduced him to her husband.

'The person who found the Doctor assumed she'd been raped,' the policeman volunteered after the two men had shaken hands and Treasure had settled in a chair beside his wife. 'The first patrolman to arrive at the scene thought the same. That was because she was nearly naked.' He looked at Molly. 'She was wearing just a bra. It might have been the murderer's intention to rape her, but he didn't for some reason.'

'Perhaps he was disturbed,' said Molly, swallowing, and smoothing down her skirt in a reflex action.

'That or she managed to scare him, or anger him in some way, madam. So he killed her before . . .' He shrugged instead of completing the sentence, then continued. 'It could be he never intended rape, of course. We're not sure yet where the actual assault took place. Or the death.'

'It wasn't where you found the body?' Molly asked.

'We don't think so. But it could have been close by. You weren't in the vicinity of Dr Wader's cottage for any reason after you left the Hall?' Lodger looked from Molly to Treasure.

'I'm afraid we don't even know exactly where her cottage is, Inspector,' said the banker, bending down to retie the lace of one of his brogues.

'At the bottom of the old part of Salt Lane, sir. That's a turning to the left off the High Street, if you're coming from the church. Just opposite the town hall.'

'Then we weren't anywhere near it, Mr Lodger,' offered Molly. 'We didn't come into Chiversley at all on the way back. We took that turning off Shaftsborne Road. The one with the metal bridge.'

'Thyme Lane that is.' The policeman nodded. 'And you didn't see anyone else who'd been at the dinner party?'

'No,' said Molly looking at her husband.

'And you were together for the rest of the night?'

'That's right,' said Treasure. 'Can I get you a drink, Inspector?'

'Not at the moment, thank you, sir.' He looked up from his notebook. 'I understand Mr Utteridge-Flax and Dr Wader had a disagreement after dinner last night.'

'Hardly that. In truth it ended as the opposite. You see they're both beneficiaries of the Utteridge trust. They'd been having some difficulty agreeing how the trust funds should be managed in future. They accepted just before we broke up that I should become the third beneficiary, providing a sort of adjudicating vote. The two of them had to agree to that. It was a magnanimous decision on both their parts. To let in someone else whose attitudes neither of them knew. So on balance there was much more agreement than disagreement, Inspector.'

'I see, sir. Thank you. As third beneficiary I understand

you'll be taking the place of the late Ambrose Picton?'

'That's right.'

'But you're not a beneficiary yet?'

'No. Only a beneficiary-elect. It'll take a week or two to process the appointment.' He rearranged the angle of the wooden fly box he had placed on the table beside him.

'You've been talking to Terence Natt, Inspector,' said Molly.

'Mr Natt and others, madam. It's been a busy morning. The trust is a bit unusual isn't it, sir? Instead of trustees there are beneficiaries who can liquidate the funds any time and take the money for themselves?'

'That's true. There's one stipendiary trustee. Mr Natt. He's paid to administer the trust. But you're right that the beneficiaries can clean out the fund if they choose. Theoretically for their own benefit. They have to do it together though.'

'Together meaning however many beneficiaries there are at the time, sir?'

'Yes. Two at the moment.' His hands sprang apart. 'Oh no, of course, since Jill Wader's death—'

'Only one, sir. Yes. And is it so theoretical? They really can legally appropriate the funds for themselves if they choose?'

Treasure frowned. 'Yes, but it's wildly unlikely.'

'You know Mr Graham Brown, I believe, sir?'

'We've met a couple of times. At lunch yesterday, and when he was helping after the convent fire.'

'Would you say he has ambitions to become a beneficiary?'

'I'd heard some talk to that effect, yes.'

'May I ask from whom, sir?'

'Why d'you want to know?' His hand went to fingering the box again.

The policeman matched Treasure's unblinking stare. 'Would it have been Miss Christine Stonning?'

'It might have been, yes.'

'Might have been, sir?' Lodger questioned in a strained voice as though the prevarication pained him.

'All right, it was.'

'Did you get the impression that if Mr Brown did become a beneficiary, he and Mr Utteridge-Flax would see eye to eye on how the funds should be used? More than say Dr Wader and Mr Utteridge-Flax had done?'

'That's a very theoretical question. I really don't think I can give you a reliable or proper answer.' A tartness had crept into the banker's tone.

'Very well, sir. Had either of you met Sir Lucius and Lady Bittern before last night?' His gaze moved from Treasure to Molly, and back again.

'No, not either of us,' said Molly.

'But they gave a dinner in your honour?'

Treasure shifted in his chair. 'My wife is something of a celebrity, Inspector. It's not unusual for her to be fêted by strangers. I go along for the food.'

'I understand all that, sir. About Mrs Treasure being Molly Forbes the actress. Very famous actress, too.' Molly blinked slowly as Lodger continued. 'Except you're also a celebrity, sir. In the business world.' This was delivered more as a bald statement of fact, not as a compliment like the other. 'And I gather the dinner last night was more in your honour.'

'A bit in both our honours, perhaps,' said the banker carefully.

'Wasn't it in the hope that in the course of the evening Dr Wader and Mr Utteridge-Flax would agree to your becoming a beneficiary? And wasn't that just what happened?'

Treasure shrugged. 'It happened, yes. And it may have been some people's hope.'

'Such as Lady Bittern's would you say, sir?'

'Possibly.'

'And Mr Natt's?'

'Equally possible.'

'Since it was Mr Natt who pressed the existing beneficiaries to agree to your being elected.'

'Yes.'

'Helped in the case of Mr Utteridge-Flax by Miss Stonning pressuring him?'

'Not pressuring, Mr Lodger,' said Molly quickly.

Treasure leaned forward in his chair. 'Since you're so well informed, Inspector, I wonder why you need to ask these questions.'

Lodger gave a thin smile – so thin it did not involve his

parting his lips. 'We like to get things confirmed, sir. People's impressions of the same event are often different.'

'How interesting,' said Molly, as if she really meant it.

'If the trust should be wound up, sir, you know Sir Lucius and Lady Bittern stand to benefit?'

'That they could do, yes. By being offered the trust's shares in the brewery? If you consider that a benefit.'

'Wouldn't you sir?'

'Depends. They'd need to borrow a considerable sum to buy the shares. Then before you could say they'd benefit or not, you'd have to know what they intended to do with the shares.'

'They'd control the brewery, wouldn't they?'

'The brewery is not particularly profitable. The interest on the money they'd have to borrow would almost certainly exceed the value of the current dividends from the shares.'

'Wouldn't other breweries be interested in taking over Utteridge Ales?'

Treasure paused before answering. 'Again that would depend on the price, as well as on the attitude of the Monopolies Commission. And again on whether the Bitterns wanted to sell. They could just as easily decide to build up the business.'

'Build it up more than Sir Lucius has done since he's been Chairman?'

'He'd have more incentive if he and his wife were in total control.'

'But it's most likely they'd sell?'

Treasure leaned back, his hands smoothing the arms of the chair. 'Forgive me, Inspector, but I fail to see the bearing of any of these conjectures on what's happened.'

'Conjectures, sir?'

'Yes, the relevance of who may become a beneficiary of the Utteridge trust or what might happen if the Bitterns got control of the brewery. Surely you're investigating a murder and attempted rape by some marauding maniac? What's that got to do with subjects discussed at the dinner party we were at last night?'

'The victim attended it too, sir.'

'And she was murdered in a wood later, after being safely

escorted home by the host. I should have thought the police would have been busy checking the whereabouts last night of every known and suspected rapist in the West Country. I mean, do you have evidence that remotely links what happened to Dr Wader with anyone else at the dinner?'

'What evidence we have to date, sir, is confidential to the police. Whether we reveal any of it to others depends on circumstances.'

'I see.' Treasure glanced at Molly. 'Well, I'm sorry, but whether my wife and I choose to answer any more questions that could implicate our friends must also depend on circumstances. Like your coming a bit cleaner with what you're getting at.'

Molly brought her hands together loudly. 'I'm sure you could both use a drink of some kind now,' she interjected brightly, getting up from her chair, and treating the policeman to a dazzling smile. 'A cold beer perhaps, Mr Lodger? There's plenty in the fridge.' She pushed back the three-quarter-length, buttoned sleeves of the crisp white blouse she had on, emphasising the shape and smoothness of her forearms.

'Thank you, madam, that'd be very welcome.' The Inspector half rose.

'No, don't move either of you. It won't take a second. Beer for you too, darling, I expect?' she asked as she neared the door.

'Yes, please.' Treasure grinned at Lodger as Molly left the room. 'My wife obviously believes cold beer will work better than oil on troubled waters.'

'Very diplomatic too, sir.'

'I don't mean to be obstructive, Inspector,' Treasure continued in a less irascible tone than before. 'But you ought to understand our position. We were guests last night. It's hardly appropriate for us to blindly implicate our hosts or the other guests in a murder. Another thing, one of the guests was the Bishop of Shaftsborne, a close friend for more than twenty years. It's going to be very hurtful and possibly embarrassing for him if it gets about there's a suspicion of a . . . a connection between what happened at the dinner and the murder.'

The policeman pulled on one of his ears, then exhaled deeply before he said: 'One man at the dinner, and another involved in the beneficiary business were seen separately in the vicinity of the victim's cottage last night, sir, after the dinner.'

Treasure's eyebrows lifted. 'The one at the dinner being Sir Lucius, I suppose, who drove her home?'

'No. This is in addition to him, sir. But he was seen by the same witness.'

'Reliable witness?'

The policeman hesitated again. 'A neighbour. Elderly maiden lady. Lives in the last house across the road from Dr Wader. The houses on the neighbour's side stop at the edge of the wood.'

Molly had returned balancing two tankards and a glass on a silver tray. 'The beer looks so good I nearly poured one for myself,' she said. 'Lemon juice has fewer calories though,' she completed with a sigh.

'The Inspector was just telling me that two men—'

'I know. I heard,' Molly interrupted.

'You haven't arrested anyone have you?' said Treasure suddenly.

'No, sir. One gentleman's been interviewed already. The one who was at the dinner. The other's still helping one of my officers with our enquiries. At Shaftsborne Police Station.'

'That sounds ominous,' said Molly, passing him a tankard.

'No more than routine at the moment, madam.'

'Did your witness see Dr Wader take her dog into the wood, Inspector?' Treasure asked.

The policeman swallowed some beer. 'Yes. After she'd been dropped by Sir Lucius in his Jaguar.'

'And Miss Stonning was in the car with them?'

'Yes. Soon after the car left, the Doctor came out with the dog on the lead. She went across the road to the wood. She'd put a mac on over her dress, to protect it probably. And a silk headscarf.'

'It was such a pretty red dress. Silk jersey,' said Molly quietly. 'We talked about her buying it. And the trouble she had getting shoes to match. Have you found her clothes?'

'Most of them, madam. In the wood. Scarf, mac, her dress and some of her underclothes. Her shoes are still missing.'

'Didn't the witness think it odd when Dr Wader didn't come back?' asked Treasure.

'Thought she'd missed seeing her, that's all. She didn't hear the dog barking either, her eyesight being better than her hearing.'

'Does this elderly lady sit in the window all the time, Mr Lodger?' asked Molly, who had gone back to her chair.

'More at night. Her bed's near the window. She's a semi-invalid. Doesn't sleep that much, only off and on.'

'Did either of the two men go into the house?'

'One of them did. Into the garden at least. The witness can't see the drive or the front door. They're hidden by trees. Anyway, she saw him come out again, and later she heard a car drive off.'

'He was in a car?'

'She assumed it was his. It was parked where she couldn't have seen it.'

'And the other man, Inspector?'

'He was walking, sir. He lives in the next street. Witness thought she first saw him coming out of the victim's gate, but she couldn't be sure. She did see him cross the road in the direction of the wood. This was about a minute after the victim had gone there too.'

Treasure drained his tankard. 'From which it's reasonable to assume, Inspector, that Mr Graham Brown may be some time yet helping your officer with his enquiries.'

Lodger gave a slightly wider than usual smile though his lips still didn't part. 'That's about it, sir, yes.' He turned the pages of his notebook. 'The other thing I wanted to ask you about him, sir, is to do with stamps.'

Chapter Fourteen

The Shaftsborne General Hospital had been opened by Her Grace the Duchess of Norfolk in 1893. There was a brass plaque saying as much in the cramped, busy and basically unaltered reception area, with its shiny white tiled walls. For most of the working week the space resembled the booking hall of a Victorian railway station during the rush hour. This was especially so just before two o'clock on a Sunday afternoon. Two o'clock is the start of visiting time.

Sister Mary Maud was leaving the hospital not visiting it, and clutching the Marks & Spencer shopping bag that one of the nurses had kindly given her. She was waiting composedly where Canon Stonning had left her – seated on the end of a single row of otherwise unoccupied grey plastic chairs beside a locked doorway with a marbled Gothic arch and under a notice that said 'Geriatric and Urological', followed by an arrow. The arrow pointed straight at Sister Mary Maud's head but she was oblivious to this. She was careful to keep her feet well under the seat to avoid their being trodden on, or run over by wheelchairs and stretcher trolleys.

The shopping bag held all the little items – some her own but mostly Sister Patricia's – that Sister Mary Maud needed to take back with her. There wasn't much in the bag, but Sister Mary Maud hung on to it tightly. The nurse had warned her not to let it out of her grasp because there were a lot of thieves in the hospital. Sister Mary Maud squinted about her, but there was no one who looked poor enough to be a thief. If there had been she'd have found something in the bag to give him, or her – along with a homily.

It wasn't for herself that she was protecting the contents of the bag, and certainly not for the dear departed Sister Patricia. They had had nothing that was truly their own, no worldly goods, since taking their vows. They only enjoyed the benefit of things that ultimately returned to the common use of all the members of the Society of Blessed Mary Magdalene – which since yesterday meant just Sister Mary Maud and the Reverend Mother.

Sister Mary Maud gave a little sigh, blew her nose, looked about her, then made a tiny sign of the cross for Sister Patricia.

'Cup 'a tea, dear?' asked the beaming lady helper in the blue overall with matching beads. She was pushing a refreshment trolley with a silver urn on it.

'No thank you,' Sister Mary Maud replied. She had accepted a cup earlier from another helper, and she had had two with her lunch in the ward before being discharged. She couldn't risk a fourth cup. It might mean having to go to the ladies and missing Canon Stonning while she was in there. After collecting her, he had disappeared to have a word with someone official.

'Chocolate digestives? Mars bar? Nothing at all dear?'

She shook her head. In any case she had no money to pay. The other lady had understood, addressed her as Sister, and insisted on giving her the tea for nothing. Much as she would have enjoyed a Mars bar (not a whole one, of course, not all at once), one shouldn't trade on people's generosity.

She hoped the Canon wouldn't forget the parcel with Sister Patricia's clothes in it. Or let it be stolen. The habit was quite a new one. Certainly not more than five years old. Reverend Mother would certainly want it to be used again. It would want shortening of course. She fingered her own outer clothing. It still felt damp to her – which was not surprising since she'd been hosed down from several directions. The nurse had said it was quite dry but she probably wouldn't know about such thick material. Sister Mary Maud made up her mind to have it properly dried *and aired* later.

'Sorry to have kept you, Sister. Rather a lot of-of-of paperwork, d'you see?' Canon Stonning had appeared through the crowd from the direction of a glass booth marked 'Administration'. He still had the brown paper parcel under one arm, and in addition he had acquired a large manila envelope. He was dressed in grey flannels, and a fawn cotton jacket over his clerical

138

collar and stock, with a quite jaunty leather peaked cap on his head. He preferred not to wear a cassock for driving in case he caught his toe in the hem – something he had once done with frightening results. 'We can go now,' he said. He considered the notice above the Sister's head. His facial muscles flexed. 'Yes,' he muttered uncertainly, helping her up.

They weaved their way slowly to the main exit, the parcel of Sister Patricia's clothing providing a useful buffer against the main and contrary flow of people.

'These new doors are automatic,' said the Canon, just before they hit him in the shoulder.

'Will Sister Patricia be all right?' asked Sister Mary Maud as they stood on the paved forecourt outside, waiting to cross the private road to the carpark opposite.

'Oh, right as rain,' the Canon answered too promptly, then frowned. 'That is, I have her death certificate here,' he added solemnly, waggling the envelope, and adjusting the parcel under the same arm. He grasped Sister Mary Maud's elbow with his other hand. 'Molyneux will be-be-be seeing to everything.' Molyneux was the Chiversley undertaker as well as its principal builder. 'Off we go then, merrily,' cried the Canon, one foot outstretched. His companion pulled him back just in time to prevent them both being run over by a motor-bike.

'You er . . . you all right, Sister?' asked the Canon later, when they were belting themselves into his small Fiat. 'Bit of a scare back there. Young idiot. You look a bit-bit-bit puzzled?' He meant confused but didn't say so, while studying her again out of the corner of his eye. He hoped she really was well enough to be discharged.

Sister Mary Maud pulled the plastic bag closer to her chest. 'There's something I've forgotten. At least, I think I've forgotten.'

'Want to go back?'

'No.' She shook her head several times. 'I mean forgotten about the other night. Something I wanted to remember. It nearly came back just now.'

'Give it time.'

'It's very kind of you to fetch me, Canon. On a Sunday too.'

'Got me out of doing the washing up after lunch.' He beamed

expansively. The kindness had involved little extra effort. As warden of the convent he'd had to see about the official documents on Sister Patricia, and he had preferred not to leave that till Monday, his day off. 'Lots of people coming to tea, too,' he said. 'To welcome you back.' This wasn't strictly true since they had been invited anyway to talk about the consequences of Dr Wader's death, but it fitted as a little compliment. 'Feel-feel-feel up to that do you?'

'I think so. Thank you. Will Reverend Mother be there?'

'I expect so. She's nearly recovered too. A little tired still, perhaps. You and she will be staying on at the vicarage for a while, and-and-and very welcome. Till we've got the undamaged bit of the convent ship-shape. Fit to live in again.' At least that was the tentative arrangement. It was equally possible that the two surviving nuns would be retired to the convent of another sisterhood in the diocese. 'Now what did I do with those keys?' He tried every pocket, and found them in the ignition. 'Ah!'

'Will your niece be at home too, Canon?'

'Certainly.' He started the engine. The traffic indicator began flashing to the left which it had been doing when he had turned off the engine earlier. 'Mr Utteridge-Flax and Mr Brown are supposed to be coming as well. And Mr Natt. And Sir Lucius and his good lady have promised to look in if they can. The more-more-more the merrier.'

The Canon let in the clutch as his hand came off the gear lever with a flourish. He drove a car as though he were conducting a symphony orchestra. He braked at the exit onto the road, looked left and right, his head and shoulders bent far over the wheel, the peak of the cap touching the windscreen. Then with the indicator still flashing to the left, he accelerated the car off to the right, rolling his whole body in that direction too.

A motor-bike – a red one this time – swerved around the Fiat from behind, tyres squealing. There was little real danger, but the roar of the other engine, the shout of the rider, and the jerk as the Canon braked the car hard, stalling it in the middle of the road, all made for an upsetting experience.

'You all right—' the Canon began.

'But that's it,' cried Sister Mary Maud shrilly, interrupting him, and positively bouncing in her seat with the pleasure of re-discovery. 'It was a red one. The same as it was in the winter. The other time. When Dr Picton died. I'm sure. But this time it was in the carpark, not the churchyard, you see? I think I can just remember the number.' She closed her eyes and started reciting letters and numerals.

'A car, d'you mean, Sister?' the Canon demanded, but abstractedly as he started the engine again. The indicator was still flashing left as once more he propelled them to the right, but since all the other drivers in the vicinity had stopped in self-defence it didn't matter.

'-2-8-4-A,' the Sister completed. 'Or was it B at the end? No it was A, I'm sure. A red motor-cycle. Do you think we should tell someone?'

'We didn't know till after lunch. Uncle had gone to Shaftsborne already. Will they arrest Graham, d'you think? They won't, will they?' questioned the agitated Christine Stonning, looking pretty if flustered on the sunlit terrace of the Treasures' house. 'I hate to barge in like this,' she went on, taking off her sun-glasses. 'We don't know each other that well, but you're both so sympathetic.' She embraced Treasure with eager spontaneity, and more warmth perhaps than the advertised slight acquaintance justified, but his response was certainly as friendly. He had stood up and gone forward to greet her on her arrival, which had been largely unheralded, although he and Molly had heard a car pull up in the drive. Now Christine bent to kiss Molly on both cheeks.

'You're welcome, Christine. Sit down, relax, and tell us all about it,' said the actress with an understanding smile. She had remained seated at the round white table with a big orange beach umbrella shading it. 'You'll have some coffee, I'm sure.' The Treasures had just finished lunch. 'Could we have another cup please, Mrs Cass?' The unexpected caller had been let in by the rubicund and embarrassed housekeeper who had followed her through to the terrace.

'Surely, madam.' Mrs Cass retreated indoors feeling less guilty than before about having admitted the visitor.

'Graham's been with the police some time?' Treasure stated more than asked when they were all seated.

'Since eleven, his mother said when she rang the vicarage just now. But he couldn't have done that to Jill Wader. He just couldn't, could he? He's so sweet and . . . well . . . so ineffective.' Christine looked from Treasure to his wife.

'Presumably the police have been to see you?' said Molly.

'Not since they came after breakfast. To ask about the drive home last night. What time we left Jill. Oh, and a bit about what happened at dinner. But nothing about Graham.' Nervously, she ran a hand through her hair.

'We've had a policeman here too,' Treasure offered. 'He told us that Graham went to Jill's cottage at nearly half-past eleven. After she'd taken the dog out.'

The blonde model shook her head vigorously. 'It's not true. He didn't go to her cottage. That's only what some stupid old busybody told the police.'

'The busybody was mistaken you mean?' put in Molly. 'Thank you Mrs Cass,' she nodded at the housekeeper who had returned with the cup.

'That bitch ought to be prosecuted,' said Christine hotly. 'Graham had been working late in the church vestry. He was going over the convent inventory for the fire insurance. All the convent papers are kept in the church safe. He walked home down Salt Lane, that's where Jill lives. At the bottom, right outside Jill's house, he crossed the road. It might have looked as if he came out of her gate, but he didn't.'

'Did he cross the road to go into the wood?' asked Treasure.

'No. Only to use the path that goes round the wood there. All the back gates of the houses in Jubilee Avenue let onto it. The ones on that side. The Brown's place is just past the Edicombs'.'

'And it was Mr Edicomb who found her?'

'That's right, Molly.' Christine moved her chair away from the table and into the sun, at the same time putting on the sunglasses which had huge unframed lenses.

'But there is another path right opposite Jill's place? One that goes straight into the wood?' said Treasure.

'Yes. The one she must have taken. But Graham didn't.'

'Do you know why he was taking such a circuitous route home?' the banker pressed.

'He wasn't. It's actually a bit quicker for him that way, although there's not much in it. His mother told me he uses Salt Lane because it's nicer than Jubilee Avenue. Because of those pretty Georgian houses at the top.' She pushed away the hair from her face again in what seemed to be a reflex not a conscious action, for it exposed the cruel scar on her forehead. 'I know it doesn't sound very convincing but it's the truth. Even I know Graham always goes that way,' she completed.

'If it's any consolation he's not the only man the police are interviewing,' said the banker.

'Charles Utteridge-Flax you mean? They've finished with him. Or he thinks so. He was at the vicarage before lunch, talking to Uncle. He was at the ten-thirty service. He admits he went to Jill's place on the way home from the dinner. He wanted another word with her about your becoming a beneficiary, Mark. But she wasn't there. Since her car wasn't either, he assumed she'd stayed on for a bit at the Hall. He waited a few minutes then drove away again.'

'But she really hadn't got back by then?' said Molly.

'That's what the old woman says.'

'And Lucius dropped her off first? Then drove you on to the vicarage?' Treasure asked.

'Yes. It was I dropped her off really. I was driving the Jag till we got to Jill's place. Poor Lucius, he wasn't bargaining on having to drive after dinner. He went terribly slowly when he took over in Jill's drive. He was sure he was over the alcohol limit. He even went a back way from Jill's to the vicarage, to avoid going through the main part of the town.'

'What was wrong with Jill's car? Has it been fixed?' asked Molly.

Christine shrugged. 'Lucius got it going this morning, apparently. He's pretty handy that way. But not late at night.' She crossed her long legs under the tight mini-skirt she was wearing. 'If only I'd stayed with Jill. Walked the dog with her. She said she'd be taking it out.' She shook her head. 'But it never occurred to me.'

'I'm sure plenty of women walk their dogs at night around here,' said Molly.

'They do. You don't expect to get even accosted in Chiversley, let alone molested. It's not like London.' She paused, one hand stroking a black-nyloned thigh. 'Poor Jill. I'm so terribly sorry.' There were tears welling in her eyes now as she went on, looking at Treasure: 'And it's just not fair their picking on Graham. I'm sure it was a sex maniac who did it. Most probably someone from outside the area. With a car. Who's probably hundreds of miles away by now.'

'That seemed the obvious explanation,' Treasure said. 'The police accept that too, but only as a possibility. They also believe what was decided after dinner could have made a motive for murder.'

'Murder and rape?'

'She wasn't actually raped,' put in Molly.

'Only because the swine didn't have time, or he was disturbed or something.'

'Or just wanted it to look like a sex crime,' said Treasure.

Christine's big eyes opened wider. 'The police think that?'

'Could be, and one has to admit it is a possibility. That's basically why they think it could have been someone at the dinner.'

'But Graham wasn't at the dinner.' It was as though the fact had only just occurred to Christine.

'Someone at the dinner, or someone involved with the Utteridge trust who could benefit from Jill's death,' Treasure corrected.

'So of course Charles would be suspect,' said Christine pointedly, and appearing actually to have ignored the obvious implication of the last comment. 'Especially since he went to Jill's. Did they know he'd quarrelled with Jill during the evening?'

'They asked us about that, yes.'

'And what about Terence Natt? I'll bet they could prove he stands to gain in some way by Jill's murder.'

'I expect the same could be made to apply to Lucius, and in the widest sense even to the Bishop and your uncle,' said Treasure with an expression and an open gesture with his hands to show he didn't really give such propositions any credence.

'Well, I can't vouch for the Bishop,' Christine replied it seemed in the same vein. 'But uncle was home, and Lucius came into the vicarage for coffee when he dropped me. He didn't leave till after twelve. Poor Jill must have been dead by then.'

'Have you any idea what it was Sister Patricia told Jill about the stamps?' Treasure asked next. 'Could Graham have figured in that?'

Christine frowned. 'That could be the problem. There was something . . . something odd about the stamps.'

'Involving Graham?' said Molly.

'It's difficult to say.' Christine leaned forwards, her hands crossing to smooth her upper arms in a self embracing movement.

'Except he seems to have been in charge of the stamp business.'

'As a small money raiser for convent funds. I'm sure there can't have been anything dishonest about it.'

Treasure leaned forward too, his hands on the table. 'Christine, would you have any idea why he telephoned Mrs Garnet in Shaftsborne on Friday evening, telling her to burn a letter from Sister Patricia as soon as it was delivered yesterday?'

'Oh, God. Does that have a bearing on the murder? Did the police tell you this?'

'Yes. And probably they didn't intend we should tell anyone else. But never mind.'

'And did Mrs Garnet burn the letter?'

'I'm not sure. I think she probably did.'

'But there has to be an innocent explanation. You didn't say whether the police think the stamps are linked to the murder?'

'They seem to. Through the fire, which they now think was arson.'

Christine swallowed and her gaze lowered as she said: 'Maybe Sister Patricia sent the wrong stamps. Or perhaps they weren't good enough. Or . . .' her words petered out.

'Or perhaps they were too good,' the banker put in bluntly. 'Look, you and I both know Graham got very edgy about the Sunday school stamps on Friday. At lunch. So much so he was onto the convent as soon as he got back to the bank. Sister Mary Maud told us.'

'But the Sunday school stamps couldn't have been important.'

'Only if he was jumpy about all the stamps produced at the convent. And it seems he may have been.'

'Reverend Mother may know something. Or Sister Mary Maud. She's recovered. Uncle's gone to fetch her.' Christine paused and remained pensive for a moment. 'There has to be a simple explanation why Graham told Mrs Garnet to burn that letter. Maybe he wanted to keep the convent's name out of any enquiry.' Her face brightened. 'Yes, I'm sure it's something as simple as that.'

Chapter Fifteen

'I'm sorry to ask you to a meeting on a Sunday, Mr Treasure,' said Natt, through a positive barrage of whistled aspirates. He closed the front door of 1, Abbot's Way which he had opened himself in answer to the banker's ring. 'Things are moving at a pace, you understand? And one that has quickened considerably this afternoon. In the last hour. Oh dear me, yes.'

Treasure wondered if the lawyer's breathlessness was advertising the growing toll this tempo was taking on him – or simply that he had come to the door too quickly: he thought probably the latter. But the figure in front of him was a good deal less assured than the Natt of previous encounters.

'I'm afraid Sunday meetings with lawyers are common enough in merchant banking,' said Treasure, following the other man through the lobby to the stairs.

Natt stopped and turned about, one hand pushing the spectacles higher up on his nose. 'That would be in the takeover world, of course. Needless to say that's not a . . . not a habitat familiar to us in this area. Though I would venture to suggest that the circumstances today are nearly as dramatic.' He seemed to commune with himself for a moment. 'Yes, as I told you on the telephone, a group of us were taking tea at the vicarage when . . . when Charles Utteridge-Flax made his astonishing announcement. We all agreed that you and the Bishop should be consulted immediately. I really am most grateful to you.' Remaining at the foot of the stairs he leaned further back towards Treasure and offered in a more confidential tone than before: 'The meeting is entirely unofficial, of course. Unfortunately the Canon is not available because of clerical duties, but the Bishop is here. He arrived a moment ago. He can't stay very long. Not on a Sunday. He's preaching this evening at Yeovil. He's in my office with Utteridge-Flax.' For the second time he pronounced the last name with an incredulous look and a slow shake of the head, much as George Washington might have done when alluding to Benedict Arnold after West Point had been surrendered.

It had been only fifteen minutes before this – at four-thirty precisely – that Natt had telephoned Treasure from the vicarage. In response to the lawyer's plea, Treasure had agreed to drive the short distance into the town and join the hastily convened meeting. Indeed, when he heard the purpose of it he had found the invitation compulsive. He had left an equally intrigued Molly brushing up her lines for the next day's filming – bank holidays being like any other day to a TV production company on location with expensive hired equipment, as well as star performers.

When Treasure and Natt entered the lawyer's office on the upper floor, it seemed that the two men already in it were suffering each other in embarrassed silence – the kind that prevails before a meeting when the subject for that meeting is best avoided, until all the participants are present, but when this very constraint makes all other subjects inapposite.

John Larpin was sitting bolt upright in a Hepplewhite-style carver chair at one front corner of the desk. Utteridge-Flax was similarly settled at the other corner. Both were formally dressed – the Bishop immaculately so in a dark suit, silver pectoral cross on purple stock below the clerical collar. Utteridge-Flax was in tweeds and a wool shirt and tie, heavy attire in view of the continuing warm weather, but an ensemble that somehow lent gravitas as well as weight to his appearance.

'If I might recapitulate what Charles announced to us at tea, so that there's no misunderstanding,' Natt began, sitting himself behind the desk after Treasure had greeted the other two and settled in a chair between them. 'As the present sole remaining beneficiary of the Utteridge trust, Charles proposes to exercise his . . . his assumed right to have the trust terminated and its assets liquidated. He requires the funds thus generated to be transferred to Anglo-Afro Hospices, less a million pounds which is to be settled on the Friends of St Timothy's Church,' he looked up from the notes before him to interpose, 'that's for the church's restoration and maintenance.' He looked down again. 'And less also an adequate provisional sum to cover . . . er professional fees involved in the winding up of the trust.'

There was silence after Natt ended with this delicately phrased reference to his own cut of the spoils.

The Bishop was the first to speak. 'Charles is legally entitled to take this . . . this action?' he questioned, after having temperately but, by the hesitation, evidently decided not to qualify the word 'action' with ones like 'monstrous' or 'high-handed'. He was looking at the lawyer and not at Utteridge-Flax.

'On the face of it, Charles can take any action he chooses. Counsel's opinion may well advise to the contrary, however,' Natt replied carefully. 'The trust deed specifically permits the beneficiaries acting in concert to wind up the trust.'

'With due notice?' asked Treasure.

'With no notice specified.'

'And since it happens there's only one beneficiary, it's legal for Charles to act in concert just with himself?' This was the Bishop again.

'That could prove to be a fine point in law.' Natt made a steeple with his hands. 'It could only be resolved by the courts in what would most likely prove to be protracted proceedings. Protracted and costly.' It was difficult not to recognise the burgeoning expectancy in the voice of a lawyer suddenly prompted to contemplate legal fees of exquisite and incalculable magnitude.

'Although there's only one beneficiary, there's another one elect,' said the Bishop looking at Treasure.

'Mark Treasure can't be formally elected for two weeks, and then only by me.' Utteridge-Flax intervened quietly and speaking for the first time. He was leaning forward slightly, hands clasped over his stomach, feet crossed and tucked under the chair. 'It's why I've decided to . . . to strike now, as it were. To liquidate the trust. So there can't be any new beneficiaries you see?' He swallowed. 'I'm sorry, Mark. Nothing personal you understand? I'm having to steel myself to do this. But I'm confident I'm acting within my legal rights. I've checked with the trust deed. Done the homework.'

'Since this morning? Since Jill's murder? What you're proposing wouldn't have been agreed if she'd been alive,' said Treasure.

'I think it would have been, given time. I think she would have come round to my plan. You too, Mark,' Utteridge-Flax replied, evading the earlier questions. 'I'm saving time, that's all.' His voice became more solemn. 'And time is of the essence for the Aids victims I'm committed to help.'

Treasure frowned. 'In your own interests, in view of what you're proposing, you're confident the police won't suspect you of being involved in Jill's death?'

'Quite confident. They've interviewed me at length. I told them I looked in at her house on the way home last night, but I left before she got back. I was at the school by eleven-thirty. I understand she didn't get home till then. Mrs Bellis, the school housekeeper, saw me come in. So I'm totally in the clear over that.' He paused, then added ominously. 'I think you'll find the police believe they have the murderer. The unfortunate Graham Brown.'

'Good heavens,' exclaimed the Bishop. 'Since when?'

'I sincerely hope they're wrong about him, Bishop,' Utteridge-Flax replied. 'We all do. But I can tell you they're not interested in me any more. Or anyone else.'

'Is this true, Terence?' the Bishop turned to the lawyer.

Natt looked uncomfortable. 'There's been no arrest, Bishop. And I think Charles is precipitate in what he says. But the police certainly seem to have Graham Brown high on their suspect list.'

'You're acting for him, aren't you?'

'Not since this morning, Bishop,' the lawyer's discomfort was increasing. 'It seemed more appropriate for him to retain someone . . . someone more experienced. A specialist.'

'In the criminal law you mean?' enquired Treasure.

'Precisely. A Shaftsborne solicitor has accepted the responsibility.'

Treasure wondered whose idea the switch had been, the lawyer's or the hapless Brown's. He suspected the former's. He also found the reason unconvincing since he doubted there was any lawyer in Shaftsborne with a mainly criminal practice.

150

'Since the Bishop is pressed for time, I wonder might we return to the business in hand?' Natt enquired, and quite clearly to relieve his enduring disquiet.

'I think we should, yes,' Treasure agreed. 'Your plan's an audacious one, Charles,' he went on. 'I'd almost say it's outrageous, but in fairness it probably isn't quite that. Even so I'm sure it'll be more complicated to execute than you expect. Unless, of course,' he added, gazing even harder at Utteridge-Flax, 'it's not so much a plan as a bargaining ploy.'

Utteridge-Flax's reaction to the last comment was a disappointment to the speaker. The man's wooden expression had scarcely altered. 'I don't need to bargain,' he said stiffly.

'I think you may find you have to. Specifically with the Inland Revenue, even if you refuse to do so with us.' Treasure countered promptly and with a good-humoured smile. 'Do you intend to have the money raised from the sale of the trust's assets transferred directly to Anglo-Afro Hospices?'

'Yes, less the million pounds that'll go to Saint Timothy's.'

Treasure's brow wrinkled. 'If the trust is to be wound up,' he said, looking now at Natt, 'the shares in Utteridge Ales have to be offered in advance at asset value to the oldest surviving male descendant of Daniel Utteridge. If there isn't a male descendant, they have to be offered to the oldest married female descendant on the same terms. You confirm that as trustee?'

'Certainly I do,' said Natt.

'On the face of it, that would mean Sheila Bittern will be offered the shares. But Charles intimated to me on Friday that he considers himself Daniel's rightful, if not exactly his legitimate male descendant. I think he ought to tell us whether he now intends to set about proving that. Whether he has a better claim than Lady Bittern, and can demand the shares be offered to himself.'

'But won't they be his in any case?' asked the Bishop with a perplexed look.

'As the single beneficiary of the trust, they're his immediately, yes. But *before* the trust is wound up, the trustee must offer them to Daniel's designated descendant at asset value. Today that would be at a bit over two pounds a share. Whoever gets them on those terms will, as controlling shareholder, be free to sell them on again to anyone he or she chooses, at market value. That's after paying the trust for them, of course.'

'To sell them to another brewer for instance?'

'That's right, John. At a conservative estimate, the market value will be about three pounds a share. Since there are more than five million shares involved, the profit on any sell-on will be substantial.'

'You mean that Charles could be aiming to get two bites of the cherry?' asked the Bishop again.

'That's up to him. And I don't believe he's told anyone what his intention is yet in that respect.' Treasure paused to allow Utteridge-Flax to speak. When the other chose not to, the banker continued. 'As a beneficiary of the trust, Charles has so far said he intends to have all the funds of the trust transferred to Anglo-Afro without ever touching them himself. If we challenged his right to do that in the courts we could lose. He'd only be switching funds from a moribund charity to an active one, and he appears to have the authority to do it. Many Chancery Court judges would approve such a move. Even applaud it. There'd be no personal tax liability either. At least I don't think there would be. But if Charles proves he's allowed to buy the shares himself, and does so, he could then make a hefty private fortune on the next sale, intending to keep it, and—'

'But as sole beneficiary of the trust, surely Charles effectively owns the shares already? Can you sell shares you own to yourself?' interrupted the Bishop.

'If you have two clear legal personas as in this instance, yes, you can.' It was Natt who had answered the question. 'And again in this case we are treating more with a right and entitlement than with simple ownership. The matter is complicated, but Mr. Treasure is correct in his assumptions.'

'Thank you,' said the banker. 'And in my view, if Charles does become the buyer of the shares, that would make his basic motive challengeable in law. It's highly possible that in that circumstance, Terence Natt here as trustee would have grounds to prevent the wind-up of the trust in the first place.'

Everyone was already staring at Utteridge-Flax in anticipation when he began to speak: 'I've no intention of claiming an entitlement as Daniel's descendant,' he began. 'I mean so that

152

I can prove a right to buy the shares from the trust. I'll admit I've thought of doing that. But it wouldn't have been to make a fortune for myself. Only to have more money to give to the hospices. I accept, though, it'd make me vulnerable to legal action. And delay the winding up of the trust—'

'It would unquestionably do that,' put in Treasure firmly.

Utteridge-Flax nodded. 'I shall still claim a moral victory. For my mother. Vindicate what she had to do. So when people read about what's happening to the trust, they'll know I could have claimed to be Daniel's descendant. I may still try to revive the Chiversley title. But that'll take time too. As for the money, I'm not interested. Not for myself. I'll try to persuade Sheila to give some of her gains to the Hospices. That's if she sells the shares.'

'It may be her husband you'll need to persuade,' said Treasure. 'The shares will be in his control, assuming they're offered to Lady Bittern before she's given birth to a son.' He paused briefly, watching Natt's reaction. 'Even if she has a son, it would probably still be up to Sir Lucius to decide on how any funds are dispersed.'

Natt cleared his throat. 'All that's true. It's another Daniel Utteridge condition.'

'So it seems in any event that Charles can realise his intention, and liquidate the trust?' asked the Bishop slowly.

'Unless we can persuade him otherwise, or unless Mr Natt as trustee chooses to challenge his decision,' said Treasure.

'Would you like me to leave now so you can discuss—' Utteridge-Flax began, half rising.

'Not so far as I am concerned,' Treasure interrupted.

'And I must leave myself in a minute or so, in any case,' the Bishop added, then, taking his lead from the banker, he added. 'I think Charles should stay.'

Utteridge-Flax dropped back into his chair.

'Charles is aware that as trustee I shall take learned opinion on whether to challenge his intention in the courts,' Natt now offered solemnly. 'That is, his intention as now expressed. I am not a rich man. Such a challenge would be costly. If I should lose, and I would put the chances at fifty-fifty, then the judge might order the costs to be paid by me and not by the trust.'

'Because Charles's purpose appears close enough to the founder's expressed intentions?' questioned the Bishop earnestly.

'Precisely,' the lawyer responded.

'Excepting that Daniel Utteridge certainly never imagined you'd be reduced to one beneficiary,' said Treasure. 'And I'm still doubtful that helping Aids victims can be described as a principal aim of the Anglo-Catholic movement within the Church of England. That's why I think if the trustee challenged you, Charles, the legal chances of his winning would be rather better than even. Perhaps a lot better.' He leaned back in his chair, debating with himself why Natt was now volunteering a different view – although one possible reason for this did occur to him. 'It's a great deal of money to let out of the Church's control without a fight. I'm sure the Bishop agrees.'

'Of course I do,' John Larpin nodded vigorously. 'Which doesn't mean I don't agree with Charles's responsible and selfless intention.' It was a difficult position for a bishop.

'I'll not be persuaded to drop my plan,' said Utteridge-Flax firmly.

'I'm not suggesting you would or should,' Treasure replied easily. 'Only that there's room for some . . . some modification on your part. That's in return for the trustee's really very charitable decision not to oppose you legally. I think that's reasonable, don't you?'

Utteridge-Flax shifted in his seat. 'Perhaps,' he said. 'It would depend—'

'Good,' Treasure countered briskly. 'So let's get down to cases shall we?'

Chapter Sixteen

'That's the licence number all right, Sergeant. And it's a red Honda,' said Detective Constable Rawlins as the unmarked Ford they were in cruised slowly past number 17, Mafeking Street, Tidmouth. They had reached the sprawling seaside resort in a forty-minute drive from Shaftsborne. At five o'clock on a bank holiday Sunday, most of the traffic had been going the other way.

'Turn round at the bottom, then come back and park opposite,' said Detective Sergeant Hardacre, stubbing out his cigarette, and glad something had gone right for the first time that day.

'Are we going in now? Front door only?' asked Rawlins.

'You want to send for reinforcements or something? Like an SAS squad?'

'No, it's just he could be dangerous.'

'Or an innocent member of the public, and this could be a wild-goose chase.' The Sergeant watched blankly as Rawlins reversed into an alley prior to driving back up the way they had come.

'Except if this Sean Ribble was working with Graham Brown and Dr Wader, before they fell out, and Brown killed her, Ribble could be an accessory to murder.'

'Lot of assumptions there, Steve, apart from the one about Brown and the Doctor. Ribble may have nowt to do with any of it. Could have been visiting a girl friend in Chiversley on Friday night. Or stopped for a leak in the carpark when the nun spotted the bike.' He smirked. 'Lucky in that case she didn't spot him too.'

'She told Canon Stonning she thinks that bike was the second one parked in the churchyard the night the organist died.'

Hardacre sniffed hard. 'What she thinks won't rate much in court, lad.'

'And Ribble's got form as well,' Rawlins tried again.

'As a juvenile.' Hardacre hissed in air through his clenched teeth. 'Fact remains it's only supposition there was a third villain there that night. The nun could be making a mistake too. She's a hundred and twenty years old isn't she?'

'Eighty-eight, actually. With a good memory for numbers. My gran's the same. She got this one right.'

'What's your gran got to do with . . . Oh, I see.' The sergeant lifted himself slightly off the seat before pulling at the crutch of his trousers. 'Anyway, the idea Brown and the Doctor were in cahoots is just Detective Inspector Lofty Lodger's pet theory. There's no proof. Nor that Brown murdered her. Only circumstantial stuff.' The car had stopped. 'OK. Let's get this over with.' He undid his seat belt and opened the door.

Mafeking Street was lined on both sides with houses in flaking stone and stucco – two-storey terraced dwellings, with bay windows, paired porches, and what had originally been scraps of garden in front, protected by low walls and cast iron gates. Most of the walls and the gates had long since disappeared, and the scraps of gardens had been paved over to provide residents' parking – for those residents who owned anything to park. The cars and small vans narrowly accommodated in this way had most of them seen better days – like the curtains in the house windows. Number 17 was, if anything, seedier-looking than its immediate neighbours. The motor-cycle parked in front shared the space with a small wooden handcart chained to a bolt in the wall.

There was no doorbell, only a black knocker in the shape of a lion's head which DC Rawlins rapped firmly three times.

The woman who opened the door was short, fat, blowsy and fifty or so. She had uncombed mousey hair standing up in an uneven halo, belligerent eyes, brightly but carelessly painted lips, and bad teeth. She was clasping a huge ginger cat in both her arms, and was dressed in a long crumpled cotton dressing-gown and red slippers with bobbles on – except one of the bobbles had just been knocked off by the door and was lying inside the threshold.

At the sight of Rawlins holding out his identification card the woman squinted at the card uncertainly, gave a decorous pull to close the neck of the dressing-gown, rearranged the cat slightly, and said: 'If you're Jehovah's Witnesses we're Roman Catholic.'

'We're police officers, madam,' said Rawlins. 'Does Mr Sean Ribble live here?'

'Why?'

'Because we'd like to speak to him. Does he live here?'

She leaned out a little, then looked slowly up and down the street. 'He's out.'

'When will he be back, d'you know?'

'He never said.' She looked down at the cat as if expecting it to provide confirmation.

'Are you related to Mr Ribble? His mother are you?'

'Landlady. And that's all.' She pulled at the neck of the gown again. This and the new set of the mouth were evidently meant to underline the propriety of her relationship with her tenant.

'And your name is?'

'Mrs Enid Clack. Widow. And not from round here, I'm not. Not originally. Not this sodding town. From London I am. Me husband moved us here ten years ago because it was cheap. Then he died on me.'

'Thank you, Mrs Clack.'

'This Mr Ribble's bike, is it, madam?' asked Hardacre who had moved to stand beside the machine.

'Was. He's sold it. New owner's coming for it tonight. I got the key, and I gotta collect the money. What's he done?'

'Nothing we know of, madam. You're sure he isn't in?'

'I said so, didn't I?'

'Would you mind if we took a look at his room?'

'He *has* done something.' The vermilion lips closed again tightly.

'The room, Mrs Clack? We could get a search warrant, you know?' Hardacre was unsure they had grounds for doing any such thing, but the ploy usually worked.

'All right, come in. Top of the stairs, first on the right.' She stood to one side to let them pass. Rawlins picked up the stray bobble and gave it to the owner. The cat made a hissing noise at him. 'Ta. Quiet Nelson,' said Mrs Clack. 'Watch out for the loose rod. Near the top,' she offered, showing that one kindness deserved another.

The narrow hall, stairway and landing were all dark and smelled of damp and other things less easy to define, but bordering on the nasty. The room the policemen entered was bright in contrast: its sashed bay window overlooked the street. The space was sparsely furnished – just a single divan bed with a rumpled duvet, a cheap wooden wardrobe, a matching chest of drawers and one plastic stacking chair. The floor was covered in marbled linoleum with an oblong of carpet by the bed. The carpet was turning up at the corners. The walls were decorated with coloured pin-ups of nude women with pathologically overdeveloped breasts. There were two posters advertising motor-cycle events stuck on the inside of the door.

But what impressed itself on both men was not what the room contained but what it didn't – such as any personal belongings except for a T-shirt and a pair of underpants lying discarded on the floor.

The door to the wardrobe was open and showed that the interior was empty, like both drawers of the chest, one of which had been pulled out and overturned on the bed.

'Looks like he left in a hurry,' said Hardacre, stooping to pick up a narrow strip of torn paper with bars and some figures printed on it in brown. 'And loaded.' He handed the paper to Rawlins. It was a bank money band. The printing read '£1000 in £20 notes' under the smaller legend 'Southern Bank plc'. 'See if there's any more like that lying about. And anything else interesting. I'll just have another word with the landlady.'

Mrs Clack was in the kitchen at the back of the house. She was standing at the cooker stirring the contents of a black enamel saucepan with a wooden spoon. The contents looked like porridge and reeked of fish – a richer version of the upstairs smell. Nelson was curled up on the table next to a loaf of bread and an open packet of butter, with the end of its tail in the butter. The cat was watching its mistress through half-closed eyes.

'You didn't tell us Mr Ribble had left for good, Mrs Clack?'

'You never asked me. Anyway, he said he'd most probably come back. Got a ciggy have you?'

'Think so.' He produced his packet and offered it to her.

'Ta.' She bent down and lit the cigarette from the burning gas ring, then jerked her head backwards after singeing the front of her hair.

'You know where he's gone?'

'No dear.' She wheezed. 'Blimey, this ciggy's strong.'

'Only strong men smoke 'em. Did he leave in a hurry?'

She grinned. 'Bloody great hurry. Shoved his stuff in a pair of them palisade things. You know, what bikers use? Paid me the week he owed, and a week in advance. To keep the room. Then he left. He give me the bike keys, like I said.'

'When did he leave?'

'Hour ago.'

'Was he on foot?'

'No. On his bike.'

'But his bike's outside?'

'His new one, he got yesterday.'

'D'you know the make and licence number?'

'No.'

'Or where he bought it?'

'No.'

'D'you know where he was going?'

'No.'

'Where are you to send the money for the old bike?'

'I'm not. I'm to keep it for him. In the TSB. Till he says.'

'Why did he leave in such a hurry?'

'Phone call. Someone phoned him. He was out the back.' She nodded through the window at the small walled area of cracked concrete and scrub that comprised number 17's rear yard. 'He was gone ten minutes after.'

Hardacre looked about the room. 'You've got a phone here then?'

She started a laugh that developed into a long wheeze and then degenerated into a frenzied cough, turning parts of her face a bluish colour. 'Phone?' she said, after she had recovered. 'Blimey, we haven't got an inside lav yet. That's where he was, see? Out the back. Like I said.' She inhaled deeply on the cigarette. 'He's got his own phone. Battery one. Takes it everywhere. He works for one of them delivery services. Express.'

'D'you know who the call was from?'

She rubbed the side of her nose with the handle of the wooden spoon. 'A woman. He called her darling. I heard that. He's a one with the women. Not me mind,' she added sternly and, in Hardacre's estimation, unnecessarily. 'See the pictures did you? Kinky I'd say. Still, takes all sorts.'

'Did you hear the woman's name?'

'Not this time.'

'What about other times? Recently?'

'There was one he spoke to Friday evening on the phone. Before he went out again. I think he'd been with her in the afternoon. Not here. I'm particular about that.'

'But they'd met somewhere else?'

'I'm only guessing. He smelt of scent when he came in.'

'And this could have been the woman he spoke to on the phone today?'

'Could have been.'

'And her name was?'

'He called her Sheena, I think. Or Tina. I'm not sure.'

'Could it have been Sheila?'

'Might have been.'

'What time did he get back Friday night?'

She thought for a moment. 'He didn't. Not till yesterday afternoon. With his new bike.'

'Who brought the old bike back?'

'Bloke who's buying it. He'd been trying it out.'

'So Sean was out all Friday night?'

'S'right. Not against the law is it?'

'Of course not. The money he gave you today. Notes was it? Could I see them?'

She left the cooker, wiped her hand on her dressing gown, and pulled out the table drawer. 'There they are.'

The four new-looking twenty-pound notes had consecutive numbers. 'Pays you forty a week cash does he?'

'Yeh. Gets a cooked breakfast for that too. You're not telling the Social Security? Remember I'm a widow. The pension isn't—'

'I'll not tell anyone.' Hardacre was copying out the numbers of the bank notes as Rawlins came into the kitchen. 'Anything?' the sergeant asked him without looking up.

'Another money band. In the upturned drawer. Nothing else.'

'Mr Utteridge-Flax is going to close the convent. He said so. It was during tea today at the vicarage. Everyone seemed shocked. I'm glad Reverend Mother wasn't there. She went back to bed after lunch. She's very tired still, and quite old, you know,' said Sister Mary Maud to Molly Treasure in a concerned half-whisper.

The two were sitting in a centre pew of the now seemingly empty St Timothy's. Evensong had ended a few minutes before and the little congregation had already dispersed. Even Canon Stonning had left promptly. He was due to read the same service at two other churches at six o'clock and six-thirty in villages some miles away.

Molly had tired of practising her lines and had walked up to the church for exercise, not for the service – and with the vague intention of learning more about Utteridge-Flax's announcement from someone who had actually been present when he made it. She had slipped into the church during the singing of the last hymn.

'It'll take some time to rebuild the convent in any case, don't you think?' said Molly.

'Oh, the Canon had said we might be able to move back in a month. To the parts that are not damaged. But then he's such an optimist. With all the water from the hoses it's bound to be very damp for a long time.' Sister Mary Maud took off her spectacles and began polishing them with a clean but frayed, large white linen handkerchief. 'Reverend Mother thinks that now there are only two of us, we may have to join the—' she took a quick breath '—the Community of the Sisters of Saint Michael and All the Blessed Saints and Holy Angels. They're not far away from here. But it's such a big mouthful, isn't it?' Despite the mildness of the irreverent comment, her lips made a shocked O-shape, her eyebrows rose, and her head sank into the shoulders as she darted a childlike guilty smile at Molly.

'I'm sure nothing's going to happen in a hurry,' said the actress.

161

'And I'm also sure it's far from certain that Mr Utteridge-Flax's plan will go ahead.'

'Oh, but I believe it should do. All that money he mentioned is doing nothing otherwise. I'm sure we shan't need it. Well, nothing like all of it. Not now we have all Sister Patricia's things too.' She brushed some dog hairs off her lap. 'We're very careful, you see. I couldn't really understand why some of the others were so against Mr Utteridge-Flax. All those sick people with Aids. We should help them if we can.'

'What did Christine have to say?'

'Poor Christine, she'd had to go out by then. Before tea. She and I had a little chat when I came back from the hospital. Such a dear, sweet girl. She's so upset about the police keeping Mr Brown. I told her it can't be about the stamps. Lady Bittern had as much to do with the stamps as Mr Brown, and the police aren't keeping her anywhere.'

'Lady Bittern had as much to do with Sister Patricia you mean?'

Sister Mary Maud leaned forward, nodding. 'Oh, yes. She's always in the printing room. Very artistic, you know. Since she was a little girl. She came to tea today. Not her husband. She still thinks Sister Patricia probably did start the fire. By mistake, of course.'

'But you said all the others think it could have been the owner of the motor-cycle? The motor-cycle you think you saw twice? If the same person was involved the night the organist died, he certainly needs investigating.'

'The police are doing that. They told the Canon they would, after he'd reported what I told him. They can find out the name and address from the number of the motor-cycle,' Sister Mary Maud explained, wonderment in the words. For her, a vehicle trace was a modern advance that nearly rated alongside airmail. 'So Mr Brown may not—'

'Excuse me. I'm so sorry to interrupt, but I have to catch the bus back in a minute. Are you the Reverend Mother, perhaps?' asked a small, nervous, elderly woman standing in the aisle and who had evidently had to pluck up the courage to speak at all. She had appeared from the back of the church and was addressing Sister Mary Maud from behind Molly.

'Reverend Mother is resting,' said Molly, turning round to speak. 'This is Sister Mary Maud. Can we help you?'

'It was the Reverend Mother I wanted to see. My late husband met her once. Oh, I should have said, I'm Florence Garnet, from Shaftsborne. I keep a secondhand bookshop there.' The speaker was kneading one leather-gloved hand over the other which was clasping the strap of a fairly capacious handbag. She was carefully dressed in an unmodish, matching green jacket and skirt, and a brown straw hat decorated with imitation cherries in unlikely colours. 'That is, we do books and philately,' she went on. 'I was at the service. I was hoping to speak to the Reverend Mother alone. It's . . . it's—'

'Confidential?' asked Molly with an understanding smile. 'I'm afraid we can't disturb Reverend Mother, but I'm sure Sister Mary Maud—'

'But you're Molly Forbes, aren't you? I should have known,' Mrs Garnet interrupted. 'They said you were down here. I'm terribly sorry. I never expected—'

'Making a film for the television,' put in Sister Mary Maud in a proprietorial sort of voice, leaning across her companion.

'That's right. My husband and I have a rented house in Chiversley,' Molly confirmed. 'If it helps at all, he and I know a little about the stamps Sister Patricia's been sending you. The ones arranged through Graham Brown.'

'You do? Oh that's a relief.' Mrs Garnet was opening her handbag. 'Did you know they've arrested Mr Brown?'

'I knew they've been questioning him all day.'

'I'm sure he hasn't done anything wrong. Not that terrible murder. Not Mr Brown. I'm sure of that.' After looking about her, she produced a small transparent envelope from the bag. 'These are the stamps Sister Patricia posted to me on Friday. I was going to give them back to the Reverend Mother. I hadn't paid for them.'

'Sit down a minute, Mrs Garnet,' said Molly. She and Sister Mary Maud moved along to make space. 'We understood you'd burnt the stamps.'

Mrs Garnet sat on the very edge of the pew, her arms tucked tightly to her sides, both hands now gripping the strap of her bag while she still held the envelope between a thumb and forefinger. 'That's what I told the police, yes. But really I still had them. I was muddled, you see? I hadn't meant to tell them Mr Brown had phoned. To tell me to burn the envelope when it came. It just sort of came out when the policeman started to ask questions. And when he asked if I'd done what Mr Brown had said, I . . . I said I had. That was in case it got Mr Brown into trouble, if I hadn't. Done what he said, I mean. Oh dear, I must sound very stupid.'

'Not at all,' said Molly. 'And if you want to give the stamps to the police now, I'm sure they'd understand.'

'Oh, no.' Mrs Garnet shook her head vigorously. 'Not till I'm sure they won't use them against Mr Brown. Now I've had time to think about it. They're Prince James Island, you see? 1853 facsimiles. There's been trouble about those. Not these ones. Other ones. It's why I brought these to give to the Reverend Mother. For her to decide what to do with them. They're really convent property. Mr Brown hasn't sent the invoice for them yet. Thirty pounds it would have been.'

She offered the envelope to Molly who took it and asked: 'And would they have just gone into your stock?'

'No. They were a special order. For Mr Hechler. He's a big dealer. In London. Except his Mrs Davenport hasn't rung yet saying to send them. And my invoice. She usually does that. It would have been for sixty pounds. That's for the six facsimiles.'

'Mrs Davenport is from Mr Hechler's office?'

Mrs Garnet looked confused. 'I don't think so. Not the same office anyway. I had to ring her back once. Last year that was. I remember it wasn't the same number as Mr Hechler's. That's why I put her number in my book.' She looked at her wristwatch. 'Goodness, I'll really have to go. I'll leave the stamps with you then. I'm so grateful.' She stood up. 'I hate anything to do with the police.' Then, looking toward the altar, she added. 'So did my husband. God rest him.'

Chapter Seventeen

'Christine says Graham Brown hasn't been formally arrested. Not yet,' Treasure told his wife after switching off the cordless telephone he was holding.

Sunday was one of Mrs Cass's nights off. The two were in the kitchen. They had been clearing up after supper when Christine Stonning had telephoned. Treasure remained seated now at the pinewood table in the centre of the room, and carefully emptied the Prince James Island stamps from their envelope.

'How was she allowed to speak to him?' Molly asked, closing the dish washer.

'She wasn't. She spoke to his solicitor. His new one. Name of Jilters. She sent her important message through him.'

'Funny way to propose. Through a solicitor. Especially one called Jilters.'

Christine had surprised Treasure by announcing that she had offered to marry Brown. 'It wasn't a proposal,' he corrected. 'It was an acceptance.'

'Except he hadn't asked her to marry him.'

'She knew he wanted to.'

'Very convoluted,' said Molly, drying the inside of a wooden salad bowl with a paper towel.

'I think the whole thing does her enormous credit,' her husband responded, spreading the stamps out in front of him on a linen napkin. 'She said she wants the news made as public as possible.'

'But it's not going to stop the police arresting him, is it?'

'No. It could be a mild deterrent, I suppose. I mean it's certainly a stout show of solidarity. Of belief in the chap's innocence. In the circumstances, most women as attractive as she is would be busy denying links with murder suspects, not forging them.'

'You don't say? Well bully for Christine. Hope she doesn't live to regret it.'

'If he's convicted?'

'No. I meant if she has to marry him.' Molly suppressed a chuckle. 'I really can't credit he's guilty of anything, but he's one of the least alluring men I've ever met. And I don't think Christine really cares for him either.' She leaned over her husband's shoulder to look at the stamps. 'They look authentic enough, but too pristine, would you say?'

'That's because they were printed the day before yesterday. By Sister Patricia. Everything else about them is genuine enough, though. They were made from the original dies, with probably the original inks. The paper is no doubt genuine. The glue as well, I should think. But despite all that, there's no argument about their being facsimiles. It says so clearly enough.' The word 'Facsimile' appeared in black letters diagonally across the face of all six blue stamps. 'Doesn't do anything to enhance their appearance, of course.'

'Which is fairly dull to begin with,' Molly said. 'But presumably they're better than the official ones the Governor of the island sent back earlier.'

'You really should have handed them to the police, of course.'

'No, to Reverend Mother. That was what Mrs Garnet wanted, but Reverend Mother can't be disturbed. Doctor's orders.' Molly gave the breadboard an extra determined wipe before putting it away. 'Anyway, there wasn't a policeman handy in Saint Timothy's. Sister Mary Maud insisted you should decide what to do with them. She said that's what Reverend Mother would want. They're both completely gone on you, of course.'

Treasure's lifted eyebrows evinced what could have been either pleasure or surprise. 'Well, I really can't see what harm the stamps can do Brown. They might even do him a bit of good. Jilters believes the police are working on the theory that Brown and Jill Wader were in collusion to sell forged stamps.'

'Which they arranged to have printed in the convent?'

'Yes. That they fell out when they got wind on Friday that

this chap Hechler was being investigated. That was probably through Mrs Garnet.'

'But when I talked to her, she didn't seem to know Hechler was suspected of anything dishonest.'

'Either Mrs Garnet is an innocent at large, or the complete opposite. You said she admitted her husband didn't like the police.'

'That's right. You suggesting he was a crook? That she's carrying on the tradition?'

'Well, she told the police she'd burnt these stamps when she hadn't.'

'There was good reason for that.'

'Based in courage or duplicity? From what you've said about her, it doesn't seem she'd be capable of either. Incidentally, Jilters says the police seem sure Brown hired this Ribble chap to burn down the convent.'

'He's the motor-bike thug they tracked through Sister Mary Maud?'

'Yes, but he was tipped off, and he's skipped. Loaded with money from the Southern Bank. But they don't know which branch. Not yet. They do know a third party was involved in dealing with Hechler. A woman.'

'Who they think was Jill?'

'Could have been Jill.'

'What's she supposed to have done?'

'Hechler's been paying for the stamps in two stages. First to Mrs Garnet. A nominal amount, and presumably above board. The second payment was in cash. That's where the other woman came in. She instructed Mrs Garnet on the phone when to send the stamps to Hechler, then presumably she collected the big cash payment.'

'How do the police know about the two payments?'

Treasure shrugged. 'Christine says they've deduced it after putting together statements from Mrs Garnet and Hechler. She's certain they're wrong about Brown being guilty, but she's not so sure now about Jill being innocent.' He held up one of the stamps to the light.

'That's ominous,' said Molly.

Her husband narrowed his gaze as he studied the stamp. 'I

still can't understand how these stamps were any use to Hechler with facsimile on them.'

'I suppose it won't come off?' asked Molly, looking over his shoulder.

'Shouldn't think so. It's printing. Well, overprinting. Or else it's stamped on, and that should be just as permanent.' He put the example he had been holding back with the others.

'With one of those rubber stamp things they use in post offices? And a pad?'

'Yes. There was a pad on Sister Patricia's work desk. I saw it. In the usual flat tin box. The ink is always permanent. Indelible.' He paused and gave a sniff. 'So let's make sure this is.'

'Dare we?'

'Only cost us five pounds to the convent funds to find out. And that's only if we ruin a stamp.' He got up and moved to the sink. 'Is there a sponge?'

'Cotton wool's better,' said Molly producing a small ball of it from a drawer. 'Let me do it.' She wet the cotton wool at the tap, rinsed it, then washed it gently over one corner of the stamp.

'Water-based ink,' Treasure pronounced a minute later, when the word facsimile had been completely washed off the stamp's surface by Molly's ministrations.

'And I haven't hurt the stamp at all,' said Molly.

'Because it's a permanent printing, of course.' He shrugged. 'So that's how it's been done. Sister Patricia ran off the stamps, duly cancelled them with the rubber stamp, and sent them off to Mrs Garnet—'

'Who sent them on as directed by the second woman on the phone,' Molly interrupted. 'And the word facsimile was washed off later. And assuming the second woman wasn't Jill, and I don't agree with Christine that it could have been, does that make everyone at the Chiversley and Shaftsborne end of the chain innocent?'

'Well, pointing in that direction, perhaps. I wonder why Sister Patricia didn't twig it was washable ink on the pad? The pad would have dried out daily.'

'So she'd have to dampen it? With water?' Molly questioned.

'No. It would have been from a bottle of probably washable

fountain pen ink. But then she'd have known the cancellation wasn't permanent.' He paused. 'Of course, the pad would only be used occasionally. And at predictable times.'

'Like last Friday. When she'd finished an order for special stamps?'

'Exactly. So that someone else who knew about the order could drop by and soak the pad.' He shook his head. 'No, that doesn't sound right.'

'What if someone brought the pad each time?' Molly suggested. 'It may even have been something Sister Patricia expected, say if she didn't have her own pad and didn't care to ask Mr Brown, or whoever was responsible, to buy one? You know how careful they all are.'

'So you think a pad could have been loaned when needed? Which wouldn't have been that often. And from a logical source perhaps?' Treasure mused aloud. 'That's possibly it. Hardly affirms your beautiful thought that everyone at the Chiversley end's innocent after all.' He frowned. 'They use those pads in banks as well as post offices, of course. Brown could have dropped one in on Thursday or even early Friday. He's the obvious source.'

'Banks don't use pads with ink that washes off,' said Molly knowingly. 'I'll bet your bank doesn't.'

'That's right, of course. But if it was Brown, he did a switch. Simple enough. He only had to fool Sister Patricia.'

'Jill Wader was a regular at the convent, of course. At week-ends and in vacations. Sister Mary Maud said Sheila Bittern was always dropping in on the printing room. Charles Utteridge-Flax goes there. So does Mr Natt. To the convent anyway. I'm sure solicitors use rubber stamps. So really it could be anyone.'

Treasure wagged a finger in dissent. 'But, come to think of it, not Jill Wader. Not this time. Not if our theory's right. She didn't get here till late Friday night.'

'But if Jill wasn't tied in with the stamp business, does that mean her murderer can't be either?'

'No it doesn't. The convent links the two things, I'm sure of it.' Treasure started to put the stamps back into the clear plastic envelope. 'Her death had something to do with her being

169

a beneficiary of the trust. The police obviously believe that too. Her apparent obduracy over change was blocking someone else's plans.'

'And that was enough to get her murdered?'

'Think how much money's at stake.'

'But the stamps aren't part of that?'

'On the contrary. The stamps could have been providing seed money. Whoever murdered Jill has needed heavy funding. To pay for a plan that's been running for some time. Remember, the death of Ambrose Picton, the organist?'

'That was a heart attack. It came on while he was being roughed up by those motor-bike yobbos. But the judge didn't say it was murder.'

'He might do now.' Treasure paused, closed his eyes, then quoted: ' "My life is in the hands of any fool that provokes me." John Hunter said that, in 1791. He was the doctor who first defined angina pectoris.'

'Heart disease?'

'Yes, and incidentally died of it. The yobbos who roughed up Picton could have been briefed to do it by someone who knew about his heart condition. If so, it was incitement to murder.'

'And Picton was also a beneficiary.'

'More opposed to winding up the trust than Jill was, apparently.'

'And she was removed next.'

'The night after Ribble, the third yobbo, burned down the convent. That destroyed the evidence about the Prince James Island stamps, and incidentally any other exotic stamps Sister Patricia may have produced in the past.'

'Innocent work so far as she was concerned. And Mrs Garnet was just as innocent?' Molly questioned.

'Probably, though I wouldn't vouch for the late Mr Garnet, and certainly not for Hechler in terms of what's been happening to the stamps once he got them. Especially now we can show the police how easily he's been able to turn facsimiles into the real thing.'

'So Ribble could have been in Hechler's pay?'

Treasure shook his head. 'I'd say more likely in the pay of whoever got Hechler's second large payments.'

'The person with the plan to end the Utteridge trust? Using the stamp money for funding? So could Ribble have been paid to murder Jill?'

'Very possibly. Her death reduced the beneficiaries to one.'

'The only one who wants the trust wound up?'

'I still don't understand why whoever's behind it all couldn't have waited to see if I'd vote for a wind-up. Once I became a beneficiary.'

Molly pulled out a chair and sat at the table too. 'I think it was because of the last things you said before we left Chiversley Hall. You made it seem you were more likely to keep the trust going than to close it. That was my impression. Someone desperate to have it closed wouldn't have banked on you.'

Treasure pulled a face. 'I hope you're wrong.' He paused, thinking of the implications if Molly was right – that his words could have been responsible for Dr Wader's death. 'In any event, Graham Brown wasn't there.'

'Charles Utteridge-Flax was. Could he have murdered Jill? Or arranged to have her murdered? He's so obsessed with Anglo-Afro Hospices. I know it's a good cause, but people with real obsessions do irrational things, even insane ones.'

Treasure thought for a moment. 'I don't believe he's the sort of man who'd hire anyone to do his dirty work.'

'So he wouldn't have hired Ribble?'

'That's right, but he could have done the murder himself. He was at Jill's house after dinner. The school housekeeper could have been tricked into giving him that alibi. Or he could have gone out again without her knowing. On foot perhaps. It can't be far to walk from the school to that wood.'

'But if he killed Jill, Picton's death may not have been related. It may have been just what the judge said—'

'An aggravated accident without intent to kill,' he interrupted, folding his arms across his chest. 'Still a windfall to someone who was looking to wipe out the beneficiaries.'

'Does accident fit with the burning of the convent?'

'No it doesn't. Ribble's presence for both events is too much of a coincidence. He almost has to have been programmed by whoever engineered the fire and both the murders.' He pursed his lips. 'Somehow I don't believe that person can be Charles.

It's the hospices that are important to him, not what happens to the shares in Utteridge Ales.'

Molly frowned. 'I don't follow.'

'Charles is obsessed with his plan, as you say. But with me as the third beneficiary, he was well enough aware a lot of money could have been available for hospices with Jill's agreement.'

'Without the trust being wound up?'

'Exactly. And without the shares in Utteridge Ales having to be sold.'

'To the Bittern's?' said Molly pointedly.

'Yes. He might not have got everything he was hoping for, but there was clear room for compromise. That must have been why he agreed to my becoming third beneficiary. If he'd been as dangerously fixated as we think, he wouldn't have accepted me.'

'But he was taking advantage of Jill's death today by saying he's winding up the trust. Or he was until you talked him round at the meeting with Mr Natt and John Larpin.'

'John and I got him to agree to freeze things. For the time being. That's all. To give everyone some breathing space.' He rubbed his cheeks with his hands. 'But, going back to what you said about his taking advantage of Jill's death.' He shook his head. 'There's no doubt he did that. Even so, it only makes him an opportunist. I don't believe he's a murderer.'

Chapter Eighteen

'I never done no murder. I said that before,' Ribble insisted again in a slovenly, adulterated Dorset accent. He inhaled anxiously on the cigarette he'd been given while continuing his ceaseless shifting on the chair.

'Your two friends, Joss Sutters and Knuckles Crabbe, they say the same, Sean. About themselves that is. Not you. We wouldn't want to mislead you there. They're not saying the same about you at all, lad. Not now, they're not. Not when they were both seen last night. Sutters in Nottingham Prison. Crabbe in . . . yes, in Maidstone.' Detective Sergeant Hardacre stroked his chin as he spoke, looking down at the faxed sheets in front of him, spreading them about as he referred to them, and running his open hand down his neck. He was on the other side of the table from Ribble in the interview room at Shaftsborne Police Station.

The room was on the ground floor between the cells and the charge room. Although high-ceilinged, it was small and cramped, with one barred window filled with opaque glass, a closed glazed skylight above the door, and a burning strip light suspended crookedly from the ceiling on blackened, uneven chains. The long white lamp was buzzing loudly. Besides the table and four chairs, there was a low cupboard against the wall to Hardacre's right, with a tape recorder on top of it. DC Rawlins was seated at the end of the table, squeezed in there near the tape recorder. He had a notebook open in front of him. So far Hardacre had been doing all the questioning.

It was seven o'clock on Monday morning. Ribble had spent the night in a detention cell. He had been brought from Portsmouth the evening before. The Portsmouth police had taken him and his motor-cycle off the overnight car ferry to Cherbourg just before it sailed. Hardacre and Rawlins had questioned him briefly already without much result. This had been shortly after Ribble's arrival in Shaftsborne. Their present and better-briefed interrogation had started thirty minutes earlier.

'I wasn't with them that night. I told you.' Ribble had given up insisting he didn't know Joss and Knuckles. Hardacre had proof that he did know them since they had now admitted knowing him. They were all three paid-up members of the same local chapter of the Devil's Angels motor-cycle club.

'Which night was that, Sean? The twelfth of March you mean? A Monday? When you robbed the church in Chiversley?'

'I dunno. I told you I wasn't there.'

'The others are saying you were, Sean. Like the witness who now says it was your bike parked with Joss Sutters' Honda in the churchyard. Looks like they'll all be speaking against you at the appeal and the new trial. For murder it'll be this time. With you in the dock. Sutters and Crabbe are looking to have their sentences reduced at least. Can't blame them for that really.' He glanced across at Rawlins as if for confirmation. 'Not now they've admitted you were the ringleader. That they never knew the real score that night. That was because you never told them, they're saying.'

'They're lying. It's a poxy fit-up.' But Ribble's thin, drawn face had paled. His cheeks had hollowed more than before under the blond stubble. The hair on his face was nearly the same length as the new growth on his shaved head – except for the inch high, rampant, Red Indian-style mane, dyed orange, that ran from the centre above the forehead to the base of his neck. 'So where's my brief? You promised I'd get a brief this morning?' He lunged forward stabbing out the cigarette butt in the tin ashtray on the table.

'All in good time, Sean. A lawyer's been requested. Be here soon, no doubt. Bit early in the morning for lawyers, this is. Bank holiday too. We'll not let that bother us, though.' After loosening his tie, the shirtsleeved Yorkshireman scratched at his left armpit. 'Sutters and Crabbe didn't need to wait for lawyers last night. Nor need 'em. Not by the look of these statements. Couldn't wait to get even with you. Not after they heard the latest. You really set those lads up, didn't you?' He looked up from his reading. 'They didn't know the organist had a bad heart. Not in advance, they didn't. Because you never thought to mention it. You just roughed him up till he dropped dead. All three of you. Not nice that wasn't.'

'I never roughed up no organist.' He half choked on the words while all the nerves in his body seemed to be taking it in turns to twitch.

'Ah, but the other two lads say you did. You told 'em it was to get the safe keys out of him, not bring on a heart attack that'd kill him. You did say you were being paid to get that safe open though. Now they know why you still got money for a job they thought had gone wrong. Not much money, of course. Not so far as they were concerned. Just enough to keep their mouths shut when they got collared. Not enough in the new circumstances. Not now they know the new circumstances. You should have given them a fair share, lad.'

'I did—' He broke off the sentence sharply, wrapping his arms around his chest, squeezing them tight, and rocking himself on the chair.

'You did give them a fair share? So you admit paying them? Not enough for a murder though. Not since they were the ones who went to jail. Not while you're living it up on the outside. New motor-bike. Nearly two grand in twenty-quid notes in your pocket. Who paid you, Sean? Who sent you to murder the organist?'

'He wasn't murdered,' Ribble shouted suddenly, his breathing shortening as though he'd been running.

'That's better. Good as murder though. Since you'd been told what would happen. What you should make happen.'

'I wasn't told nothing.'

'But we know you were. By the person who sent you to the church. The one who paid you. That's the real villain, of course. You going to tell us who it was, then? It'll go a lot easier for you if you do tell us. At your trial.'

Ribble stayed silent, eyes closed, his arms still tight around his body, the arc of the rocking becoming longer.

'We think it was the same person that paid you for the other job. The convent. We know you set fire to the convent Friday night.'

'I never.' But the change of expression had registered the opposite. The eyes had opened and the rocking had stopped abruptly. This was the first time the convent had been mentioned.

'We know better, don't we Steve?' Hardacre nodded at Rawlins.

'That's right, Sergeant. Got a witness to that,' the Detective Constable replied.

Hardacre leaned well forward in his chair. 'And did you hear, a nun died because of that fire, Sean? Heart attack again. In hospital she was at the time of death, but there's no doubt the fire was the cause. So the charges are building up, Sean. Two deaths and a third we haven't come to yet. All down to you, unless you tell us who paid you? We know somebody did.'

'Nobody paid me for nothing. It's a diabolical liberty keeping me here. I want that brief. I haven't done nothing.'

'Cigarette, Sean?' Hardacre pushed the pack and a box of matches across the table. Ribble grabbed both, took out a cigarette and lit it with shaking hands. Both policemen watched him carefully, then the Sergeant said, 'But you've already admitted you murdered the organist, Sean. It'll be on the tape.'

'I never—'

'But you've told us you did, lad. And we know you started the fire. Now all you can do to make things easier for yourself is tell us who's been paying you. It was a woman, wasn't it? Paid you for the two jobs and warned you on the phone yesterday to scarper.' Hardacre waited for a response but there wasn't one, only a sullen look. 'Fond of women, aren't you Sean?' he continued after a pause. 'Well-developed ones. Like the pin-ups in your room.' He paused again. 'Her name's Sheila, is it?' Again he waited a moment. 'Posh bint, is she? The one who's been paying you? Likes a bit of the rough trade though? On the side?'

Ribble blew out smoke. There was a sly look in his eyes. 'Don't know what you mean.'

'Oh, it's very simple. Up-market bird, married, takes a fancy to a good-looking, working-class stud like you. Nothing to it.

Nothing you couldn't handle. Except she was after more than sex. She wanted a bloke frightened to death, and then a building burnt down. And she didn't want to take the rap if there was one, like now. But she's paid for the privilege. Two ways probably. When you met her Friday afternoon. Isn't that right Sean?'

'Get stuffed. No bird's paid me for nothing.' He looked as if he was going to add something, then didn't.

'So the money in your pocket yesterday, and the money you paid for the new Suzuki – we know that was cash – where'd you get it all, Sean?'

'Ever heard of saving, have you?'

'Go on. You couldn't save that much in five years, lad. Not if you were the busiest motor-bike courier in England.'

'I sold me old bike.'

'Privately. Not to the dealer. We talked to the dealer. The bloke you sold it to came round for it last night. We talked to him too. Mrs Clack couldn't hand over the bike. We've impounded it. Evidence. So she didn't get the money either, I'm afraid. But the man had it with him. Said you told him it had to be cash. Anyway, it means you never had it, so don't try telling us you did.' He sat back in his chair.

Rawlins cleared his throat. 'Where were you at eleven-thirty Saturday night, Sean?' he demanded.

The tension went out of Ribble's face. 'In London. Wembley. Rock concert. Nine of us went. They'll tell you.' The puzzled expression seemed to be spontaneous. 'Why d'you want to know that?'

'We're asking the questions, lad,' Hardacre put in roughly. 'So how well do you know Lady Bittern of Chiversley Hall?'

'So long as I'm not in your way, Mr Treasure. Or your lady. Mrs Cass said you wouldn't mind. My regular May Day holiday job this is. Whether the Captain's here or no. Doesn't do to let it go through the summer, see? Sun does more harm than the wind does in winter. Most people don't understand that. Nice bit of cedar this. We supplied it fifteen year ago.'

The speaker, a beaming, stocky Roy Edicomb, was standing in front of the wooden summer house at the bottom of the

177

Treasures' garden, close to the river. He had a white carpenter's apron on over his open shirt and flannel trousers. Although he was ten years older than his wife, the check cap now covering his prematurely bald head stopped the difference from seeming even greater, at least it did in Mrs Edicomb's view, which is why Mr Edicomb rarely went out bareheaded. There was a large paint brush in his left hand, and a small, uncovered drum of wood preservative in his right. He had just picked up the drum by its handle, and was peering intently at its thick orange contents, as if he had lost something in it. There was a step ladder set up near the structure behind him.

'You certainly won't bother me, Mr Edicomb, and my wife's away filming.' It was nine o'clock, and Treasure had been coming up from an early session on the river carrying a fishing rod. He had arranged to meet Inspector Lodger quite soon. 'Mrs Cass tells me you're senior carpenter at Wheelers, the garden furniture makers? That's near the brewery isn't it?'

'It is, Mr Treasure. Biggest suppliers in this part of England we are. Not that that's saying a lot, but we make good stuff. Stuff that lasts if it's looked after.' He nodded approvingly at the summer house which was pentagon shaped and the type that revolves on a plinth.

Treasure examined the edifice. 'It wouldn't be my idea of a holiday to paint that over with preservative.'

'Two coats, too.' Mr Edicomb's smile got wider, the cheeks dimpling, and the eyes showing earnest dedication. 'Won't take that long though. The Captain pays me a retainer like. That's when he's on an overseas posting. Like he is now. In Washington. I was in the Royal Navy too. He likes me to keep an eye on all the woodwork about the place. Makes a change from being at Wheelers all day.'

'Don't your children expect you to take them to the seaside or anything?'

'They've gone already. Choir outing today, see? Coach left at eight. The wife's gone as well. Deserves the break.' The last phrase sounded a touch thankful as well as generous, suggesting perhaps that she was not the only deserving one.

'I believe I've met your two children, Mr Edicomb.'

'Go on, sir?'

'They sold me some very attractive Sunday school stamps. In aid of the choir fund.'

'Oh aye?' Mr Edicomb offered carefully. He was either dissociating himself from the sale or, like Graham Brown earlier, he was doubtful about the validity of the cause. 'Think I know the stamps. Got them from the wife probably. Used to be a Sunday school teacher.' He took a stained wooden stick from his apron, stuck it into the orange mixture in the drum, and began stirring slowly.

'They were printed in the convent I gather.'

'Ar, wonderful lot of things they used to do there. All over now, I'm afraid. Even before the fire. Only two nuns left now. That's since the one died Saturday.' He shook his head, then rested the drum on a middle step of the ladder and continued stirring.

'Your wife or the children don't collect stamps?'

'Nothing like that, no.' He made it sound as though the practice might be unhygienic. 'The wife used to keep chickens,' he added in a compensatory tone. 'She gave it up though. Not worth the candle, she said. Right, too.'

'Mrs Cass told me it was you who discovered Dr Wader's body.'

Mr Edicomb stopped stirring. 'Terrible thing, sir. Worse thing that's ever happened to me, I can tell you. In the whole of my life.' Leaving the stick in the drum, he took a handkerchief out of his trouser pocket and blew his nose fiercely.

'It was her dog that alerted you?'

'That's right.' Mr Edicomb folded over the handkerchief and blew again even more fiercely. 'Hay fever,' he said, by way of apology. 'We were in bed by then, of course. We knew Thackeray's bark. That's the dog. Golden retriever. We looked after him sometimes. Dr Wader kindly used to pay us to do that.' He paused in memory of the dead woman, or the ceased payments, or possibly both: there seemed to be no end to the income supplements enjoyed by the Edicomb family. 'I dressed and went out with the torch. Just as well. Might have needed it for protection. That's if I'd met the murderer. It's a big heavy torch. Rubber. Good as a truncheon. We all have them in the Avenue. People in the Community Watch that is.' His shoulders squared at this reference to his quasi-constabulary activity.

'Pity Dr Wader didn't have one too,' Treasure observed.

'That's right. I'd told her that. You can't be too careful, I said. But she relied on the dog. Well, that's fair enough you'd think, wouldn't you? And his lead, of course. Chain lead it is. She always took that when she walked old Thack.'

'For protection or to restrain the dog?'

'Sort of protection. She didn't need to put Thack on any lead. Not when he was with her. Never left her side. More's the pity dog nor chain didn't help her Saturday night. Fiend he must have been that did that to her.' Mr Edicomb shook his head slowly from side to side. 'They're saying now the police are sure it was Graham Brown. Codswallop that is. Graham wouldn't hurt anybody. His mother's fair going out of her mind. The wife was in with her last evening.'

'They haven't arrested him?'

'No. But the word is that they will do, right enough. All because he happened to pass her house at the wrong time, and old Miss Quigley opposite saw him.'

'You know Miss Quigley?'

'Yes, poor lady. Martyr to arthritis she is. Sits up in that window all the time, minding other people's business. Can't blame her I suppose. Not really. Not in her sad condition. She's done Graham Brown no good though.' He looked at his wrist watch. 'Well, I mustn't hold you up, Mr Treasure. Done with the fishing for today have you?'

'No, I expect I'll go back to it later. I'm meeting someone in the town. At the Feathers.'

Mr Edicomb rubbed his knee. 'Watch out for the beams there, sir. Old oak they are. Genuine. Gentleman of your height can do himself a mischief on them.'

Chapter Nineteen

'It'll not get Mrs Garnet into trouble, sir,' said Detective Inspector Lodger, as if he meant it. 'A lot of people say the wrong thing on impulse when they're interviewed by police, then regret it later. But often they feel they can't go back on anything. Then they're in a panic.'

'I'm sure that's right, in the majority of cases,' said Treasure, temporising, and without wishing to upset the Inspector's premise. According to Molly, Mrs Garnet had been in no sense close to panic.

'What she'd said to us was silly, of course, but we're glad of the evidence, whatever the route,' the tall policeman continued. 'Thanks again. And for the other information. I'll give you a receipt for these.' He put the stamps back in their envelope, then leaned forward to move his coffee cup along the low round table in front of him to make room for his notebook.

'I'm quite sure she isn't aware the overprinting's removable, and I'm equally sure she's been acting in the role of innocent pawn,' said Treasure, again without volunteering comment on Mrs Garnet's deeper motivations – like the one bedded in her husband's detestation of policemen. 'I'd be willing to bet Graham Brown's been in the same position.'

'On the stamps, sir. Perhaps.' Lodger's tone was less encouraging this time.

They were in the front lounge of the Feathers – an open area on the ground floor across from the main reception desk, but partially screened by a wrought iron trellis. Afternoon tea was served here, but it was seldom occupied by anybody in the morning except briefly by departing guests waiting for the arrival of transport, or for porters with their luggage, or for other departing guests. It was empty now except for the two men. Treasure had agreed to meet the Inspector here at nine-thirty. When the banker had arrived on time, Lodger had been waiting for him with coffee already ordered.

'We'll have to see Mrs Garnet again, of course,' the policeman continued, handing Treasure his receipt. 'It should be fairly painless though if she's ready to co-operate.' Incautiously, he leaned well back in the long, low armchair, found the position impracticable, arched forward again energetically from the waist and ended up looking at Treasure between bent knees. 'On a different subject, sir. You must have talked to Dr Wader a lot at Chiversley Hall on Saturday. I remember you told me you sat next to her at dinner, for instance?'

'Sure. And she and I talked a good deal before and after the meal as well,' the banker replied.

'Did she say anything at any point to suggest she might be meeting someone later that night?'

'No. I think I'd have told you if she had.'

'You're quite sure of that, sir?'

'Certain. You've got the idea she'd arranged a meeting?'

Lodger gave a pained expression. 'There are reasons that strongly suggest she might have done. Naturally Mr Brown denies she'd made any arrangement with him. Mr Utteridge-Flax says the same.' With his weight on his elbows, the speaker lifted himself to the front of the chair, and straightened his back.

'They being the two who went to her house after dinner anyway. Or close to it in the case of Brown,' said Treasure.

'Precisely, sir. And if they're both telling the truth—'

'You think there could still have been an arrangement with someone else she knew?'

'We've had to look to that possibility.' The tone didn't suggest that the search had been exhaustive so far.

'Why couldn't it have been a total stranger who followed her into the wood, intending to rape her?'

'Because, as far as we can tell, there's not much chance anyone could have followed her into the wood. Except for Mr Brown.'

'Because they'd have been seen by Miss Quigley from the

house opposite?' Treasure asked. 'But her line of sight didn't cover all angles of approach surely? For instance, the path behind the houses in Jubilee Avenue, the one Brown was making for. I just drove down Salt Street to look at it. Anyone coming from that could have turned sharp right into the wood, probably without being seen by Miss Quigley.'

'Without necessarily being seen by her, sir. It would have been risky all the same.' The still uncomfortable Lodger crossed his long legs – another fairly elaborate exercise in the circumstances, made more so by the closeness of the table.

'Even so, Miss Quigley couldn't actually see Brown either, after he left the road,' said Treasure. 'You told me so yourself. So she can't swear whether he went along the path as he says, or into the wood.'

Lodger nodded, with some reluctance. 'If it wasn't Graham Brown who strangled her, we think it was someone who entered the wood from the other side. From Shepton Way. There's a small lay-by there, where the path comes out. It's not likely she'd have walked up that far, not the whole width of the wood, not at that time of night, and not just to exercise the dog. So she wouldn't have been seen by anyone who was driving along Shepton Way, or parked in the lay-by.'

'So someone coming from that side would have had to know her movements and her habits?'

'Either that, or he was meeting her by appointment.'

Treasure drank some coffee. 'Or he was a vagrant in the wood who attacked her on impulse. To rob and rape her.'

The Inspector clasped both hands in front of his crossed knees, levering himself forwards into a more confidential proximity to his companion. 'She had a dog with her. Vagrants are usually chary of dogs, especially big ones. The victim wasn't carrying a handbag, the commonest inducement to unpremeditated robbery.' He paused for a moment as if debating whether to go on, then he did. 'And rape never seems to have been in question. You see, her clothes were removed after death.'

'After death?' Treasure repeated, looking puzzled. 'So he was one of those kinky people who—'

'No, sir. We don't believe he was that either. There was no indication of sexual interference of any kind.'

'So why did he strip her? Must have been for some kind of gratification?'

'We think it was just a crude effort to throw us off the scent.'

'To make you think it was a stranger? A vagrant or a sex maniac? In that circumstance, wouldn't it have made more sense actually for him to have raped her?'

'And leave physical evidence easily traced if it was a man in her own circle of friends?' said Lodger. 'Someone at that dinner, for instance? One of the men we've been questioning?'

'I see, yes.' Treasure rubbed his forehead. 'Could have been . . . an impotent stranger, I suppose?'

'We thought of that too, sir.'

Treasure looked up at the beam in the ceiling above his head. 'Or if not an impotent man, then a strong woman?'

'Ah, now why did you say that, sir?'

'No special reason. I suppose I was just thinking laterally.'

The policeman looked disappointed.

'What about this chap Ribble, the motor-cyclist?' Treasure went on.

'We've got him in custody.'

'Well done. If he was involved where Sister Mary Maud says he was, could he also have been the murderer?'

'No. He's got a water-tight alibi for that time on Saturday night.'

'Pity.'

'But he's tied in with the other happenings all right. And since they revolve around the trust and its beneficiaries, we're pretty certain the murder does too.'

'Not the work of a vagrant, Inspector?' said Treasure regretfully.

'Not the work of a vagrant, sir,' the other responded.

'Goo' morgin, Camom. Nife agem,' said the old crone who had answered the door. Her mouth was sunken in repose, as though she had no teeth, and certainly none had been evident as she had uttered in a mechanical, lip-sucking way, showing difficulty with the conquering of most consonants. She was dressed in a flowered overall, and thick woollen stockings that sagged above the ankles onto the tops of fur-lined suede boots. The stockings and boots seemed conspicuously unseasonable – though perhaps not as comically inappropriate as the spirited recording of 'The Arrival of the Queen of Sheba', from Handel's *Solomon*, which had accompanied their owner's appearance at the door, the music billowing down from the upper regions of the house.

'Morning, Sarah,' the Canon replied breezily, tipping his biretta, then letting his hand drop to fiddle with one of the higher buttons on his cassock. 'This is Mr Treasure. We've come to call on Miss Quigley. Is she-she-she receiving?'

'Loute and clee-ah, Camom.' Both edges of the woman's now tightly closed mouth next stretched ear-wards as her eyes lit up and her body quivered with mirth at her own drollery. 'I'g bepper amoumce you.' She turned and shuffled off toward the stairs, leaving the front door open, the padding of her boots drowned by the crashing of cymbals and drums as the music from above reached its final crescendo.

'Sarah's the maid,' the Canon vouchsafed to Treasure quietly. 'Been with Miss Quigley over fifty years.'

'Fippy-poo,' Sarah bellowed triumphantly over her shoulder from the landing half-way up the stairs. 'The Camom's here. Does he come ub?' she hollered, though the music had stopped, her head turned in the other direction. There was a faint affirmative sort of noise from somewhere on the upper floor. The maid turned her head back again. 'You cam come ub,' she supplied. Then her head swivelled away once more, like an umpire's at a tennis match. 'Dare cubbink ub,' she cried, heavenwards. All this effort had made her breathless. She remained standing on the landing, grasping the balustrade for several moments more.

'We'd better shut the door,' said the Canon, ushering Treasure into the hall. The house was four square – a modest, late-Georgian villa, hipped roofed, walls of dressed stone and standing in a small garden that had probably been a large one till the owner had sold off land for building. The last exigency was witnessed by the row of small modern bungalows sprouting on one side, the first of them almost indecently close. On the other side the house was set next to the wood, divided from it only by the pathway to the backs in Jubilee Avenue. The front door, set in the centre, led into a large tiled hall. This was furnished unpretentiously with well-designed, early Victorian pieces that seemed to have matured as antiques since they and the house had been new, a century and a half before. The furniture in other rooms was to give the same impression. The stairs were of polished oak, uncovered, and noisy to mount.

'Come in, come in, Canon. You'll take a glass of sherry? Who's this with you?' Miss Quigley questioned in a cultured, squeaky and sharply penetrating voice from her wheelchair on the far side of the front bedroom. She seemed frail and was certainly ancient, with grey hair caught back in a bun above a face so parched and wizened, it had less the look of flesh than gnarled woodbark. The neck was scrawny but held high, sprouting like a daisy stem from below the white lace collar on a blue velvet jacket. From the waist downwards she was wrapped in a tartan travelling rug.

When the Canon had made the introductions, the visitors accepted the two vacant chairs at the card table set against one of the two sashed windows. In the main, the room was furnished as a bedroom not as a sitting-room, but in addition to the usual accoutrements of a lady's boudoir, in the corner behind Miss Quigley stood some complicated sound reproduction equipment. This was contained in black plastic boxes embellished with a great many dials and control knobs. There were closed racks of compact discs too, and elsewhere in the room loudspeakers had been placed at no doubt critical points.

Miss Quigley's wheelchair was on the side of the table that gave the best outside view. 'So you're the merchant banker who's going to be the new beneficiary?' she said to Treasure. 'I've heard about you from Reverend Mother. You have a celebrated wife. Actress.' She glanced quickly at the Canon as if to stem an expected complaint from that quarter. 'Nothing wrong with being an actress,' she added loudly, as if the cleric might be hard of hearing. 'There might have been in my day, of course.'

'Miss Quigley was born in the-the-the last century,' said the Canon approvingly.

'I'm ninety-six,' the lady offered, in keeping, Treasure felt, with the custom of this numerically exact household. Her hand went up to tidy a non-existent wisp of straying hair. The hand was as wrinkled as the face but with knuckles painfully enlarged by arthritis. 'You want to ask me about the trust?'

'Yes. But only incidentally. I'm more interested—'

'I knew Daniel Utteridge's daughters, of course,' Miss Quigley interrupted. 'Those who survived to any sort of age, that is. One died in childbirth. Another of cholera. She was a nun. Didn't know either of them.' She gave a delicate sniff. 'The next to oldest daughter was the Reverend Mother at the convent when I was a girl. Well, you'd expect that with the father putting up the money. Ah, thank you Sarah.'

The aged maid had appeared balancing a full decanter of pale sherry and three crystal sherry glasses on a silver tray. She finished her traversing of the room with sudden and alarming haste, depositing her burden on the card table with a noisy breath of triumph. 'There you are,' she enunciated with perfect articulation, and a glistening display of National Health dentures evidently reserved for special occasions. 'Shall I pour?'

'Thank you, no, Sarah,' her mistress demurred with asperity, removing the stopper of the decanter herself.

'Please yourself,' the other replied, turning about and shuffling away.

'I expect you knew your neighbour Jill Wader,' said Treasure.

'Hardly. I watched her a good deal. From here. I don't go about at all. Not at present. My legs, you see? Fortunately my eyesight and hearing would do justice to a person half my age. Or so the doctors say.' After this lively, objective testimonial to the robust condition of some of her faculties, Miss Quigley lifted the decanter a fraction with a shaking arm, then put it down again with a bump.

'Allow me.' The Canon half stood, took the decanter and began filling the glasses.

'What sort of a man was Daniel Utteridge, I wonder?' Treasure asked. 'Did his daughters ever say?'

'A saint according to those of them who were nuns. A tyrant and a social climber if you listened to the married ones. One of them told me that in her old age. When she was a widow.'

'He achieved his goal at least. A peerage,' the Canon observed.

'I wonder what he'd do with the trust fund now the convent is running down?' said the banker.

The old lady considered for a moment. 'If he were alive, no doubt he'd do what Charles Utteridge-Flax wants to do. Switch the money into fresh good works, in the hope of getting an even higher honour from the Queen.' The eyes narrowed. 'That's what Charles himself is hoping for, of course. He's as good as told me so. Knows he'll never prove he's entitled to be the second Lord Chiversley. But he'd expect a knighthood at least for being so generous to this black hospice charity. You know it has a royal patron? Oh, yes.' Her chin lifted in a gesture of extra affirmation.

'Killing two birds? I hadn't thought of that. Is he personally so ambitious?'

'Not for himself, Mr Treasure. It's to vindicate the girl he calls his natural mother. Probably correctly. I knew her well. Before she ran off. Madcap girl.' Like the Reverend Mother, Miss Quigley pronounced the last word always as 'gel'.

'It's possible he could get his way. Because of Dr Wader's murder.'

'I know. He's presently the sole beneficiary, of course. Have you come to talk about that? I expect so,' Miss Quigley continued without waiting for a response. 'I was the last to see her, you know? Dr Wader I mean. Well, of course you would know. I told the police.'

'And-and-and about seeing Charles and Graham Brown,' said the Canon, passing round the glasses.

'I couldn't help but see them all. That's her house opposite. You can see bits of it through the trees. And the lamp-post in front. I spend most of my day and night listening to music and looking through this window.'

'You should get a television,' said the Canon, sipping his sherry rather noisily. 'I'm always telling her that,' he completed to Treasure.

'Nonsense. Horrid invention. This is my television.' Miss Quigley waved at the window.

'You couldn't see where Utteridge-Flax and young Brown went after they crossed the road,' said Treasure, leaning to one side so that he had the same view of the street as Miss Quigley.

'Charles drove away. I saw the car when it passed. He'd

parked it this side of the road. It was his car, I'm sure. Brown went home or into the wood after he called at Dr Wader's house.'

'He insists he didn't go to her house, Miss Quigley. That you were mistaken in thinking he did,' the banker said.

Miss Quigley toyed with her glass. 'Is it important?'

'They're very likely going to arrest him on-on-on suspicion of murder,' the Canon advised gravely.

'Then I won't swear to it.' She tasted the sherry, then licked her lips. 'But I don't believe he's telling the truth, all the same. Or else he's . . . mistaken.' She gave Treasure a rueful smile.

'Was there anything else you mentioned to the police that you wouldn't absolutely swear to,' asked the banker.

'I forget what I told them now.' She paused. 'Oh yes, I recognised Lucius Bittern's car. There were three people in it when they drove into Dr Wader's. Two when they came out. That must have been accurate. Lucius had driven her home with your niece, Canon. That's what they told me afterwards.'

'Did you see who was driving when they arrived?' Treasure put in.

'It was a woman. One of the two. Not Lucius. He was in the back.'

'Behind the passenger?'

'Yes.' She put a finger to her brow. 'Let me see. He was leaning forward. I think he had a hand on her shoulder. Yes, and she was in red. And the one driving had on a white wrap. She was wearing it when they left again. That was when she was a passenger.'

'But you couldn't identify the women when they arrived?'

'Certainly not. When they left, it was easy to construe that the one in red must have been Dr Wader.'

'How long was it till the car came out and drove away again?'

'Two or three minutes. Not more.'

'And it didn't drive past your house.'

Miss Quigley's face clouded. 'I'm sure it didn't. Except if they were going to the vicarage—'

'Christine told me they took the long way round. To avoid the town,' the Canon provided. 'Lucius was concerned about

189

the amount of alcohol he'd drunk,' he added, solemnly eyeing his now empty glass and then the decanter.

'But he was driving then,' said Miss Quigley with a frown.

'I know,' The banker's face was also furrowed. 'And Dr Wader came out shortly after with her dog?'

'As I knew she would.'

'She was dressed in a mackintosh and scarf. Did you by any chance notice her shoes?'

'No . . . Yes, I did,' she corrected. 'They were red. Bright red.'

'You told the police the dog was on the lead.'

'Yes.'

'Was that normal?'

'For it to be on the lead?' Miss Quigley hesitated. 'D'you know, it wasn't?' She fingered the cameo brooch on the lapel of her jacket. 'Now I think about it, that was quite unusual.'

Chapter Twenty

'When you said you wanted to meet Miss Quigley, I thought it was to do with-with-with Sheila Bittern. To find out if Sheila had been to Jill Wader's house after the dinner. But is that right? I mean, how could she have? Or was it something to do with the stamps?' The Canon raised both hands in a gesture of despair. 'Dear me, I seem to be getting very muddled over the whole business. Perhaps it was the sherry.' He peered through the car windscreen with a deeply worried look on his face. It was as though the landscape outside was unknown to him or had changed dramatically since he had last seen it – except they were approaching his own house which he had left only half an hour earlier. He lifted his biretta and smoothed his largely bald head before covering it again. 'This is a splendid motor,' he said, leaning back in the seat again, and testing the depth of padding in the armrests with his elbows, but only gently, as Treasure drew the car up outside the vicarage. 'You'll come in for a moment?'

'Better not,' the banker answered in a preoccupied voice. 'Christine isn't here is she?'

'I fear she went to Shaftsborne. Very early. To see that solicitor. The one who's acting for Graham now. We were expecting her back for lunch, but she rang to say she'd be going to London instead. I don't know why.' The Canon looked at his watch. 'Goodness, it's-it's-it's very nearly noon. You wanted to see her? She might come back tomorrow.'

'Then I'll see her then.' It was the banker's turn to look perplexed. 'There's something I ought to warn—'

'Whatever's the matter with Sister Mary Maud?' the cleric interrupted. 'Has she gone mad?'

It was true that the Sister was hurrying toward them from the direction of the convent in a state of what appeared to be unrestrained jubilation if not actual abandon. The hand she was waving in the air was clasping something small but evidently precious. The other hand had hold of Lazarus's lead. Lazarus wasn't on the lead. He was following his minder at some distance and at a much more orderly pace than hers. He had slipped his collar. Sister Mary Maud was dragging it along the path at the end of the lead, unaware that Lazarus wasn't in it.

'I've found it,' she cried as she came up with the two men who had by this time both got out of the car. 'It was in the hop. Or do I mean the jump? The big receptacle they're putting the debris in.'

'The skip?' Treasure provided because he could see one on the grass outside the convent chapel.

'That's right. Oh dear. I seem to have mislaid Lazarus. Reverend Mother will be . . . No, here he is.'

The dog had dawdled up by this time with an unconcerned look in his tired eyes. He sniffed at his collar, then settled down beside it. He began licking one of four distinctly blackened paws, looking up at his audience between libations as if in hope of tribute for such laudable industry.

'What is it you've found?' asked the Canon, his gaze on the Sister's clasped hand.

'In the . . . the skip? Yes. So unlikely too. It's so small, you see?' she continued excitedly. 'But they're throwing everything in there. So we had a little rummage. Lazarus and I. It was on the top. Such luck.'

'What was?' the Canon tried again.

'Didn't I say? Why, the ink pad. Sister Patricia was quite sure it had been lost in the fire. She told me. In the hospital. It bothered her so much. It was in her special care, you see?' She opened her hand. The palm, covered in what looked like carbon black, was holding a small, thin, oblong tin box. There was printing on the box top but since it too was mostly covered in grime it was difficult to decipher any legend. The Sister opened the top which was hinged. 'It's not damaged inside. The pad, I mean. Although it's rather dried out. Isn't that amazing? How it's survived. Oh, if only Sister Patricia could have known it was safe before she died. She really was so upset about it.'

'Well she'll-she'll-she'll know now. It'll make her rest more easily, no doubt,' said the Canon, with an air of more than just professional piety.

'Why is the pad so special?' Treasure asked, his interest entirely terrestrial.

'I can't remember,' answered Sister Mary Maud. 'Sister Patricia did explain. I'm afraid I wasn't paying enough attention at the time.' She closed the lid carefully. 'It was something to do with the ink being hard to get, or officially approved.' Her eyes lit up. 'That was it. Officially approved by the Post Office. For cancelling stamps. It was why we couldn't have one of our own. Only the loan of one. Or was it to save expense? It always went back after Sister Patricia had used it.'

'Who took it back?' said Treasure.

'Why, the same good lady who brought it. Sister Patricia told me that too, although it was all supposed to be a secret.' She smiled benignly at the Canon. 'We couldn't do without . . .' Her hand suddenly went to her mouth in a gesture of dismay. 'Oh dear, I'm afraid Lazarus has done something on the front wheel of your car, Mr Treasure. I hope it won't hurt the rubber. Dampness is so bad . . .' She hurried forward, snatching up the dog collar and undoing it as she went. 'Naughty Lazarus.'

'Why Mark, how very jolly to see you.' But despite the apparent enthusiasm, Sheila Bittern's greeting lacked ebullience. She had answered the door dressed in a not very clean, green kaftan dress which served to emphasise rather than diminish her Rubenesque proportions. There was a tea towel in her right hand. 'We're a bit at sixes and sevens, I'm afraid. Lucius is going to London after lunch.'

'I remember his telling me. It's why I'm here. I need to see him before he leaves.'

'About the trust is it?' Her face brightened. 'Old Charles has got a ruddy nerve, saying he's going to wind it up. Terence Natt seems to think he might get away with it, too. It'd suit us, of course.'

'Meaning you'd take up the brewery shares? If that were

after your baby's birth and it's a boy, he'll be very rich when he comes of age, and potentially richer still.'

'Well, between you and me, it's going to be a girl,' she said, as if the information was of no real consequence, and while rubbing at a spot on her front with the tea towel. 'It could make her rich too, in the end, of course. I shan't be profligate in my lifetime. There'd be plenty to go round after all, especially if Lucius arranges for the brewery to be taken over. Is that what you meant?'

'Yes.' And meanwhile, Lucius will have the sole disposition of his wife's entitlement, Treasure added to himself, but without saying so out loud. Instead he observed: 'I believe Terence Natt thought I'd agree to a wind-up too. When I became a beneficiary.'

'Yes, he did. It's why he wanted you to be elected. He told me so. Said he'd decided our purposes were the same. Or could be. That was after he'd talked to you.'

'Thank you for telling me.' He was impressed by the lady's candour which he persuaded himself was genuine not calculated.

'I expect Lucius will tell you the same. Well, anyway, you can ask him. He's in his study over there. I'll show you.' She moved across the hall with the banker. 'You're welcome to stay for a pot-luck lunch.'

'I don't think I can. Thanks all the same.'

'Some other time then. Soon.' She pushed open one half of the study double door, then had to stand back to let the visitor through. 'It's Mark, darling. Nice surprise. I'll leave you to it. Got to see about the grub.' She closed the door behind Treasure.

Bittern rose from where he was sitting at a large partner's desk. He seemed neither pleased nor displeased at the intrusion, only puzzled. The room was in the same state of deterioration as the rest of the house. There were a great many business papers in front of Bittern on the desk and more in a black leather document case open at his elbow.

'I'm sorry to call unannounced. It's important,' said Treasure a touch stiffly.

'Glad to see you,' Bittern replied. He was dressed in a dark blue pin-stripe suit. 'Do sit down. Cigarette? Drink?'

'Thank you, no.' The banker took the chair nearest the

desk. 'What I have to say shouldn't take long.' He swallowed hard then began to speak rapidly. 'Did you know that for the past eighteen months, maybe longer, Christine Stonning has been making a fortune selling stamps that were forged in the convent?'

'Surely not?' Bittern's face had clouded. 'I didn't know. Then again, why should I? But I find it hard to believe. Impossible. The stamps they printed there were all facsimiles.'

'Turned back later into perfect forgeries by washing off the cancellation.'

The other's face hardened. 'You can prove that? That Christine was involved?' He reached for a cigarette from the box on the desk. 'You've got some of these stamps?'

'Yes. I gave them to the police this morning. They came from Mrs Garnet, a dealer in Shaftsborne. She'd been told to burn them by Graham Brown, but she hadn't.'

'So surely it was Brown, not Christine—'

'Brown had been organising the printing and distribution of what he thought were facsimile stamps for legitimate uses. He's been doing it for years without getting anything out of it for himself. Nothing except appreciation. The convent and Mrs Garnet had been getting a nominal amount of money, and that's all they've ever got. It was after her accident that Christine effectively took over the operation for profit with a crook called Hechler.'

Bittern blew out smoke noisily. 'She did that from here? But—'

'From here and London. Mostly London. As Mrs Davenport, she phoned orders for stamps required to Mrs Garnet who passed them on to Brown who passed them to Sister Patricia. When the stamps were ready the Sister posted them to Mrs Garnet who'd be told by Mrs Davenport, again by phone, where to send them and when. All apparently above board, and certainly proof against investigation. Christine did take a hand in the production by fixing it so the word facsimile was printed on the stamps in water-based ink.'

'She's told you that herself?'

He shook his head. 'Sister Mary Maud did. Unintentionally. Brown vaguely knew that Christine was lending inked pads and other things to Sister Patricia to save the convent expense. He didn't realise the pads were part of a deception. He didn't twig either that Christine was involved in anything questionable till late Friday afternoon when she suddenly had to come clean with him. Or nearly. That was when she told him to get back some stamps from Mrs Garnet due to arrive by post next morning. Instead, he phoned Mrs Garnet and told her to burn them. He didn't realise their importance.'

'But Sheila told me the police had him in for questioning about the stamps on Saturday. If he was innocent, why didn't he blame Christine then?'

'Because he decided to protect her. Because he's madly in love with her. But the police were close to finding out the truth. They'd planned to go over the convent printing room on Friday, but agreed to delay it till Saturday. The reason for that delay was quite innocent, but the consequences were profound. On Saturday the police would have discovered the number of limited editions Sister Patricia was equipped to produce. That's why the place was burned down on Friday night.'

Bittern shook his head. 'Brown arranged that?'

'No. But Christine did.' Treasure was carefully watching the other's reaction. 'That was why it was even more important the police should never have an inkling about her stamp activities. She even promised to marry Brown so he'd go on keeping his mouth shut. That worked too, until Mrs Garnet gave her away.'

'How?'

'Once, in the early days, Christine left a message for Mrs Garnet to call her back on a London number. It was careless, and she never did it again. Christine always used the name Mrs Davenport, but Mrs Garnet had made a permanent note of the number that first time. It was the number of Christine's flat. She's had it changed since, perhaps because she realised the size of the error, but the police traced the old number back to her when they got it from Mrs Garnet. That was this morning.'

There was silence for a moment, then Bittern said: 'And you're still saying Christine burnt down the convent?'

'That she arranged it, yes. Through a young thug called Ribble who appears to have been as much under her spell as Brown. And they're not the only ones. Some men do as she tells them for money, some do it for sex, some it seems for both. Ribble probably fell into the last category.' He saw the other man's gaze grow in incredulity. Bittern stubbed out the cigarette and made as though he was about to speak, but he stayed silent until Treasure had completed with: 'She'd also had Ribble hassle Ambrose Picton into the heart attack that killed him.'

'You can't prove that.' But Bittern's tone was closer to a plea than to a rebuke. His eyes had dropped to studying the hands that he was clenching and unclenching before him on the desk.

'I can't prove it, no. But his two cronies can and have. The ones who are in jail already. They named him as ringleader and paymaster when they were told the case could be reopened with a more serious charge. That Ribble could be accused of murdering Picton. Christine will be an accessory, of course. And to the arson charge as well. She's been careful never to figure as the principal.' He considered for a moment before adding slowly: 'I expect she'll plant the main blame for Jill Wader's murder onto someone else too.'

Bittern looked up sharply, his face ashen. 'She wasn't involved in that. She couldn't have been.'

'Certainly it lacks the finesse of some of her other crimes. It wasn't so long in gestation, perhaps, although she had to act pretty quickly to arrange the fire the night before. She drove to see Ribble about that. Near Tidmouth, on Friday afternoon, taking ready money with her. A lot of it. She must have finally made up her mind about killing Jill after dinner here on Saturday. I believe because of something I said. It's why I feel responsible for what happened. Why I'm determined Jill's murder's going to be solved. You'll help, of course?'

'To clear Christine. In spite of what you say. Good God, the police know Brown did it. You're crazy to think anything else.'

Despite the words, Bittern's protest was feeble compared with Treasure's firm response. 'Brown couldn't have done it,' the banker said. 'He wasn't even an accessory. Not this time. Stripping Jill's body wasn't just careless, of course. It was stupid too. It was meant to mislead the police into thinking rape had been intended but it did the opposite. Tell me, why didn't Christine drive your car to the vicarage after you left Jill's house? I gather you'd been scared of being stopped by the police and breathalysed.'

'That's why she did the driving to Jill's place, yes.' The tone was now sullen. He reached for another cigarette.

'But why not back from there to the vicarage?'

'Well obviously it was such a short drive.'

'But through the town again with the most risk of your being noticed by police.'

'I didn't go the direct way.'

'Not up Salt Street to the High Street. You went in the opposite direction. Down to the T-junction with Shepton Way.'

'That's right. Then round the back, up Abbot's Way.'

'You didn't have a quite different reason for taking that route, and for doing the driving yourself?'

'No. Why should I?' He inhaled sharply on the cigarette.

'Except that Christine wasn't in the car then, was she? So she couldn't have driven?'

Bittern's reaction was almost as though he had been hit in the face. 'I don't know what you mean. I don't see why—'

'By the way, what was wrong with Jill's car?' Treasure interrupted sharply. 'I gather you fixed it easily enough yesterday morning.'

'Dirty plugs.' He stubbed out the cigarette savagely so that the end disintegrated in the ashtray.

'Are you sure? It wasn't because Christine had removed the cylinder head? Or something like that? When she went to the loo ahead of the party breaking up? So Jill's car wouldn't start, and you'd have to run both of them home because all the other cars had gone?'

'That's total nonsense. Your imagination's run away with you.'

'Why do you suppose Jill put her dog on the lead to go in the wood that night?' Treasure persisted.

'Did she? How should I know. I wasn't there.' There were beads of sweat on his brow.

'Neither was I there, but I know why the dog was on the lead. It wasn't Jill who had charge of him. It was Christine, dressed to look like Jill, and Christine couldn't risk having the dog run away, or go berserk later. It had to be on the lead from the start. As for Jill, she was still in the passenger seat of your car, expected to pass for Christine if anyone saw you. That wasn't likely, but she was well strapped in because by that time she was . . . very dead. Did you do the actual killing? Christine put you up to it, of course. Christine, your London mistress, only it looks as though you've been sharing her with a few locals down here. Brown, Ribble, possibly even Utteridge-Flax—'

'It's lies, all lies.' Bittern's self-control had gone at last, his nerve snapped. He had stood up so suddenly that he toppled the chair behind him. 'You'll have to prove all of it.'

'I can. Easily.' Treasure stayed motionless in his seat while continuing with his quick-fire accusation. 'I can prove it all. Except which of you did the strangling when you had stopped in Jill's drive. And which of you held her down. It's the strangler who'll get the biggest sentence, I expect. The one who wrapped the cord around her neck. Although if it was Christine there'll be a plea of mitigation. That terrible accident of hers. Those injuries to the head. She's insane, of course. Not responsible. So there's no reason why you shouldn't tell the truth. Better for you. Better for her.'

The banker lowered the tone of his voice, but increased the rapidity of his words as he went on. 'It was her wasn't it? Who did the strangling? But it was you who drove the body to the other side of the wood, to Shepton Way. You met Christine there again, masquerading as Jill. Then you stripped the body and dumped it in the undergrowth, tying up the dog. You scattered Jill's clothes. But you both forgot the distinctive red shoes. Easily done, because Christine was actually wearing them. The only part of Jill's clothing she had to put on. The scarf and the mac covered everything else. Did you both realise she still had them on when it was too late? When you'd left the scene? When you reached the vicarage? The shoes haven't been found yet. Still hidden in your Jaguar are they? Or have you got rid of them? It was the missing shoes that first pointed to what might have happened. That and the dog being on the lead. The London police will have picked up Christine by now. My advice to you is to tell the truth to the police here, and quickly. She's going to try blaming you for everything if she can.'

Treasure had watched the veins on the backs of Bittern's hands harden like steel as the palms took the weight of his body. The head had sagged over the desk, and while its owner had stayed silent throughout, his breathing had become noticeably heavier and shorter.

When Bittern's head came up it did so slowly. The face was haggard and seemed to have aged ten years, the expression dulled with defeat and tinged with fear. The eyes that met Treasure's seemed already to be welling with remorse.

'You didn't mean that Charles Utteridge-Flax was also her lover, surely?' asked Molly, finishing her coffee and putting the cup to one side.

'No. But it was important Bittern should feel jealous as well as found out. He wouldn't have confessed otherwise.'

'That Christine engineered everything?'

'And that he held Jill from the back seat while Christine—'

'Don't, please,' Molly interrupted her husband with a shudder. It was after ten, but the night was balmy. They were sitting on the terrace again in the moonlight, this time side by side in the swing chair that Mr Edicomb had brought up from where it had been stored in the summer house. Molly hadn't returned from filming until just before eight: Treasure had been involved with the police until nearly that time. Lucius Bittern and Christine Stonning had been arrested separately during the afternoon.

'But how much of what you said to Bittern was backed by evidence and how much was supposition?' Molly asked next.

'There was very little real evidence, but I was convinced I had the scenario right. Right enough to bluff him into a confession.'

'And getting Bittern to admit everything saved the police a lot of time and trouble?'

'So Lodger was big enough to say. I had the advantage, of course, taking an unofficial line.'

'Which was just as well because Christine confessed to nothing?'

'Still hasn't. Bittern was her weak link. If he hadn't been weak she'd never have been able to manipulate him, of course.' He leaned back against the cushions. 'Christine's plan was plain enough. She needed to have the trust wound up, Bittern to become financially powerful as a consequence, and all so she and he could live happily ever after. Or that's what she told him.'

'You mean she'd have left him once she'd milked him of enough money? Sheila's money?'

He shrugged. 'Who knows. He was completely besotted with her. But then so were the other two men she involved.'

'But not Charles?'

'He was pretty devoted to her. Just lucky he was never put to the real test, perhaps. That she didn't need to use him as flagrantly as she did the others.'

Molly pulled the sides of her cashmere cardigan closer together. 'And the stamp business . . . ?'

'Was to raise money to fund the bigger plan.'

'And Sheila Bittern was used by her husband really just as much as Christine was using him.'

Treasure rubbed his forehead. 'If not in such a bloodthirsty way. Sheila's had a raw deal, and a terrible shock, of course. I assume she'll divorce him.'

'And good riddance. They're a pretty ill-matched couple in any case.'

'Yes. He evidently asked her to be his second wife for her money not her . . . her other attributes. She's just been a source of funds to stop his house falling down and, more importantly, the mother of a child that was intended to put millions in his control before he left her.'

'Taking a hefty slice of the millions with him.' Molly frowned. 'He was lucky the child was going to be a girl.'

'Though it's a pity Sheila told him. Natt advised her not to.'

'What you call Sheila's other attributes may not be legion,' said Molly with feeling, 'but to her credit, innocence is one of them.'

'Exactly. I was fairly sure she wasn't party to her husband's crimes before I went there before lunch today. The police had tied her in with Ribble. Wrongly, of course. They even had her down as a prime suspect for the murder.' He shook his head. 'It was what she disclosed to me about the sex of her baby, oh, and about Natt's attitude to my becoming a beneficiary. That convinced me I was right. She was so ingenuous.'

'All of which put Natt in the clear as well?'

'Oh yes. As we figured at the start, he's very much Sheila's lawyer, works in her interests, and that's it.' He pouted. 'She's welcome to him. Dull, pompous chap.'

'But honest. Like Graham Brown. And you certainly saved his skin.'

'He's worthy enough. It's people like him keep Middle England going. They always seem to be clamouring for recognition, but usually no one thinks of giving them any. Parish churches, charities, local good works in general. They couldn't do without their Graham Browns.' He took a sip of the very dilute whisky in the glass he was holding.

'So was it the chance of Brown being unfairly arrested that made you so concerned to catch the real villains?'

'Perhaps.'

'Or till you realised that Christine was making a play for you too, for the wrong reasons?' She chuckled quietly. 'That made you suspicious. It was after that phone call last night, wasn't it? After you'd thought about it. That she was playing you along like the others, for her own purposes.' She tucked her legs up onto the seat and snuggled close to him.

'How did you guess that?'

'Because she was too obvious to be plausible. It set you looking for motives. My husband prefers the subtler approach.'

'The Canon and his wife are just desolated, of course,' he said a moment later. 'I stressed to them that Christine could well have been deranged since the accident. Career ended. Convinced her looks were spoiled. It's hard to gauge what those things can mean mentally. Charles was at the vicarage too. He said the same.' Treasure looked pained. 'We both think that's what a judge is going to feel.'

'And are you going to let Charles wind up the trust?'

He looked into the middle distance, at the moon's reflection in the river. 'D'you know he wants me to decide? He's so depressed about what's happened.'

'He feels guilty?'

'I think so. He's not going to do anything until I've officially become a beneficiary.'

'Which he has to arrange?'

'Yes. I'm then going to propose we invite John Larpin to become the third beneficiary, so he can be the adjudicator. It's what should have happened in the first place. It's every bit as much a moral issue as a money one. We'll take it from there.'

'So the trust could go on as it is?'

'Not quite as it is. Charles has certainly convinced me that Daniel Utteridge would have approved our putting a lot of money into Aids relief. Miss Quigley did too, though she cited a different motivation. Whether we eventually put all the trust funds into that will need to be decided.'

'But Utteridge Ales won't alter?'

'Not immediately. Apart from requiring its non-executive Chairman to resign forthwith. Natt has that in hand already. On behalf of the majority shareholders.'

'I see. But otherwise the company won't change? It'll stay too small to be cost-whatever-it-is. Cost-efficient. Isn't that what you said?'

He smiled. 'It's been that way for a long time. It'll probably survive unchanged for another year or so. Till we decide. I'm going to have a look at it tomorrow. Got a date with the Managing Director. Natt arranged it. I must say, it sounds a very cosy outfit. Local industry. Good local employer. Excellent products. Established before the Battle of Waterloo.'

'Another bit of Middle England? Like good old Graham Brown?'

'Yes,' Treasure responded defensively. 'Bet it's a fine place to work in.'

'And what about the nuns? Will Reverend Mother and Sister Mary Maud have to be boarded out with that other sisterhood? The one with the long name?'

'Not if they don't want.' He paused. 'Definitely not.'

'When did you decide that?'

'I just did. And I'm sure Charles and John Larpin will agree. And the Canon. Why should those two old dears be farmed out if they want to stay? We don't need to rebuild the whole convent.' He took one of her hands in his. 'Just the bit with the chapel and their rooms. It can easily be made habitable. Better than habitable. Positively . . . heavenly. Yes, heavenly. We'll have the insurance money to do it with, after all.'

'But will it be cost-efficient?' asked Molly quietly.

'Too bloody bad if it isn't. Life's too short. We abandon too much in the name of expediency . . . yes, and efficiency. You can't measure contentment merely in pounds or dollars.'

'Hear, hear!' Molly exclaimed approvingly, and a touch surprised. 'It all sounds very splendid,' she said, then she looked up at him with a mischievous glint in her eyes. 'We may have to talk the old ladies into accepting the advance all the same. You know how frugal they are?'

'Advance of what?'

'Of heavenly treasure, of course,' she replied, then kissed him softly on the lips.